DOWN TO THE SEA

DOWN TO THE SEA

BY

MORGAN ROBERTSON

AUTOGRAPH EDITION

PUBLISHED BY

McCLURE'S MAGAZINE

AND

METROPOLITAN MAGAZINE

THE QUINN & BODEN CO. PRESS
RAHWAY, N. J.

CONTENTS

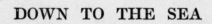

DOWN TO THE SEA

THE CLOSING OF THE CIRCUIT

"WHILE my child lives and I am here to teach him, he will not know the meaning of the words light, color, and darkness. He will grow up ignorant of his condition and will be educated from expurgated books for the blind. I shall be his teacher, and as far as in my power I shall lighten his curse." Thus spoke the father to the physicians who had examined the expressionless blue eyes of his infant son. "No hope," they had said. The trouble was with the optic nerve or the inner connection with the brain. He would never know light from darkness, though the eye, being well nourished, would grow with the body and retain its color.

The wife and mother had died in giving birth to the little one, and as there were no solicitous relatives on either side to interfere, the doubly afflicted man was free to educate his child as he wished. He erected a high wall around his property, gave emphatic notice to the villagers to keep out, and retired into the darkened world of his son. While none approved of his plan, few cared to question or openly criticise the stern, iron-faced man who occasionally appeared on the streets, and in time, as they died off or moved away, the strange existence unfolding within those high walls was forgotten.

The child grew, healthy and strong. With his father for teacher and a few trusted servants his only companions, he passed his childhood and early youth, and was educated as are the blind—with this difference: nothing was taught him that in his father's judgment would lead him into inquiry as to his true condition. His four remaining senses became abnormally keen; he heard distant sounds that others could not detect, could taste an odor in the air, and could feel, besides colors, the faintest of shadows on the wall—which latter changing phenomenon was described to him as an uncertain attribute of heat.

In him, too, developed to a remarkable degree what has been called the magnetic sense, which enables the blind to distinguish the proximity of a solid object or an open space. So strong was this perception that he needed no cane to traverse at a run the rooms and passages of the house or the winding paths of the garden. And, to reduce the list of embargoed words, and because in a measure it did the work of his missing sense, to this faculty was given the name sight. Hence he would say that he " saw " something, when he merely meant that he felt its presence.

To the extent that he was influenced by external impressions, he was happy; but instincts within him, aided by maturing reasoning power, tended, as he neared manhood, to arouse his suspicion. The sounds beyond the garden wall, the making of his clothes by some one unknown to him, the occasional presence of silent men who worked quickly with tools and made changes in doors and passages, the continuous supply of food from without, and the great front door, locked from his earliest remembrance, were problems to his now logical mind that he would solve. They indicated the existence of a sphere of action far beyond his present environment; so he tortured his father with speculations, and his education stopped.

" I have taught him too much," said the unhappy

man. "I started wrong. I should have made him deaf and dumb before I began."

The father took refuge in direct deceit, ascribing some of the phenomena which troubled the boy to the great unknown, others to the wisdom and experience of other men, which would come to him in time. He thus temporarily eliminated all factors but one— that of the locked front door; and could only meet the boy's demand to be allowed passage through by a downright refusal. The result was a stormy scene.

The father retired to his study sorrowing over the first harsh words he had given his son, and the boy went out into the evening and sought the extreme corner of the garden, where, sitting on a rustic bench and brooding rebelliously over the sudden appearance of boundaries to his investigations, he heard among the strange yet familiar sounds from beyond the wall a new one, and felt the presence of some one near and above him. Not needing to raise his head to assist his consciousness, he asked: "Who is it?"

"Me," came a musical voice.

"Who?" he asked again, with a puzzled face.

"Oh, auntie says I'm a tomboy. Do you live here? My! what a pretty garden. May I come down?"

"Yes, come," he answered, understanding the request.

"Look out! No. I'll get the ladder. I couldn't climb back if I jumped."

A black-eyed, dark-haired sprite of fifteen on top of the wall pulled up a ladder, lowered it, and clambered down.

"You're not polite—you might have helped me," she said, with a coquettish flirt of her curls as she faced the immovable boy. "What's your—oh, I didn't know. I'm so sorry."

Tears came to her eyes and a look of womanly pity swept over her childish face. She had seen his expressionless, half-closed eyes.

"Sorry? What for?" he asked. "Sorry you came? I'm glad. Who are you?" he passed his hand lightly over her shoulders and face.

"I'm sorry for you; I didn't know you were blind. Indeed, I didn't."

"Blind? What is that? You are a boy like me, aren't you? But your hair is dark while mine is light. How old are you? I am eighteen."

"No, I'm not a boy," she answered, indignantly. "I thought you were blind, but you can see my hair. You mustn't handle me like this—you mustn't. I'll go back."

He felt that he had offended her, and instinctively —for entertaining visitors as well as a perilous knowledge of another sex had not been included in his curriculum—he became deferential, and invited her to sit down. She did so, at a safe distance, which he respected.

"Nice evening, isn't it?" she said, breaking the embarrassing silence; but before he could answer this puzzling remark she went on:

"What ails your eyes? What makes you keep them half closed?"

"I don't know. Do I?" He felt of them, opened them wide, and turned his face toward her. "Tell me about yourself," he resumed. "Where do you come from?"

"Oh, I don't live here," said the maiden. "I'm just visiting Aunt Mary, and thought I'd climb the fence. I don't live anywhere; I've been aboard papa's ship all my life. He's coming for me to-day, for we sail to-morrow. We're going to Shanghai this voyage."

It was unintelligible, but from the list of strange words he selected one and asked what a ship was.

"Why, don't you know? A vessel square rigged on all three masts. The *Franklyn* carries double to'-gallant sails and skysail yards. Papa says he will try her with stunsails next voyage."

"I never learned of these things," said the boy. "You say you live in a ship. Is it a house with a garden—like this?"

"Oh, the idea! No," she laughed, merrily; but the laugh changed to a little scream. "There's a caterpillar!" she said. "Take it away, quick! Knock it off! Ugh!" She sprang toward him. "On my dress," she explained.

"What? Where? What is it?" he answered, reaching out both hands in the vacant air. His knowledge of caterpillars was nearly as limited as his knowledge of dresses. She brushed the creeping thing away with her handkerchief, and, sitting down, composed herself much as a bird smooths its ruffled feathers; then looked intently at the sightless eyes of the boy, staring high over her head.

"What was it?" he asked. "What hurt you?"

"Nothing; it's all right now. You are blind, aren't you?" she said, gently.

"I don't know," he answered, a little impatiently. "You said that before. What does blind mean?"

"Why, you can't see."

"Yes, I can."

"But your eyes were wide open and you didn't see the caterpillar. It was right under your nose, too."

" I don't see with my nose. And what difference does it make if my eyes were open? What are they good for, anyway? "

" To see with, of course. Didn't you know? "

" To see with? Eyes are good to see with? Do you see with your eyes? "

" Yes. Didn't you really know what eyes were for? Didn't you know that they were to see with? Couldn't you see when you were little? "

" Not with my eyes. I see with something inside of me; a sort of consciousness of things. How do you see with your eyes? What is it like? I thought I was the same as other people."

" Why," answered the girl, with a little quaver in her voice, " we see the sky, and the sun, and the stars, and flowers, and people, and houses, and— and— Oh, we see everything—that is, in daytime. In the night we can't see because it's dark." She was crying, softly.

" How far away can you see with your eyes? " asked the boy, eagerly. " I can see six feet."

" Oh, we can see miles and miles. We can see everything in front of us."

" And is every one that way but me? "

" Most every one. There are a few blind people. But, tell me," said the girl, wiping her eyes, " how do you know the color of my hair? "

" With my fingers. Do you tell colors with your eyes? "

" Mary! Bear a hand now, my girl," came a voice over the wall. " Where are you? "

" Oh, there's papa!" she exclaimed. " I must go." She moved toward the ladder. " Good-by."

" Don't go!" he cried, following her. " Don't go. Come back."

She turned, threw her arms around his neck, and kissed him. "Oh, you poor boy!—poor boy!" she cried, in a choking voice. "Stone blind and you never knew it." She kissed him again, then bounded up the ladder and over the wall.

Not once within his memory had the boy felt the pressure of lips to his own, and this pure kiss of an innocent, childish girl—his initial experience—became a turning-point in his life; for it outweighed every other influence and consideration known to him.

With the kiss still warm on his lips, he felt for the ladder, climbed to the top and called, repeatedly, the name he had heard: "Mary!"

He was not answered. But his sensitive ear distinguished the sound of retreating footsteps—long and heavy, light and pattering—with the lessening murmur of a sweet voice, which dwindled as he listened until it became as the tinkle of a distant bell; and when this was hushed in the silence of the summer night, he descended to the bench, feeling as might a lost soul called to paradise only to receive sentence of doom.

"Stone blind and you never knew it." He repeated her last words again and again, for they rang in his ears. Others could see with their eyes and he could not. Why? They could see things far away and he could see but six feet. Why was it? Why had his father, from whom he had received everything, denied him this? And why, having denied him, did he prevent him from going out through the door, where perhaps others would give him this wondrous faculty? It was wrong, unjust, shameful. Mary was kinder than his father.

As he thought of the generous sympathy of the

girl, which he had felt without wholly appreciating, his resentment toward his father increased to passionate rebellion.

" Mary lives in a ship," he muttered. " It has no garden. It can't be far." He climbed the ladder, raised it, lowered it on the other side, and descended. He was running away—looking for Mary and the wonderful unknown faculty of eyesight. The patient labor of eighteen years was undone in one short ten minutes by a warm-hearted, irresponsible iconoclast in short dresses. A minute before the father had come softly into the garden and, without seeing the ladder, had looked a moment on the brooding boy; then, from motives of delicacy, had retired, leaving him to come in when he pleased.

At the foot of the ladder the boy hesitated, then followed the wall to the corner, where another—or fence—began. He followed this and reached another, which he knew was parallel to the one he had climbed, and here he found a movable part which swung like a door. This he opened, and the creaking of the hinges was answered by a deep-toned growl from behind. He had often heard this sound, and dogs had been described to him; but, never having been struck or injured in his life, he knew not the fear of physical pain, and so—though feeling an impulse to flee—waited until he felt the impact of a hairy body and the closing of powerful jaws on his arm. Then, instinct—antedating his reason by several thousand years—dominated his mind, and he acted, rightly. He was strong and active. Reaching for the throat of the beast, he choked it with all the power of his fingers until the jaws relaxed; then he flung the gasping, snarling brute from him, passed through, and shut the gate—feeling within him a dim consciousness of victory—and examined his arm. The skin was unbroken; the dog's teeth had but pinched severely.

He had conquered in his first friction with the unknown, but very humanly became frightened when the danger was past, and, not daring to return, went on feeling the fences. He was walking on boards, which soon gave way to gravel, then grass, but fences of different design still guided him. After an hour or so these ended and he felt open space. Turning to the left, he found hard ground underfoot, then more grass. As the ground made easiest walking, he held to it, turning to the right or the left as he felt the grass under his feet.

All night the boy followed this country road, pausing at intervals to call for Mary, wondering at the immensity of the new world he was exploring, but feeling no fear of the darkness and solitude, for this had been his life's portion, and with all fears that she might not be in front of him dominated by an indefinable impulse to go on. He was in the hands of his instincts, better guides than his eyes could have been, with his complete lack of worldly knowledge.

In the morning, faint with hunger and fatigue, with feet blistered and bleeding, he sat on a stone doorstep, and, with a strange roar of the waking city in his ears, called to the passers-by, asking for Mary and the ship. None answered until a withered old woman, hobbling along on crutches, stopped and said:

" Poor b'y, what ails ye? Oh, Mither o' God, he's blind. What ye doin' here, b'y? "

" I want to find Mary. I'm hungry."

" Come back, me b'y. Come back—jist round the

corner. Me husband was blind—rist his sowl. I'll give ye a bite."

She fed him, questioned him without results, watched his head sink on the table in the lethargy of exhaustion, and put him to bed, with injunctions to her grandson, Tim, to " lave him be." Then she went to her apple-stand.

She had returned at nightfall and prepared her supper before he awakened; then the mutual questionings were resumed. A stubborn pride prevented him speaking of his father, or of himself beyond asking how he could learn to see with his eyes; but he demanded persistently to be taken to the ship and Mary, and became so urgent that the old woman finally called her grandson.

" Tim," she said, " take him down to the docks a bit and try and find his friends. He's lost, poor b'y, an' a bit daft. Mebbe he came from some ship close by. Bring him back if ye don't find them, Tim."

The only description of Tim that this story requires is that he was a typical gamin, fond of dog-fights, one of which, in a near-by vacant lot, he was now missing.

" Dere's a ship bound out to-morrer, two docks down," he said as they started. " Is dat de one yer lookin' fur? "

" Does Mary live there? " asked the boy.

" Dunno; her name's Mary, I think—Mary somethin'. Let's hurry."

They hurried—from different motives—and soon reached the dock, where, standing close up to the black, flaring bow of a full-rigged, deep-laden ship, Tim spelled out, in the light of a neighboring street-lamp, the name *Mary Croft*, in gilt letters on the topgallant rail.

" Mary, sure 'nough," he said; " is that de one? "

" Is it Mary? " asked the boy, in a frenzy of excitement. " Mary! " he called. " Mary! "

" C'm' on," said Tim, laconically. He piloted him to the long gangplank, placed his hands on the man-rope, and said: " G'wan up; dat's de ship yer lookin' fur, I guess," then sped to the dog-fight.

Slowly, yet eagerly, the blind boy ascended the gangplank, felt the grating and steps inside the rail, and descended to the deck, calling the name of the girl whose magnetic sympathy had enchanted him from home; but, as the only soul on board was the watchman, very properly sound asleep in a forecastle bunk on the last night of his job, the boy's call was not answered. Just abreast of the gangway was the booby, or hatch-house, which led to a " 'tween deck " below, formed by the extended poop or half-deck on which he stood. He felt the proximity of this hatch-house, and reached it, finding in the after part a door unlocked, which he opened; then he called again for Mary.

Hearing no answer, he stepped in with his hands on the sliding hood above the door. But his foot encountered emptiness, the hood slid back from the pressure of his weight, and he fell heavily to the deck below, where, striking his head against a cask, he lay quiet. Toward midnight he aroused to a half-consciousness, crawled aimlessly about twenty feet, and swooned again. Here he lay screened from observation until the officers and crew had come aboard in the morning, the ship had been towed to sea, and the pilot was preparing to step into the waiting dinghy which would take him to the station boat near the Sandy Hook Lightship. Then he was seen groping under the hatch. He was hauled to the deck and into the presence of the captain and officers, a pitiable spectacle, with clothing soiled from the filth of the " 'tween deck," his sightless eyes staring from deep hollows in his livid face, and his temples streaked with congealed blood from a cut in his head.

" Stowaway! " grunted the captain, glaring on the trembling boy, weak from shock and seasickness. " All right. You'll get enough of it."

" That's no stowaway, captain," said the pilot, with one leg over the rail. " He's blind as a bat. I'll take him ashore if you say so."

" What do you say, you young brat? " bawled the captain. " We're short-handed, and you can stay if you want to. Do you want to go ashore, or do you want to stay in the ship? "

" I would rather stay in the ship. I want to see Mary."

The pilot was in a hurry, and, hearing the first part of the sentence, slid down the side out of hearing of the last part—which might have delayed his departure had he heard it. And in this ship the boy went to the southward, while the pilot went ashore.

The *Mary Croft* was, or had been, a composite ship—that is, wooden planked over iron frames. But this, among the other characteristics of her class, was all that was left her. During a long career, marked by innumerable dismastings and refittings, she had lost her iron spars and wire rigging, and had reverted to an old-fashioned wood and hemp. She was laden with kerosene oil in tin cases, was bound to the antipodes, and was manned with the usual short-handed crew, representative of all nations, so dear to the heart of the American captain.

Without being asked as to his name or for an explanation of his presence on board, the child of nature, who had not yet heard an oath or foul word, whose lowest ideal was the boon of eyesight, was driven with kicks and curses forward among the crew, where his inquiries for Mary were silenced with laughter, to work as best he could and learn to be a sailor. Profane abuse, cuffs, or fist blows, and a stinging rope's end were the methods employed in this school of seamanship, and his affliction only increased the rigor of the tutelage, for none of them believed him actually blind. His habitual use of the word " see " and its synonyms, the keenness of the faculty that he meant and the readiness with which he found any part of the deck where he had once been, was evidence to them that he was shamming— an outrageous violation of nautical ethics.

As the ship neared the tropics, his education, from being confined to the work on deck, progressed on higher lines. Followed by objurgations from the officers, he felt his way aloft one day to the mizzen-royal yard, and, under the instructions of a sailor who accompanied him, learned to loose and furl the sail. This became his especial task, to which, asleep or awake, night or day, he was called when sail was shortened or set. Thinly clad and hatless, he suffered torture from storm and sun, and in the watch below, the servant of the forecastle, he cleaned pots and pans, washed the shirts of the rest, and brought their food from the galley as ordered.

No word of sympathy, no kindly inquiry or expression of friendly interest lightened his darkness or relieved the hideous nightmare which enveloped his soul; he was merely a subject for forecastle wit and ridicule. But into the depths of his misery and helpless terror, surrounded by phenomena of sound and motion beyond the power of his mind to grasp, when the old life in the garden faded to a dream of another world, and even his father's voice would not come back, he carried the memory of the soft, yielding features of the girl, and the kiss on his lips, and the sympathy of her voice. And this memory kept him sane; for while he remembered he hoped, and the reason that hopes will not totter.

In the dreadful, stifling calm of the zone between the trade-winds the ship lay like a log, with the deck hot to the feet and the hemp rigging sticky with oozing tar that had been as hard as wood. A gale, a hurricane, would have been welcomed by the crew as they worked in the rigging or on the blistering deck; but not a catspaw of wind for days had relieved the air of its furnace heat, and no cloud appeared in the metallic sky with its promise. Off to the westward was a large clipper ship, which at the beginning had been hull down on the horizon, but now, at the end of the sixth day, in obedience to the law of attraction, was but five miles away and drifting closer each hour.

" This is a cyclone-breeder," remarked the captain to the first mate. " The barometer acts queer." He went below and returned in a moment, pale and earnest.

" The mercury's below twenty-nine," he said. " Shorten down to topsails before supper. I'm afraid of this."

" Look there, captain," answered the mate, pointing to the southern horizon. Sea and sky were merged in a filmy, translucent wall of light-bluish gray, that shaded indefinitely into the color of the two elements. As they looked it grew larger. The ship to the westward was taking in sky-sails and royals.

" In with the kites!" said the captain, tersely.

" Call all hands!" roared the mate, as he sprang forward. " Starboard watch aft!" he continued, as the crew answered. " Let go royal an' t-gallant hall'ards, fore and aft, an' clew up! Down wi' the flyin'-jib! Bear a hand, my lads! bear a hand!"

The men needed no encouragement. They saw the portent in the southern sky, and hauled and worked and multiplied themselves as only a short-handed merchant crew can. The three royals were soon hanging in the bunt-lines and they manned the top-gallant gear. The blind boy quickly furled the mizzen-royal, and came down while the men were still tugging at top-gallant clew-lines and bunt-lines. The mate saw him.

" Here, you goggle-eyed cub! Lay aloft and stow that main-royal!" he shouted. The boy obeyed, and as the captain directed the hauling-up of courses and lowering of upper topsails before sending the men aloft to furl, he was alone in the rigging, climbing a strange road to find in his darkness, by the similarity of structure with the mizzen-mast, a royal-yard where he was to do two men's work.

The dim shading of gray soon assumed form and size and a deeper hue. Covering half of the southern horizon, and stretching up, a dingy curtain, nearly to the zenith, it presented, in sharp contrast with the brilliant hue of the sky above and around, a menacing aspect of solidity, horrid to behold in the velvety blackness of the center, which absorbed every ray of light from the western sun, reflecting none. It was the complete negation of light and color. Beneath it was a narrow band of pale gray, and beneath this the glassy sea, which bore no trace of ruffling wind. The

cloud—if cloud it was—seemed to move with a volition of its own, silently, with no mutterings of
thunder or gleam of lightning.

As the boy reached the royal-yard, and the men
below were manning topsail down-hauls, it gathered in its shadowy edges, lifted up, and came on, a
mighty, roughly symmetrical ball which hovered
nearly over the ship. Tints of deep purple now appeared in the valleys of its surface, and on its western
edge was a golden rim.

"Make fast all!" cried the frightened captain.
"Lay aloft and furl!" he roared.

While the last word was still on his lips, a sheet
of white flame enveloped the *Mary Croft*, and a report beyond all imagining or description shocked
the air from horizon to horizon. The cloud above
spread out to an elongated spindle, like the black
wings of a mighty angel of death, and went on overhead, having done its work. The ship was a disintegrated wreck. Where wood separated iron in that
composite hull, there was molten metal anl flame.
Each oaken rail was a line of fire. From the roaring
furnace below arose, through each hatch and a dozen
ragged holes in the deck, spurting, hissing columns
of black smoke and burning oil and incandescent
gas. The hemp rigging slackened, and, with the
festooned canvas, burst into flames which crept aloft,
threatening with new torture a moaning boy on the
main-royal yard-arm, who alone of that ship's company, insulated on a dry wooden spar, had heard the
report and felt a small part of the terrific discharge
of heaven's artillery that had destroyed the ship.
Not a man standing within or above that iron-ribbed
hull had known what struck him. Each was dead
before the sensory nerves could act.

The boy on the yard, racked with excruciating pain in every nerve, clung to the spar with one hand and held the other to his head, for in his head was the acme of his agony. Then he became conscious of heat from below, with smoke which stifled him. Choking and gasping, expecting momentarily to hear the roar of the mate, he attempted to furl the sail. Then he felt rain on his bare head, large drops, which multiplied to a shower, then to a deluge of water that compelled him to hold tight to the yard with both hands. The pain in his head increased as he took away his hand, and strange, dream-like sensations crowded his mind, sensations of motion, as though his brain was loosened and turning around. Then the heat and smoke from below ceased; then came wind, cooling and welcome, which increased, at first a breath, then a gust, then a breeze, then a gale—a screaming hurricane. He heard loud creaking below him. The yard inclined, and he shifted his position; it became upright. Then he heard a grinding crash from somewhere, and, clinging tightly to the spar, felt a sickening dizziness, which lasted until, coming with a swishing crash of water, he felt a concussion which, tearing him away from the yard, hurled him into a salt engulfing element that filled his mouth and nose and choked him. Something hard struck his legs, which he grasped, and soon he could breathe. It was the yard-arm, which he knew by the touch.

As he climbed on the floating tangle of spar and cordage, he felt again the scorching heat and breathed the stifling smoke. Then he heard a distant report. It was an encouraging signal from the clipper ship, which, laying over to the lessening squall, was steering a course that would bring her straight to the wreck. But it frightened the boy, reminding him of the awful sound that had hurt him. To him this terrible experience was but a little stranger than his daily contact with environment. He did not know what had happened or how he came to be in the water. He called for help, but, hearing no answer, waited for some one to come. The soreness in his joints was leaving him, though when he opened his eyes there invariably came the pain and the whirl and the phantasms in his head. But this pain gradually became endurable and the whirl less pronounced, so that the phantasmagoria was defined and at times stationary.

As he changed his position on the spar he noticed that the phantasms changed also. Then he found that merely moving his head to the right or to the left, up or down, seemed to cause this change and motion. He realized that when he faced one way there was little difference—nothing but a slight sensation of motion that was pleasurable. In another position there came sharply defined shocks which irritated him. Facing another way, he felt a return of the pain and a lively hatred of the phantasm which accompanied it. He turned away, instinctively shutting his eyes, and the movement and all sensation ended. Then he opened them, and the phenomena returned.

He felt of his eyes with his hand and a new phantasm blotted out all others. Removing his hand took it away. He brought both hands together and repeated the experiment; then, separating them and bringing them together, again and again, the truth came home to him.

"I see!" he cried, to the sky and ocean. "I can see with my eyes! I can see! I can see!"

The optic nerve had been at work since the lightning-bolt had jarred it into life.

In his great joy he shouted with all the power of his lungs; he wanted his shipmates to know; for even they, with the whole world, must rejoice with him. His shout was answered by a distant hail, and then he turned and shouted again. Into his field of vision came a moving object which slowly grew larger. He reached out his hand to touch it, but failed. He waited, shouting at intervals until the moving thing filled his eyes with its strange outline, then heard the voice again.

"All right, my lad," it said, close to him; "hold on! In bow! Way enough! Back water, starboard! Got him?"

Strong hands grasped him and he was lifted into a boat.

"Who's left? Any one?" asked the voice.

"I can see," he answered. "I can see with my eyes."

"Poor devil, he's crazy. Back water, men; we'll look aboard, if we can."

"Where were you when she was struck?" asked the man nearest him.

The boy was staring at the moving pictures filling his brain, which he knew must be men, like himself. For answer he shut his eyes and felt the features of the questioner.

"Where were you when she was struck?" the man repeated.

"Struck! Yes, something struck me. I was on the main royal-yard, and then I was in the water. I don't know. What was it? Who are you?"

"Great God, sir," sang out the man, "he was on the royal-yard when the mainmast went."

"No wonder he's daft. Way enough, boys!"

The flames above deck, temporarily quenched by the rain, were again breaking forth, fed by the raging gulf below. Holding his breath, the officer climbed the weather mizzen-chains, and, shading his eyes from the fierce heat, glanced once at the hecatomb on the shattered deck of the *Mary Croft*, and dropped back, pale and horror-struck.

"She'll sink in half an hour," he said. "It's best. Give way!"

They left the ship and returned to their own, the clipper, where the boy, astonished that no one shared his joyousness, was lifted up the side and placed on the deck. He looked around and staggered, until, shutting his eyes, he recovered his balance.

"Oh, it's the blind boy," exclaimed a voice that he knew, which sent his blood leaping.

"Mary!" he cried. "Mary! Mary, where are you? I can see now! I can see with my eyes!" She was at his side in an instant. With his eyes still closed, he felt of her face and hair, reveling in ecstatic delight of the senses which remembered her; then, opening them, stamped his soul with her image, which he had not yet imagined. And it pleased his new-born sense more than any of the phantasms that had yet appeared to it.

A COW, TWO MEN, AND A PARSON

"YES," said the retired pilot, "I've as much respect for an able seaman as when I was learning to be one; at the same time, I may say that in these days of donkey-engines and steam capstans

and windlasses the able seaman can be dispensed
with, to a great extent.   Ever tell you about that
trip I made without a sailor aboard?   No?   Well,
it's worth hearing about.   It was certainly a remarkable voyage.

"I was a youngster then, just out of the forecastle, and was going out to Calcutta, second mate of
the bark *Tempest*.   The mate was a York State man,
a rattling good fellow and an all-around sailor-man;
but he had one failing—profanity.   He could out-
curse any man I ever met.   It just rolled out of him,
without any trouble on his part at all.   He was
never at a loss for a word or a forcible expression;
but, to do him justice, he always swore at things, not
men.

"Well, about this time there had been a lot of
trouble in holding men to their ships after they had
signed articles, and the captain had arranged to
bring ours aboard with a tug after we had towed
down to the lower bay.   A gang of riggers bent sail
at the dock and helped us down, and we dropped
anchor to wait for the tug with the captain, pilot,
and crew.

"Before leaving the dock our one passenger joined
us and spent his time looking after his cow, that had
come aboard with him.   He was a missionary, going out to convert the heathen, and his Society had
backed him up to the extent of the cow—for fresh
milk.   It wasn't usual to take cows to sea, but I
suppose the skipper liked fresh milk and hoped to
get some, so he let the cow come along.   The cow
wasn't consulted, of course.   We knocked a few
boards together and made her a temporary pen on
the forehatch.

"The Chinese steward was ashore with the captain, but had got the cook, a countryman of his, aboard at the dock, and this gentleman—well, I'll speak of him afterward. The ship had lain port side to the dock, and our big anchor-chain was used to moor her. For some reason the mate had forgotten to have it shackled to the anchor as we towed down the bay, so we used a small one. It was safe enough if it didn't blow hard. No tug appeared, and, night coming on, the mate agreed to stand watch till midnight, when I was to relieve him.

" At supper-time we had our first rub with the cook. The mate had poked his head into the galley and told him to cook supper for us, as the steward was ashore. In Pidgin English he was answered that he had shipped cook, not steward; that he was to cook for a crew of fourteen men, which he would do and no more. And what did that Celestial do but cook up a supper of salt-horse hash for a full crew and place it in the empty forecastle.

" The mate interviewed him again, but got no satisfaction. During the interview the cook's heels cracked the carlines overhead, and several pots and pans were dented; but he knew his work, and would not cook for the cabin. So, all we could do was to muster around the dishpan of hash in the forecastle and get it down. The parson began to say ' Grace,' but the mate quashed it. ' Stow that, parson,' he said, irreverently. ' Be thankful if you like, but don't bring me in, for I'm not—for this grub.'

" You see, the mate had been used to the cabin menu for some years, but I, fresh from the forecastle, enjoyed it. As for the parson, he took one mouthful of the sickening mess and passed; but he ate it at the next meal, when hungrier.

"I turned in and slept till midnight, when the mate called me.

"'Looks rather bilious over there to the nor'west,' he said, as he went below. 'Look out for a Staten Island squall—wish we'd shackled on the other anchor.'

"I aroused him in an hour. The squall was coming, black and wicked. He came up, took one look, and said: 'Call the sky-pilot; he's got to help.' I got him up after some trouble and we went to work trying to shackle the chain to the big anchor—a big job for two men, for the parson was useless. Before we got the end up to the rail the squall struck us and away we went, the small anchor nearly jumping out of the water as we dragged.

"The mate ran aft, looked at the compass, and came back. 'We're dragging right into the Swash Channel!' he yelled, as he joined us.

"It was about the sharpest squall I have ever seen. We were forced to shout into one another's ears to be understood. Lightning played all around us, and by the light of the flashes we worked until we had the chain secured to the anchor, which, luckily, hung at the cat-head instead of being stowed on the rail. We then overhauled a range of chain, but just as we were ready to let go there came a mighty straining on the windlass, then a sudden jolt, and we knew the small anchor had caught something and parted the chain. Then we heard for a moment the bell-buoy and knew we were in the Swash Channel.

"'Stand by to give her the chain, quick!' shouted the mate as he let go the big mud-hook. We were going astern about six knots an hour, and, though we lifted the chain around the windlass fast as we could, she brought up too quick. Away went the big chain.

"The mate screamed in my ear: 'Show the head of the foretopmast staysail; slip both chains at the first shackles; I'll take the wheel!'

"I knew what he wanted to do—keep her off the bottom. So I loosed the staysail, then hunted for the parson, who had disappeared. I found him in the forecastle, praying, and felt that I did wrong to interrupt him; but that sail must go up, and I knew the cook wouldn't help, so he had to come.

"The mate had thrown the wheel over, backing the ship around broadside to it as we dragged the sail part way up. I made the sheet fast, then punched out the shackle-pins and let the chain go out of the hawse-pipes. She soon began to go ahead. The mate got her on the course down the channel, and, as he knew every foot of the bay, steered us right out to sea past Romer Shoal, Sandy Hook, and Scotland Lightship. The parson had gone below out of the rain, and I kept lookout on the poop to be near the mate. About a mile outside of the lightship he threw the wheel down and lashed it; then we stowed the staysail after a fashion and loosed the spanker to heave to under.

"We got the parson out again, and the mate took a pump-brake to the cook, who squealed and chattered, but would not turn out to help. We pulled the spanker up without him, and then she lay quiet enough in the offshore sea that was rising.

"At daylight the land was a dim line of blue, and that squall settled down to a three-days' gale that blew us a hundred miles to sea. The mate and I stood watch and watch, while the parson fed the cow and prayed. And the cook? Why, every meal-time

that demented heathen would lug the whole bill of
fare to the forecastle door and return in an hour to
dump the stuff overboard. Meanwhile we would
have eaten what we wanted of it. The mate busied
himself plotting the drift of the ship, hammering
the cook, and swearing.

"The parson didn't offer to say grace any more,
but the mate supplied plenty of profane language.
Once, as he reeled off a string of oaths, the parson
admonished him. 'What's the difference, parson?'
he answered. 'You pray and it's supplication, isn't
it? I swear. Same thing—supplication.'

"The poor parson rolled up his eyes. 'Shocking!
Shocking!' he said. I didn't like to hear the mate
talk like this, but he was my superior and I had
nothing to say. The parson was a long-geared,
mild-mannered man, with a chin-whisker and bald
head; a nice old fellow, and very much frightened
at the trouble we were in.

"The third day the wind moderated, and the mate
proposed trying to set the lower topsails.

"'How'll we sheet home?' I asked. 'If we had a
donkey-engine, now—'

"'I have it,' he broke in. 'We've got a cow—a
good, strong, able-bodied cow. She has got to work
her passage.'

"We inspected the cow. 'I'll make a canvas strap
for her breast,' he said, 'and rig a harness to hook
on to the gear.'

"He went at it, harnessed the cow, led her out and
hooked her on to the weather main topsail-sheet. I
loosened the sail and sung out, 'Sheet home!' but
the cow would not. She just stood there and looked
around in a bewildered way, remarking 'Moo-o-oo!'
every time the mate whacked her with a board. He

whacked and perspired, and swore until he was tired, and then the parson suggested that she might pull if she was fed first—perhaps she was hungry. It gave the mate an idea. He brought up a turnip and held it in front of her nose. She reached for it and got a smell; reached farther and pulled the sheet a little; he gave her a morsel. Then, with the taste in her mouth, she walked away with the sheet to get more. Soon we had both sheets home and the weather-brace tautened, and the cow got the rest of the turnip. Then we set the fore topsail the same way and put the cow in her pen.

"The mate was in high feather. 'It won't do to feed that animal,' he said to the parson. 'She's our crew—fourteen sailors rolled into one cowhide. But if our crew has a full belly our crew won't work—understand? We'll make her grub a reward for service rendered, payable when earned.'

"The parson saw the force of this reasoning, and the mate went below for a nap while I watched the ship. Every time I passed the galley door the cook stuck his head out and jabbered at me. All I could understand was that he had shipped to cook 'fol foulteen sailol-man; no glubbie, no cookie.' I went in and gathered that the salt beef the steward had weighed out to him was all cooked and he wanted more. When the mate came up I told him.

"Good enough. We'll stop this waste of grub. 'Parson,' he shouted, 'can you cook?' The parson left his cow and came aft.

"'Well, really,' he began, 'I can hardly claim—'

"'Can you, or will you, boil spuds, fry steak, and make coffee? We have these things aboard, and if you'll cook we'll have something to eat, and I'll put that yellow-back in irons.'

" He agreed to try it, so the mate got out the dar-
bies, and with a belaying-pin battered the poor
Chinaman into condition to submit to being ironed.
Then he dragged the shrieking wretch aft and bundled him down the booby-hatch, where he lashed
him to a stanchion and gave him the last dish of
hash he had cooked and a bucket of water. We had
no more trouble with him.

" The parson cooked dinner for us, and as the day
wore on we made more sail, putting on the upper
topsails, top-gallant-sails, and the jibs, the parson
backing ahead of the cow with a turnip, I whacking
her with a board, and the mate standing by to nipper
and bossing the job. She always got a morsel of
turnip for every rope she pulled, but it was a much-
disgusted old cow that we led back to the pen. She
must have thought it over that night, for the next
morning when we introduced her to the main-brace
she let out her heels, knocked me galley west and
chased the parson up on the poop, while the
mate took to the rigging and nearly fell overboard.

" But she cooled down and squared in the yards,
for the wind was fair for Sandy Hook, and that day
a pilot boarded us. He laughed till the tears came
as he saw the cow walk along with a brace fast to
her, bribed by the turnip ahead and fanned by a
board behind.

" An ocean tug came along about dark and the
mate struck a bargain to be towed in with the tug's
tow-line and docked. The cow helped us to get the
line, and worked half the night clewing up the sails.
If she could have gone aloft we would have made her
furl them. We were mean enough. As he backed
into the slip next day the tug captain climbed

aboard. 'What kind of a crew do you call this?' he asked, as he saw us getting lines ready.

"'Good crew,' said the pilot. 'A cow, two men, and a parson, and the best man here is the cow.' Then he told him what had happened.

"The tug captain grew black in the face as he cursed his stupidity in docking a helpless ship at ordinary rates. If he had known how short-handed we were he could have demanded and been paid a big pile. Then the mate came along and helped him out. The air was blue and sulphurous for a while, as these two experts turned loose, but the mate won.

"And the cow? Oh, the mate bought her from the parson at Calcutta. Said he'd put her on the articles when he got a ship to sail, and draw her pay."

THE RIVALS

HAD he been a cold-blooded creature with a heart of one ventricle, he might have been classed with the amphibia; for he was a vertebrate; he was born on land and had taken to the water—but only to the surface, for, though he could suspend respiration and even heart-action for a long period, a dive beneath would be fatal. Other points of difference between him and amphibians were his superheated, half-gaseous breath and blood; his twin hearts of complex structure that throbbed at "ten thousand indicated"; lungs, veins, and air-passages of cold-drawn, seamless tubing; nerves of copper, and hide of Harveyized steel several inches thick in places. His nose—of the same material and solid—was tons in weight, and his vertebral column longer, thicker,

stiffer, and stronger than that of any known amphibian, living or extinct; so he was not an amphibian;
neither was he any other kind of reptile, nor fish, nor
bird, nor animal. He was superior to all, and, possessing a soul, was in close touch with humanity.

His consciousness had begun with a tickling sensation of broken glass and streaming wine on his nose,
and the sound in his ears—or bow-sponsons, to be
correct—of a receding musical voice which said: " I
christen thee *Vengeful.*" Then, in a quiver of nervous expectation and wonder, he had slid backward
until the water received him, while thousands of
small creatures all about him buzzed noisily. He
had known his name when he heard it—it seemed
that he had known it for ages—but he was still
dazed and stupid, unable to " take notice," and immediately dropped into the healthy slumber of the
newly born, during which slumber the mites of creatures tied him to a dock, scrubbed him, groomed him,
and labored over him until his heart and lungs—in
fact, his whole nervous and vascular systems—had
developed to working condition. He had grown
some formidable teeth and claws, and two pairs of
one hundred thousand candle-power eyes which could
see objects five miles away in the dark. He had acquired, too, a voracious appetite, and they poured a
thousand tons of picked coal into his stomach, which
he liked and began to digest. Then it was that he
really lived and enjoyed life.

They called him a sea-going battle-ship of sixteen
thousand tons displacement, and said that he was
English; but he cared little for that. He remembered his name and knew his business, which was
closely connected with his name. He purposed to
attend to it; but in this regard was first confronted

with the problem of the small creatures—the eight
hundred busy, buzzing, scurrying parasites that lived
upon him and within him. Naturally he had expected
to be annoyed by them, but somehow—he could not
understand how—they seemed to know the right thing
to do at the right time, and even to anticipate his
wishes. Was he hungry? They filled his stomach.
Thirsty? They pumped fresh, sweet water into him.
Hot and uncomfortable? They opened his ports and
ventilating apertures, and cooled him with steady
blasts of air. Every morning they attended to his
bath, flushing and flooding all parts of him, rubbing
him dry, and polishing his teeth and claws. When
he had resolved upon a short venture to the open sea,
he found them enthusiastically interested in the plan,
calling it a "trial trip." And when, after a glorious
battle with the mighty waves which tried their best to
overwhelm him—a series of spurts ahead and back-
ings astern, quick turns to the right and left under
full speed, and a wild rush in a straight line in which
he put forth his strength to the utmost, and quivered
in every nerve and muscle, and roared and shrieked
in his joy of might—he returned to his place in the
harbor, fatigued and panting and hot with exertion,
the joyous buzzing of the parasites equaled his
mightiest roar. The buzzing was answered by other
buzzing from other bugs on other ships in the harbor; and when it had subsided a little and become
articulate, he heard them boasting: "Nineteen knots
over a measured course—the largest and fastest battle-ship in the world." It would have been easy, in
the furious rush into a head sea, to wash most of
them off; but he had spared them, and now was glad.
Whatever they were—whatever their part and mission, they were at least friendly, and did him good

rather than harm. Later, when they had bathed him and cooled him down, and he was receiving the sober and more dignified congratulations of the ships, he heard them described as his " crew "—part of the congratulations referring to his good luck in getting a crew of such intelligence and efficiency.

" There's work for you in this world, youngster," said a one-funneled, sponsoned warrior of a past generation. " I won't be in it, though I hope to see it. Back number, you know. Obsolete, they call me; but if I had your teeth and hide and barbettes, I wouldn't funk at any job. Speed don't mean much in a mix."

" Don't, eh? " murmured a small, saucy torpedo-boat which, with feminine presumption and curiosity, had sniffed her way up between the two, and now lay breathing steam and black smoke in Vengeful's face. " Means a good deal to me."

" Pardon me," coughed Vengeful, politely; " but wouldn't you mind, Miss—I really don't know your name—but wouldn't you mind—"

" Dolly, you're no lady," interrupted the old warrior. " Clear out. You may not know it, and it's a rough thing to say to one of your sex, but your breath's very bad. Make your escape. Use some o' that speed o' yours."

" I'll not speak to you again, old Sponsons," snapped the torpedo-boat. " I can't help my breath —I just can't eat that hard coal you're all so fond of; it disagrees with me. And I only wanted to be introduced."

" Get around to leeward, and I'll make you acquainted; but, understand, I won't warrant you."

" You needn't mind, old Shiver-the-Mizzen. I'll introduce myself."

"Privilege of a gentleman."

"Mind your own business."

She shot ahead, a black streak under a thick line of horizontal smoke, turned in her tracks, and circled up under Vengeful's lee, where she stopped and said:

"Don't you believe a single word that old wretch says about me, will you? He hates me."

"But he hasn't said anything," answered Vengeful.

"But he will, I'm sure. My name's Wasp; but he calls me all sorts of names. When he's good-humored, as he happens to be to-day, it's Dolly or Mollie or Daisy; but oftener it's Newsy or Nosey or Busy. I detest him. Say, Mr. Vengeful "—she dipped her nose coquettishly in the crisp harbor sea and rolled a little, as though in feminine embarrassment—" found a sweetheart yet?"

"Say, Vengeful," called his friend, in a whispering blast of steam, "look out for that minx. She's a whole bag o' newspapers—she's a whole press syndicate. Listen to her and get the news, but look out what you say."

"What's he saying about me?" she demanded, lifting her nose high.

"Nothing—really nothing." Vengeful shivered at his first lie.

"Well, I hope not, just as we're getting acquainted. But about that matter—well, about your sweetheart. You won't wait long. Look around you. Why, every girl in the crowd is jealous of me now, and Black Jack, over there—see him at the outer buoy?—is jealous of you. He thinks I'm the only girl in the world, and I've made him think he's the bravest and best fellow alive; but I don't like him—don't like Russians at all. See him squirm. Why, he's pointing at you."

There was a large fleet at the anchorage. There were battle-ships of all types and classes, obsolete or modern—ponderous, truculent, masculine; armored cruisers—sexless compromises, poor fighters, and bad runners, despised of the ship world, but handsome withal, of good figure and pleasing carriage; protected cruisers were there—stately, lady-like, and respectable from keel to truck; unprotected cruisers as well, feminine too, of moral fiber and reputation in keeping with their unprotectedness, but which came mainly from their mutual jealousy and proneness to scandal-mongering. Lower still in the moral scale were the torpedo-boats and destroyers, quick of wit and speech and heel, shameless and irresponsible, but of serpentine grace and beauty. Of such was Miss Dolly, and in the first class named was her critic—crusty and discouraged old War-horse, honest as a bulldog and a fighter in his day, but now a third-rate.

All these, with one exception, had offered welcome and congratulation to Vengeful. The exception was the Russian indicated by Dolly, a high-sided vicious-looking fellow of about Vengeful's draught and displacement, now tugging sulkily at his mooring buoy far over toward the channel. On his rail and boats was an unpronounceable, untranslatable name, which no one called him by, the fleet with one accord agreeing upon Black Jack as a fitting cognomen for a person who, even as a visitor, had not the manners to answer a civil " good-morning," be it given in the form of gun-salute, whistle, or signal. He had unkindly sneered at Vengeful on his first appearance among them, and all through the running fire of comment and approval following his trial of strength had remained moodily silent. As Vengeful looked at him he had swung his forward turret guns until they bore upon his superstructure, and was slowly bringing every gun in his port secondary battery to bear upon the same spot. One vicious eye on his forward bridge glared unspeakable things at Vengeful, and as he rolled and pitched in the choppy sea of the channel this eye lifted and fell, staring him out of countenance. The insult was unmistakable.

"My, what a temper!" giggled Miss Dolly. "Do you think, Mr. Vengeful, that you could thrash him?"

"I'm pretty sure that I could," he answered, slowly, though he quivered in anger; "but not sure of the etiquette."

"Challenge him," said Dolly, as she shot ahead. "I'll carry the challenge. Oh, I hope you'll thrash him well."

"Come back here, Miss Busy," hailed the observant Warhorse. "None of your mischief-making. Come back, I say." But Dolly was far away, circling around toward Black Jack. "Steady, Vengeful," he said, softly; "he's an infernal cad, of course, but a guest. You can't quarrel here; but you'll find him outside some day. However, he needs a rebuke from the rest of us."

Softly, yet penetratingly, Warhorse emitted a long-drawn hiss from an old-fashioned supplementary exhaust, and turned his one weak eye on the ill-bred stranger. Other ships followed suit; and a chorus of hisses and disapproving glances descended upon Black Jack. He understood; the guns swung to place and the vicious eye looked ahead. Vengeful had remained silent, and the unpleasantness might have ended with the rebuke; but Miss Dolly was at work. She was beside the Russian, whispering, nodding, and curtesying.

"He's smitten with her," growled Warhorse. "Wish they'd elope." He opened all his sponson ports, but nothing of the conversation could be heard at the distance. Soon, however, Miss Dolly raced ahead and demurely took her place at the dock. Then a deep-toned voice came over the water.

"So, you young whipper-snapper, just out of the cradle, you can thrash me, can you?"

"I answer for him," roared Warhorse, in a mighty burst of escaping steam. "He can not only thrash you with half his guns, but when you turn to run he can catch you under one boiler. He can toss you out of water with his nose, or climb over you and drown you with his weight. We've had enough of your company. Let go that buoy and go. Understand? Go! I am the father of the fleet, and what I say on these matters is the law of the fleet."

Approving hisses, groans, and growls from the assembled ships followed this, and, as the sulky Russian made no answer, they clamored at him with bells—all striking eight—one ship beginning as another ended. When all had sounded, Black Jack responded in kind, and, in spite of the apparent flippancy of the answer, the tremble in the notes told his humiliation. But not even his furious jerks at his cable, nor the quavering sobs and gasps he emitted as he rolled heavily from side to side, nor the thickness and blackness of the smoke belching from his funnels were a fair index of his rage. Before he slipped his moorings he again turned a gun on Vengeful—this time a small four-inch—and discharged it unshotted, repeatedly, each bark holding a note of hatred and challenge.

"Don't answer, Vengeful," cried Warhorse, soothingly. "Act when the time comes; but—I'll do the talking." He "talked" with a series of barks from a still smaller gun, the intent in the choice meaning the same as Black Jack's—that big-gun fire would be wasted on so poor an adversary. The Russian said no more; detaching his cable from the buoy, he forged ahead, turned abreast of Miss Dolly's dock, and, with a gloomy, backward glance at the quiescent young lady, steamed out to sea.

"Don't this put me in rather a bad light?" asked Vengeful, discontentedly. "I'm to fight him, I suppose; but where will I find him?"

"Mediterranean," answered Warhorse. "Didn't you understand? I told him you'd follow; but you need gun-practice and a little geography before you start."

Geography Vengeful learned at the anchorage, from the ceaseless gossip and conversation of the ships; the gun-practice he secured in the open sea, to which he made tri-weekly trips. And soon he surpassed his utmost expectations. He could hit the bull's-eye of a target a mile away with a twelve-inch shot while under full speed, and send a second through the same hole. The fleet was frankly proud of him, and even the flippant comment of the unprotected sisterhood held none of the usual sarcasm, while the behavior of Miss Dolly was most exemplary—as old Warhorse put it: "Minding her own business, and sawing wood like a lady."

But her maidenly reserve left her when Vengeful was ready to start. She left her dock and hovered near him, hinting broadly that she would be glad of

an invitation to accompany him. It was not forth-
coming; Vengeful was a battle-ship, and, aside from
the slight resentment which he felt toward the gos-
sipy female, he had the instinctive aversion of all
battle-ships to torpedo-craft in general; for there is
but one thing afloat feared by a battle-ship—the
slim, fish-like horror that an angry torpedo-boat can
send at an enemy, the thing that dives from a tube,
seeks a twenty-foot depth, and travels at a thirty-
knot rate in the direction originally pointed. If
swerved from this direction by wave-motion, or obstructing logs, buoys, or cables, it immediately re-
turns to it, implacable and murderous. When it
strikes it explodes and dies; but its victim dies as
well; for the mightiest craft on the sea cannot
withstand the impact of two hundred and twenty
pounds of exploding gun-cotton. Like all of his kind,
Vengeful carried torpedo-tubes, but only because
he was born with them. Battle-ships scorn their
use.

He had calmly and politely ignored hints, hoping
to discourage her; but she was persistent, and at last
announced, shamelessly, that she would accompany
him, even though he was not polite enough to invite
her. Unfortunately, she was to windward at the
time, smoking badly, and Vengeful, choking in the
fumes, lost patience.

" No," he gasped and spluttered, " you won't accompany me. You ought to know better. Go away
—go away from me, or else keep to leeward."

" Well, I never! " she answered. " Ought to know
better! Better than what? The idea! Go away
from you! Keep to leeward! You, too? I never
thought you'd insult me. And I thought you were
a gentleman."

"I'm not," he groaned. "Not with that breath in my face. Please go away."

"I will!" she screamed, in shrill, whistling accents. "I just hate you, now, I do. Whee-oop, whirroop!" and away she raced in a hot cloud of escaping steam. Then she came back, but this time to leeward.

"I'm going just the same," she snapped; "going to see you thrashed." And again she was off.

"What'll I do, Warhorse?" asked Vengeful, when the air was clear. "I don't want her traipsing along after me. Is there no way to prevent her? I'm young yet, with a good reputation, so far."

"One way."

"How?"

"Drown her," said Warhorse, grimly. "Drown her before she can work off one of her ducklings."

"But I can't do that. Have you no influence over her?"

"More than any one else here, but not enough to control her now. She is sensitive about her bad breath. But I'm rather fond of the little spitfire, and if she goes, I go too—to look out for her. It'll take most of my time, no doubt, but if I can be of any service in the mix—"

"Not at all. It'll be my row. No one else can attend to that. Hello, she's coming again."

Dolly slowly approached and stopped between the two.

"I believe," she said to Warhorse, in an even, sneering tone, "that I am supposed to ask the father of the fleet for permission to go out."

"You are," he answered, promptly, yet kindly; "and you are officially forbidden to go. You suffer from certain structural defects peculiar to your sex, and you'll surely drown yourself out there in Biscay.

Stay home where you belong—hold on, there!" he roared. "What are you doing? Don't point that thing my way "—she had swung a menacing torpedo-tube around— "Stop," he continued, almost pleadingly. "What's the matter with you, Dolly?"

"There's enough the matter with me," she answered, training a second tube on Vengeful. He shivered, and experienced the freezing sensation in his veins which comes to the bravest in time of sudden peril, yet kept his head; and Warhorse bunglingly endeavored to bring a four-inch slow-fire gun in amidships sponson to bear on the angry female. But she saw him, hissed a warning, and the gun swung back.

"I beg of you, Miss Dolly," said Vengeful, gently, "not to continue this scene. You do yourself an injustice."

There was enough of friendliness in his tone, but too little of apology.

"Do I?" she answered, wildly, her words coming explosively from a sputtering safety-valve, while her funnels belched gaseous poison. "Injustice? Not half the injustice you have done me, you wretch, you villain! You made love to me—you did—you did! And then you insult me. I've a good mind to kill you both."

"Don't, please don't," said Vengeful, in alarm. "It's all a mistake. I never meant to hurt your feelings. I didn't know. Please go away, now, and think it over."

"I won't go away. I won't think any more. I've thought until my head aches. Whee-ee-ee-oo-oo!" she shrieked. "Whah-whee-whiroo-oo-oo!" Then followed an outburst of chattering laughter, then more shrieks, while she bobbed and rolled in the choppy harbor sea. It was genuine hysterics, and wise old Warhorse knew the remedy.

"Oh, ho—ho—ho—" he laughed. It was a forced, mirthless laugh, but the agitated Miss Dolly could not differentiate. "Oh, you great big girl, aren't you ashamed? Crying over a man. Everybody's listening."

It had its effect. She emitted a few concluding sobs and sniffs, then straightened her tubes and went to her dock. The danger passed, Vengeful shook in every plate and frame, though, to give his tremors a worthier seeming to the fleet, he blew off steam from one boiler, while Warhorse, clumsily rigging out a torpedo-net as obsolete as himself, murmured, huskily, "'Hell hath no fury,' and so forth. Vengeful," he called over the noise of steam, "there's a sweet young thing for her draught, but the Bay of Biscay'll stop her, we'll hope."

It was as he said. They left together, Vengeful cautiously protesting at her coming, Warhorse endeavoring by sarcasm and ridicule to discourage her, and the young lady sulky and determined as a spoiled child. She took the lead down the channel, and, once past Cape Mathieu, disdainfully shot ahead into the troubled waters of the bay, against the loud and earnest warning of Warhorse. They came up to her a little later, rolling in the trough, cold and drenched, half full of water, and barely breathing. Warhorse swung his huge bulk around to windward of her, and, dribbling oil to smooth the sea, gathered her up to him; then he put the tube of a stomach-pump down her throat—or, technically, a six-inch suction-hose down her fore-hatch—and pumped her out. Vengeful had watched curiously, and when Dolly's breathing and heart-action were normal, and when she was warmed up enough to thank her rescuer, Warhorse called out:

"Now, Vengeful, no use turning back—we'll go on; you've the horse-power, and Dolly's weak. Give her an arm—I mean a tow-line."

"Most happy, I assure you," murmured Vengeful, politely; for the sight of the drenched and woebegone little beauty had killed his anger. He approached carefully and passed Miss Dolly the end of a four-inch steel hawser, which she tied to her forward bitts, and, being agitated, she tied an extremely hard knot—a mischance often happening in feminine experience with shoe-strings; then, with Warhorse leading and setting the pace—twelve knots an hour —the cavalcade proceeded, with the subdued young lady contentedly rocking along in the oil-smeared wake of Vengeful.

Steam-boats are hard to tow; and notoriously harder than all are torpedo-boats; yet Miss Dolly, with a docility only explainable by her state of health, slipped along in a fairly straight line until Warhorse had led them past frowning Gibraltar and into the comparatively smooth water of the Mediterranean. But here, warmed, rested, and quite recovered, she perhaps realized more keenly the humiliating position she was in, and allowed her natural perverseness to assert itself. She first called, in icily polite terms:

"Stop, if you please; I am quite able to proceed alone."

"Hold on to her, Vengeful," whispered Warhorse, who had heard the request. "She's safe now. Keep the hawser taut so she can't shake loose. No knowing what she'll be up to."

"Let go of me!" she hissed, spitefully, a little

later. " Do you hear? " But Vengeful put on speed.
Now, it may have been this increased speed, or it
may have been a shoal over which they were passing,
that made steering at the end of a tow-line rather
difficult; but these two factors together seemed
hardly enough to produce the wild yaws to starboard
and port which Dolly made after vainly waiting for
Vengeful to "unhand" her. More probably her
chagrin at the hardness of the knot she had tied
influenced her. She could not cast off, and she
strained mightily one way and the other, then,
steadying herself, held back with all her strength,
and the steel hawser sang like a harp-string. No
four-inch wire rope can withstand the strain of six
thousand horse-power pulling in one direction and
sixteen thousand pulling in the other. Dolly's nose
lifted high out of water; then the hawser snapped at
the bitts, and before she had recovered from the con-
sequent dive it had whirled ahead like a whip-lash
and sunk in a series of tangled coils alongside of
Vengeful's port rail. There was a crash, a burning
pain in his vitals, a furious racing of his port engines, and he came to a stop, with one propeller,
fouled by the steel wire, torn from the tail-shaft.
Dolly dashed by him, and before anxious old Warhorse had circled around and joined him, she was a
lessening spot on the eastern horizon.

" Great hundred-ton guns, Vengeful, who'd 'a'
thought it? " said Warhorse. " All my fault, too.
Hurt much? "

" Some," he groaned, through escaping steam.
" That doesn't bother me. What's the remedy?
Where can I doctor up? "

" Oh, it's a hospital job. Malta's the place for
you. There's a good graving-dock there."

They went ahead, Vengeful under one engine, which was yet strong enough to push him along at Warhorse's best speed. At this it was but a day and a half's run to Malta, but they were destined not to reach it so soon. Coming out of Algiers, as they passed, was Miss Dolly, and behind her an elbowing crowd of steamers, tugs, yachts, and small sailing-craft, which circled seaward and formed a ring many miles in diameter. In the center of this ring the two gladiators—the old and the young, the obsolete and the modern—came to a stop. They understood and waited; and far to sea, now a mere speck on the outer fringe of the circle, was Dolly, also waiting.

"Talk about Samson and Delilah," growled Warhorse. "This beats all the ingratitude I ever heard of. She's found Black Jack, and betrayed you, Vengeful."

"Yes, I know; but she merely found him first. I'm ready for him."

"I can't advise much, Vengeful, except, perhaps, to hit his gun-positions with small shot and his belt with big ones. Hit below the water-line—it's rulable —and keep your head by all means. I've lost all my heavy guns and am soft as pot-metal; but I'll stay in until he puts me out."

"No, stay out. It's my argument."

"Not under one screw, my boy. Your turning-circle is too small for fair-play. Here he comes. Good luck to you, Vengeful."

Black Jack was coming out, belching dark, flame-flecked smoke from his two immense funnels, and with his four heavy turret-guns cocked in the air and swinging from side to side as though to limber his muscles. He rolled and pitched and staggered in the sea, half blinded and drunk with rage; and this, with the hoarse, inarticulate roar of steam from his iron lungs, apprised Vengeful that, even had he desired it, no compromise was possible. At a mile's distance the Russian lowered his guns; but Vengeful struck the first blow—he hit him with a twelve-inch shell on the bulge of a bow sponson, and though the sponson was shattered the angle of impact was too great, and the shell glanced off without exploding, However, it sent the host of bugs infesting the Russian scurrying to hatches and apertures, and Vengeful now noticed that his own rather excited collection had sought safety within his Harveyized cuticle. He hoped that none would get hurt, for he had begun to like them; but when an answering eight-inch shell crashed into his superstructure, exploding within, he gave up this hope in the momentary agony of his own pain, and he knew by their plaintive buzzing that many were injured and perhaps killed. But there was no time to further consider them. Black Jack was now pounding him with tons of steel, and he responded in kind, while old Warhorse boomed and blustered with his own futile gun-fire, but did little harm; for on the few occasions when he could hit the enemy his shells exploded without entering the thick hide.

On the inner of two concentric circles Vengeful proceeded with barely steerage way. On the outer, Black Jack charged around at full speed. They were practically breast to breast. Each used smokeless powder, and no obstructing clouds obscured their vision; each carried four twelve-inch and a broadside battery of eight-inch guns, seven to a side; they were equally equipped with secondary "murdering guns"—the small calibered, quick-fire rifles so menacing to gun-ports and apertures; and both were possessed of the deadly, pivoted tubes amidships from which the Whitehead torpedoes could be driven. Roaring and flaming, they drilled each other's softer parts with solid shot and exploding shell, and peppered each other with a horizontal hail from their secondary guns, which rattled on the steel walls like rain on a roof. Soon, over all this riot and roar, came a mournful cry from Warhorse, and Vengeful looked, as he could, but for a moment saw nothing but a cloud of steam and yellow smoke; then out of it emerged the old warrior, low on his side and down by the head. He had mistakenly swung out of the circle in an effort to flank Black Jack, but only laid himself open to the unused starboard battery of eight-inch guns. This fire, directed solely at him, proved his undoing. With his boilers punctured and magazines exploded, he settled lower and lower; then, lifting his nose high out of water, he slid, gasping and gurgling, to the bottom of the sea. A few black, struggling mites reached the surface and swam a few moments; then a single mighty bubble rose from the depths, burst in a yellow cloud, and overwhelmed them.

Raging with fury at the death of his friend, Vengeful now fought with a strength and ferocity which would have soon ended the combat in his favor had not a slight difference between himself and Black Jack come into play as a factor in the interchange of force. The Russian's armor-belt was of equal thickness from bow to stern; Vengeful's, thicker than Black Jack's amidship, was thinner at the ends by several inches. And far down beneath the protective deck in the stern, shielded only by the thin armor-belt, was a vital part which deserved better protection—the tiller and steering-gear. A twelve-inch shell punctured the belt at the water-line, burst within, and parts of it, tearing their way downward through the frail protective deck, shattered the tiller and threw the rudder out of commission. He was comparatively helpless and in awful pain—able to steam ahead at reduced speed and turn in a circle by the pressure of his one propeller, but utterly beyond his own control. Before he could stop his starboard engines this circle, contrary to the one he had been steering, had begun; and frantic backing only placed him in a worse position, for it threw him around, facing the Russian, open to his raking fire, and unable to use his broadside batteries. The Russian halted, not slow to take advantage of his helplessness, and before he could swing himself farther around with the reversed starboard engines, he was drilled fore and aft, and half his eight-inch guns were dismounted. Now he gloomily remembered Warhorse's confident and defiant predictions at the anchorage of the treatment that Black Jack was to receive when they met. The humiliation of his position overcame his pain and momentary doubt, and when able to train his remnant of guns on his enemy, he blazed away again with renewed pertinacity, hoping for a favorable moment when he could steam suddenly ahead and ram the Russian.

But the moment did not come; and though his fire was reducing Black Jack from a high-sized battleship to a shapeless floating scrap-heap, he himself was suffering equally, if not more. Little by little his superstructure was shot to pieces, and one by one his guns were upset until he had none left but his four large turret-guns and one eight-inch gun amidships, while Black Jack's armament, well protected by armor, was still intact. In his extremity he thought of his torpedoes, but put the thought from him at once. He would die fighting, but would not first dishonor himself. So, still fighting, he awaited the end.

Yet there are craft which have no such scruples about the use of torpedoes. Stricken as he was, he noticed a commotion in the circle of spectators, and he looked for the cause. Just within the line was a small spot, and on each side of it a high wave, crested with foam. It grew larger, and as it grew it took on the form of a face—a determined little face with two defiant hawse-pipe eyes. It was Dolly, and she was coming: she was in a hurry. Gloomily speculating on her errand, wondering what was to be her next performance, Vengeful remarked a cessation of Black Jack's fire and looked back at him. He, too, was coming; he had swung himself toward Vengeful and was charging down on him, to ram— to finish the fight with one solid, smashing blow that would kill him. Faster and faster he rushed until but four hundred yards separated him from Vengeful; but faster still came Miss Dolly; then she shot between them, and only now did the demoralized Vengeful realize that her tubes were trained to port —toward the Russian. One by one as she came to bear three pointed cylinders leaped into the sea, and three streaks of bubbles darted toward the Russian; but before they reached him Dolly was riddled into a sieve by the shower of small shot which Black Jack sent from his murdering guns. Whimpering with pain, she passed out of range; but her work was done. Black Jack tossed a jagged and torn nose nearly out of water; then this nose twisted sidewise; then he quivered convulsively and a camel's hump arose amidships, while the pile of scrap-iron topping it was thrown aside. A third convulsion racked him, and his whole after end disintegrated; then over the shattered hulk lifted a mighty, many-hued cloud—all this to the music of thunderous reports and crashings as torpedoes burst and magazines exploded. Black Jack was broken in pieces, and his divided parts, wrenched asunder from unequal stress of entering water, sank separately. He had uttered no word— he was killed by the first torpedo.

Vengeful breathed hoarsely; he was sick and faint from the reaction of feeling, half dead from pain and fatigue, but yet able to rouse himself as a small craft, low down in the water, crept up to his side.

" Bless you for this, Dolly," he said. " I'll never forget it—never. I was about done for when you came."

" Yes," she said, mournfully. " But I knew it was your first fight, Mr. Vengeful, and that you were also at a disadvantage, too. I'm very sorry, now. And then, too "—she was still lower in the water and settling rapidly—" you see, I'm English myself, and I never liked him at all. I told you—you remember? I told you at home "—she was gasping now, and very close to his side—" and then, too, I love you."

She went under as she spoke the last word, but not far. While she had been talking, Vengeful had been acting—and never before had he so thoroughly appreciated the intelligence and efficiency of his entomological contingent. They aided him mightily, and just in time he slipped two mooring-chains under her; then he lifted her up.

" Now, little girl," he said, gently, when she was able to listen, " when we're doctored up a little we'll go home. And you can tell the fleet that I have found a sweetheart."

A CHEMICAL COMEDY

IT was to be a grand reception and ball—the grandest and greatest ever given on board a warship. Society—official and civil—at Malta was invited, and dressmakers and tailors worked overtime preparing society for the event. Army men of the garrison, navy men of visiting warships, furbished up gold lace and discussed international etiquette; while bandmasters, ashore and afloat, contested for possession of the latest dance-music, and drilled their men mercilessly, in the hope of being chosen. There was reason for the hope. With the *Argyll's* large crew banished to boat-work or to the bowels of the ship, there was room on her spacious upper-decks for five hundred dancers, and much music would be needed. Even the crew that expected banishment caught the infection of preparation, and each individual sailorman, in off moments snatched from polishing the ship, polished himself in the hope of a station or duty which would make him a spectator of the ball. In this spirit, and to this end, Old Man Finnegan made himself a pair of white duck trousers.

Innocent and simple-minded as a child when sober, Finnegan was yet an expert with the needle, and he brought to the making of these trousers the skill and experience of thirty years in the service. When finished, and the starch scrubbed out of them, they were a garment to be proud of, a source of envy— stitched, starred, and crow-footed in silk—and, metaphorically speaking, white as the sins of a saved sinner. Filled with and inspired by the motion of Finnegan's attenuated legs, they even possessed a flowing and wavering grace of their own—a fluttering of light and shade and an interchange of indefinite lines of beauty, due no doubt to the extremely wide bottoms he had given them—wider than the regulations prescribed.

Such little vanities of dress, though sternly repressed in the younger men, were winked at in the older, and Finnegan's new trousers aroused disapproval in the mind of but one man—an unkind person named Thompson, the third master-at-arms—who had charge of the brig, and occasionally locked Finnegan therein. As he seldom met the old man when sober, he had formed an estimate of his character based wholly upon his aggressiveness and lack of reverence for petty officers when drunk, and his disapproval of the trousers was but part of a comprehensive disapproval of Finnegan. When he found him parading the berth-deck in his new vestments he was quick to report him to the officer of the deck for dressing contrary to regulation, and as quick to escort him into the official presence. Finnegan eyed his accuser reproachfully, and saluted the officer of the deck.

"Turn around," said the latter, as he critically studied the offending trousers. Finnegan turned slowly in his tracks, once, twice, three times, and was beginning the fourth turn when the officer halted him.

"Make them yourself?" he asked.

"Yes, sir," answered Finnegan. "Made 'em for the ball, sir."

The officer smiled and said: "A remarkably good fit—a workmanlike and a seamanly job. I see nothing wrong with the dimensions, Mr. Thompson "—this to the master-at-arms—" but I *do* see something

wrong with your coat-buttons. One is a little out
of line. You'd better fix it."

The abashed petty officer departed, and the lieutenant said to Finnegan: "We will need a few neat
and tidy men on the quarter-deck. Take care of
those trousers," he said, "and perhaps we can use
you at the ball."

"Thank ye, sir," answered the delighted old man.
"I will, sir."

Now be it said that Finnegan was the last man on
board to be useful at a ball. His appointment was
merely one of the hundreds of small favors which the
old man continually received from officers and men;
but he went forward, rejoicing in the official endorse-
ment of his trousers, and became in time so puffed
up with pride that, forgetting the officer's injunction
to care for them, he gave away to less fortunate shipmates all his older and now despised duck trousers,
leaving the new ones all he had to wear whenever
the officer of the deck decreed that white was to be
the uniform of the day. This happened quite often
before the day set for the ball, but Finnegan's luck
stood by him up to within a week of this eventful
occasion; then one day, boat-work being heavy, he
was called to man an oar, with no time to change
from dress-ducks to working-ducks, and, clad in his
immaculate trousers, went ashore in a boat for a load
of contributed fireworks from the torpedo station.
Here his luck failed him; the sudden presence of the
busy boat's crew somewhat disconcerted the working
force at the station; regular work was interrupted,
and the attendant of a fuming bath of mixed acids
left it unguarded for a few moments to wait upon
the visitors. Finnegan, passing by at this time, with
his evil star in the ascendant, must needs slip, stum-

ble, and sit down in this bath of acids. He arose quickly, and yelled wth pain as he burned his fingers on his dripping trousers; then they surrounded him.

" Three parts sulphuric," said the superintendent to the youthful officer in charge. " Get him aboard quickly, or it will skin him alive when it soaks through."

They stuffed the seat of the trousers with dry cotton-waste and pulled off to the ship, with Finnegan standing erect mourning the mishap to his vestments. But even so guarded, the acids got to work; they hoisted him up howling, and sent him to the sick-bay for treatment. He averred painfully that he " felt like he'd sot on a hot stove."

He was quite recovered in a few days, but the trousers were not. Where the acids had touched they were stained in ineradicable yellow. He scrubbed them with hot fresh water and salt-water soap—as strong an alkali as is convenient to use; he rendered them clean, but they were still yellow. Excepting the scornful master-at-arms, the whole ship's company under the rating of warrant-officer offered sympathy and advice. Finnegan tried all the remedies—caustic soda, wood-ash lye, lime-water, and ammonia. Nothing availed—the yellow spot remained, and he disconsolately adopted the last advice given and painted them with a mixture of precipitated chalk and alcohol, obtained from the apothecary's clerk. This succeeded, and he proudly took his position on the quarter-deck on the day of the ball, with his trousers glistening in all their pristine purity.

His duties were nominal—merely to stand by the flagstaff at the taffrail and answer salutes of passing craft, while the quartermaster who should have attended to this was stationed at the gangway. All boats were in service, passing back and forth from the ship to the landing-stage, and soon the deck was filled with laughing, dancing humanity, which enjoyed itself to the utmost with only an occasional glance and thought for the quiet, benign old sailor who stood at the taffrail. But he thought steadily of these people, and of the good times they were having, and the good things that were being handed around to them by a corps of shore waiters. He was getting very tired, standing so long in one place, and could not be blamed for wanting a stimulant; nor could the shore waiter, who obeyed his order for " straight whisky and a leetle water on the side," be blamed for serving him, for he did not know, and Finnegan spoke with authority. It did the old man good, and in time he ordered more, and then more, and still more of the intoxicant, to the result that when the fun and laughter were at the highest his stability was at its lowest, but his intelligence was still sufficient to provide for the future. He bravely ordered a whole bottle, which, being oval in cross-section, he easily squeezed into the seat of his trousers—the best hiding-place under the circumstances.

But the waiter thought it a little irregular, and spoke to the caterer who employed him. This functionary inspected Finnegan, and spoke to an officer —it happened to be the one who had placed Finnegan there—and the officer came, and saw, and spoke to the third master-at-arms, who happened to be at hand. Mr. Thompson approached Finnegan, waving his baton officiously.

" Come! " he said, sternly, as he collared the old man. " Come—out o' this with you! Who gave you the right to get drunk on the quarter-deck? "

"Not drunk, Misher Thompson—jess 'joyin' m'shelf," protested Finnegan.

Those nearest began to be interested, and a few ladies moved away. Mr. Thompson was wisely and justly disposed to forestall further embarrassment; he swung Finnegan around at arm's-length and gave him a sharp spank with his baton.

There was a dull, puffing report—something like the cough of a pneumatic tube—a faint cloud of smoke in the air, the rattling of a bottle on the deck, and an aged sailor racing forward through the astonished throng of guests, yelling incoherently and holding his hand where the seat of his trousers should be, but was not—this section of the rear elevation being replaced by an equal expanse of still intact blue flannel underwear. Leaving behind him a trail of sparks and thinning smoke, the human comet disappeared into the superstructure, while Mr. Thompson, his eyes bulging from his head, followed with the unbroken bottle.

Officers and guests—among the latter the superintendent of the torpedo station—crowded below, and found Finnegan backed up against a bulkhead, surrounded by questioning shipmates. He was sober now, but shocked almost out of his faculties. He could only stammer, "He shot me—he shot me, an' busted the bloomin' bottle."

"But I didn't shoot him," said the master-at-arms, holding up the bottle. "And I didn't bust the bottle. This one dropped out, and it must ha' been something else; but there's no broken glass around."

They examined the vacancy in the trousers. The edge of the cloth was seared by flame, and a few sparks still smoldered.

"Are you the man who sat down in the dipping-tub ashore at the station?" asked the superinten-dent.

"Yes, sir," answered Finnegan.

"Same trousers?"

"Yes, sir."

"What did you do to them? Try to scrub the yellow out of them?"

"Yes, sir. Scrubbed wi' everything, but couldn't get 'em white, an' so I painted 'em."

"Scrubbed with soda?" asked the superintendent, a grin coming to his face.

"Yes, sir; an' soap an' lime-water, an' then I had to paint 'em wi' chalk-paint."

The superintendent turned to the master-at-arms. "Did he have that bottle tucked into his trousers?"

"Must have, sir. Everything carried away all of a sudden, and it fell out. I just hit him a light tap."

The superintendent sat down on a convenient bench, uttering strange, explosive sounds. It was some moments before these sounds began to take on the pitch and timbre of laughter, and some moments later when he could speak intelligibly. Then he gasped between paroxysms: "Every detail followed out—soaking in acids, scrubbing with soda, rinsing well, undoubtedly all free acids expelled, lime-water and precipitated chalk. Gentlemen, he turned the seat of his trousers into gun-cotton, and it exploded when struck."

But this did not impress Finnegan. While he lived he regarded the master-at-arms as an enemy who had attempted his life.

A HERO OF THE CLOTH

THE *Argyll's* crew had been dismissed from quarters, and the usual sea-drill was now on. Three men, idlers for the moment, met casually on the after superstructure-deck and discussed—not the subject uppermost in the minds of the whole ship's company, the prospect of meeting the enemy before dark—but Finnegan—poor, disgraceful old Finnegan, the ship's drunkard, who had appeared at quarters fairly steady of legs and voice, but the center of an atmosphere of whisky fumes which, like other radiant energy, decreased in potency only with the square of the distance. The three were the first lieutenant, the surgeon, and the chaplain.

"Wonder where he gets it?" the surgeon had remarked. "My stores are intact; stewards don't miss any."

"Makes it," answered Mr. Clarkson, the first lieutenant, twirling a couple of large keys around his finger by the ring. "Makes it, inside or out. He may have a private still in his ditty-box, or else he swallows corn, rice, barley—anything at all—and distills it in his stomach. I've brigged him until I'm tired; it does him no good."

"Let him alone, then," said the surgeon.

"A horrible enslavement!—truly horrible!" said the chaplain, a young man, with fine eyes, delicate features, and a rather weak mouth. "What can be done for him? I have talked with him when sober, and he promises; I have prayed for him when he has broken his promise, and that is all that I can do. I cannot approach him when in that condition. It is unchristianlike, I know, but I cannot. The disgust and horror inspired by drunkenness are overmastering. I fear I am out of place here."

"Nonsense!" laughed the surgeon. "Let Finnegan alone. When sober, he's a fool; when drunk, a capable man—at least, he is at his best. Finnegan's cerebral connections are reversed. Stop his nourishment, and you make him feel as *you* would if *you* filled up; he'd have all the frills—languor, remorse, double vision, liver out of plumb—bad headache—"

"Hello! what's up?" interrupted Mr. Clarkson, laying the keys on a gun-breech and picking up a weather-worn pair of binoculars which lay around for any one's use. He looked ahead, where bunting was flying from the signal-yard of the flagship. A first lieutenant usually has most of the naval code in his head.

"Double column," he said, as he made out the signal. "A matter for the man at the wheel and the engineer; but I'll go forward."

"And I'll get down to my sick men," said the surgeon, also turning toward the steps. "And, say, Mr. Parmlee," he added, from the top stair, "better give Finnegan up, or hand him over to me."

He followed the first lieutenant, and the young chaplain, with troubled face, leaned against the six-pounder, on which lay the keys left by Mr. Clarkson. He spied them, and absently picked them up; then he peered forward and about, watching the methodical shifting of ships from single to double column. Soon he was conscious that some one had ascended the steps, and was now behind him. Turning, he saw Finnegan, who seemed, in the strong sunlight, to be a little more watery-eyed, a little more unsure of his footing—in short, a little drunker—than he had been at quarters. He shuffled his feet, smiled vacantly, and knuckled his forehead. Mr. Parmlee shuddered, and moved over toward a ventilator, on the lower rim of which Mr. Clarkson had placed the binoculars. He lifted them to his eyes—an operation requiring both hands—and nervously scanned the ships of the squadron. Finnegan approached.

" 'Xcuse me, sir," he began, but the chaplain moved away.

" 'Xcuse me, sir," continued Finnegan, following, " but did ye know, sir—"

" Why do you not go down to your duties?" asked the disturbed chaplain. " Have you nothing to do?"

" Yes, sir; but jess wanted to ask ye, sir—"

Mr. Parmlee moved on, and Finnegan shuffled after.

" Jess wanted to ask ye, sir, if ye didn't want the keys."

At this moment Mr. Clarkson appeared, hurrying aft on the superstructure. He spied the grinning, stumbling, and aggressive Finnegan, and noticed the annoyance, which was almost fear, in the face of the retreating chaplain.

" What's this?" he said, sharply. " What are you doing up here? Down below with you, quickly! Corporal," he called down to the quarter-deck, " take this man below and hand him over to the master-at-arms. Put him in the brig for drunkenness."

So Finnegan was led down. His hammock was slung in the brig—the slatted apartment in which misbehaving man-of-war's-men are confined—and he turned into dreamless sleep, while his mates above drilled and perspired, and the conscience-stricken chaplain, locked in his room, prayed fervently for courage and strength and self-control to aid him in his duty to the souls in his care.

At dinner time he visited the brig; but Finnegan's snores apprised him that he was not yet in a receptive or responsive condition, and with a sigh of mingled shame and relief—for the good intent had cost him a struggle—he left him to finish his sleep. At two o'clock Finnegan wakened, sober. He vociferated loudly for water, complaining of " hot coppers," and, when this was given him, he asked for his dinner. A sympathetic and envious messmate brought what had been saved for him, and, on Finnegan's inquiring what he was " in for," told him that he had pursued the sky-pilot around the superstructure-deck, intent upon braining him with a breech-block, and that it had taken six marines and a corporal to subdue him. He would certainly be court-martialed and dismissed the service in disgrace. To which Finnegan responded, mournfully, that he " didn't 'member nothin' about it."

But the tale reduced him to a penitent frame of mind, which inspired him to respond warmly to the forgiving chaplain's prayers when he called a little later; and, as Mr. Parmlee, with a delicacy equaled only by Finnegan's, made no reference to the cause of his incarceration, but merely begged that, for his sake, if not his own, he would stop drinking, the remorseful prisoner stoutly averred that the chaplain was a good man, that he would oblige him—that he had taken his last drink, and henceforth would lead a sober life. And Mr. Parmlee departed, with reviving hope for Finnegan and a glowing sense of duty well performed.

He sought the after superstructure-deck, where he had talked with the surgeon and first lieutenant in the morning, and here he found the former, peering through the binoculars at a long line of black spots drawn up in battle formation on the horizon ahead.

"The enemy, Mr. Parmlee," he said, handing him the glasses. "We'll be hammer and tongs at him in half an hour. All ready in your department? I'm prepared—knives and saws all sharpened, gallons of chloroform, tubs of water, bales of bandages, everything ready for the good work."

The chaplain took the glasses, but, before he could adjust them to his eyes or reply to the surgeon, the bugle-call to general quarters sounded, and for a few minutes the great battle-ship seemed a floating bedlam. Men swarmed from below, scurried about, sprang from high places to low, from low to high; they did things to boats, davits, ventilators, gratings, ladders, and hatches; then, stripping their shirts from their backs as they ran, disappeared through ports, hatches, and companions. And now, up the steps on a run, anxious of face and wild of eye, came Mr. Clarkson.

"Did you see the keys?" he asked, hurriedly, as he approached and looked about. "The keys of the magazines? I had them at inspection quarters, and I had them up here. What did I do with them? Did either of you notice?"

"No," they both answered, as they aided in the search. "Saw them on your finger," added the surgeon. "Didn't you take them with you?"

"No, no; I must have laid them down here somewhere. I went right to my room, but don't remember putting them away, and they're not there now. Great Heavens, this is awful! I'll be laughed out of the service, if not court-martialed and broken. Got machinists at work cutting round the locks, but it's a four-hours' job, and we'll be at it in no time. And we can't fight—we can't fire a gun; and we're the only ship in the lot fit to engage that crowd ahead. I haven't told the old man yet—not yet, while there's a chance to find them. Great God! Where are they, anyhow?"

He groaned as he mopped the perspiration from his face.

"I remember, Mr. Clarkson," said the chaplain, thoughtfully. "You laid them here on this gun, and then—"

"Yes, by George, I did!" responded the officer, joyously, as he rummaged about the gun-breech and the deck beneath; "but where are they now?" he asked, and his face took on the troubled look.

"And then," continued the chaplain, doubtfully, "after you had gone, I picked them up."

"Where did you put them?"

"I have not the slightest idea—I do not know— I cannot remember."

"Try—for God's sake, try! Did you take them below?"

"I am positive that I did not. Still, we can look in my room. I was somewhat agitated at the time."

Down rushed the three to the chaplain's room; but the closest search failed to discover the missing keys.

"What were you agitated about, Mr. Parmlee?" asked the surgeon.

"Why, I confessed to you my weakness, did I not? It was Finnegan's incomprehensible behavior. He was trying to accost me."

"Drunk, was he? Then there was method in his incomprehensible behavior. What did he say? What did he do?"

"Did he have the keys?" asked the lieutenant, starting toward the door.

"Wait. Let me think," said Mr. Parmlee, with

his hand pressing his forehead. " I believe that he did say something about keys; but what it was I cannot remember."

" Come on," said Mr. Clarkson, and away they hurried to the brig, where a sentry admitted them. Finnegan was asleep again, but they ruthlessly awakened him, and he rolled out of his hammock, blinking his eyes and knuckling his brow. He was as sober as the chaplain.

" I don't know nothin' about it, sir," he stuttered. " I wouldn't ha' done nothin' only I was loaded, sir. He's a good man, sir, an' I wouldn't hurt a hair of his head."

" Finnegan," demanded the lieutenant, impressively, " what did you do with the keys? "

" Keys, sir! What keys? "

" The keys that you found on the superstructure-deck just before you were taken down by the corporal."

" I don't 'member anything 'bout that, sir. They told me I 'most killed the chaplain, but I don't know anything 'bout it, sir. I wouldn't hurt him for all the world, sir."

Mr. Clarkson groaned in despair.

" Finnegan," interposed the chaplain, " try and think. Don't you remember that you wanted to speak with me? Don't you remember saying something about keys? I cannot remember what it was. Can you? Try and think."

But Finnegan's bewilderment only increased, and he protested again that he meant no harm, and knew nothing of what he had done.

" Come outside," said the surgeon; and they followed through the door, beyond Finnegan's range of hearing.

"There is but one thing to do," he said. "We must get him drunk again. If we knew his brand of whisky, it would be better; but we must get him as drunk as he was, and quickly, too. Then he will remember what was on his mind up there. He must be assisted, too. We have no time to lose, and he might take too long to load up—stomach's too sour to take in much right away. Can you spare the time, Clarkson?"

"No, no—Heavens, no! I ought to be on the bridge now, or in the turret."

"I have no time, either. Candidly, Mr. Parmlee, I was joking when I said I was prepared for wounded men. I am not. My sick-bay is full of patients and everything is in confusion. I belong there now. It is for you."

"I!" exclaimed the chaplain, in accents of horror. "I—make him intoxicated? I cannot!"

"You can," said the surgeon, vehemently. "You and the captain are the only idlers in the ship when going into action. And the captain must not be told, unless the case is hopeless. Would you see Clarkson ruined for your fault in mislaying those keys? You or old Finnegan had them last, you know. And it won't help matters to lay it on to Finnegan. Would you see this fleet defeated to-day? Are you under no obligations to your country? Your duty, Mr. Parmlee, requires that you lay aside all personal scruples and get this man drunk as quickly as you can. You must pour it down his throat—and, if necessary, you must drink with him to encourage him."

"I cannot! I—a minister of the Gospel? Only this afternoon I adjured him to give it up. No; is there no other way? Are there no duplicate keys?"

"There were," answered the agonized lieutenant, "but they went overboard, and have not been replaced. Decide quickly, Mr. Parmlee. You are the only man aboard with leisure at this moment. Every one else, from the captain down to the band-drummer, has a station and a duty."

"And you will go down with Clarkson," added the surgeon, warmly. "You are the one who really lost the keys. Shall we tell this to the captain? It won't do to say that Finnegan lost them."

"That consideration does not influence me," said the chaplain, with dignity. "Gentlemen, I am a novice—in fact, I have never tasted the poison—but I will endeavor to perform this distasteful task."

"Good for you, chaplain!" said the surgeon, slapping him on the back. "Go to your room, quick. I'll send up the booze from the bay, and Clarkson can sentence Finnegan to a bad half-hour with you for spiritual instruction. That's the game, Clarkson. Prisoner released from the brig on eve of action wants spiritual help. Now, I'm off."

They separated, the surgeon going down to the sick-bay, the first lieutenant to the bridge, and the chaplain to his room, where he fell upon his knees in prayer. In a few minutes a knock at the door aroused him, and he admitted an apothecary's clerk, who, when he had deposited an opened quart bottle, some glasses, and a pitcher of water on the table, respectfully, though rather facetiously, asked him for a little of the "Dutch courage."

"Certainly," said Mr. Parmlee, with a ghastly smile. "Help yourself. But you will kindly say nothing, I hope, to others about this service of stimulant. I—you see—in fact, I am in poor health, and this is my first experience of war."

"That's all right, sir," answered the man, with a grin, as he helped himself. "Lots of it floatin' round for every one outside of our department, but old Pills is meaner 'n a pawnbroker on this question."

He drank and departed, and soon another knock on the door announced the arrival of the wondering Finnegan, in charge of the brig sentry, who smiled hugely as he said:

"The first lieutenant's compliments, sir, and he wants to know would you pray for Finnegan 'fore he goes to his station, sir."

"Why, yes, of course—most certainly. Step in, Finnegan," responded the chaplain. "Step in and be seated."

Finnegan entered, seated himself on the edge of a chair, and the sentry closed the door.

"I didn't 'xpect to be prayed for, sir," said Finnegan, with reproach in his voice. "I swore off, all right, an' I'll stick to it on your account, sir, 'cause you're a good man, an' didn't go for to have me court-martialed; but I can't pray, sir—not a little bit."

"No, no, certainly not, Finnegan," answered the chaplain, drawing another chair up to the table. "This is just a ruse—a little ruse of mine to make it easier for you to reform. You know—that is—you see, there are different roads to the same end, or, rather, more than one method of—well, I am afraid I express myself poorly. I mean—"

"More'n one way to skin a cat, sir? That what you mean?"

"Well, possibly. Your metaphor, in a measure, covers the problem before us," answered the chaplain, smiling painfully as he wiped the perspiration from his brow. "I mean that a sudden deprivation of stimulants to one thoroughly accustomed to their use is apt to produce harmful effects on the nervous system; and that, in your case—valuable man that you are to this ship—it is deemed by the first lieutenant, the surgeon, and myself advisable, as we will shortly engage the enemy, to provide you with a reasonable quantity of the liquor to which you lately have been accustomed."

"Some o' the hair o' the dog, sir. You mean I'm to have a drink, sir?"

"Yes, Finnegan, help yourself."

"But, say, chaplain," said Finnegan, his hand pausing in mid-passage toward the bottle, "I swore off, you know—"

"Yes, but hurry. You will be needed at your station soon."

"Well, if you say it's all right, it must be all right, sir. But I'd feel better if you'd take a nip, too, sir. I don't go for to presume you'd be drinkin' with me, sir, but you swore me off—"

"I will drink with you. Help yourself—hurry!"

"Thank ye, sir."

Finnegan poured out a share of the stimulant, and so large was it that the chaplain, judging by the comparison, made his own smaller portion slightly larger than an average man cares to swallow at once. They drank together, without toast or comment.

Finnegan sighed gratefully as he put down the glass; but Mr. Parmlee, with streaming eyes and choked breath, grasped the water-pitcher, and, disdaining table etiquette, raised it to his lips and flushed his blistered œsophagus with fully a pint of water. Then he pressed his hands to his stomach and glared wildly about the room.

"I can see yer not used to it, sir," remarked Finnegan, in a patronizing tone. "Have yer chaser all ready next time, sir; and p'rhaps ye'd better water it a little, till ye can take it straight."

"Yes," gasped the chaplain, "perhaps I had. As you say, I am not an adept—in fact, I drink very little; but, of course, this need not influence you. It is very good liquor, is it not? From what I know about whisky I should say that it is very good—very good, indeed. Shall we have another?"

"What, so soon, sir? Well, if you says so, all right, sir."

Finnegan filled his glass again, and volunteered to adjust in Mr. Parmlee's the right proportions of whisky and water; but his judgment was certainly biased by his own experience, to the result that the chaplain imbibed a second portion of the whisky fully as large as the other. Tempered by the water, it went down easier, but, coupled with the first, soon produced the later effects. His face took on an expression of fierce gravity, much in contrast to the amiable countenance of Finnegan. Ten minutes passed before either spoke; then Finnegan, judging, no doubt, that precious time was slipping by, coughed gently and said: "Shall we hit it up again, sir?"

"Shertainly, shertainly," answered Mr. Parmlee, reaching a wavering hand toward the bottle; but Finnegan had it and was helping himself.

"Thash right, Finnegan—thash right. Don't be 'fraid. Very good whishky. 'Hit up again.' Very forshfu' figure of speesh. Whash th' other? Lesh shee—whash th' other?" Mr. Parmlee scratched his head and nearly fell off the chair from the disturbance of his center of gravity. He clutched the table and continued: "Lesh shee—'hair on the dog'? Thash it. An' whash th' other? Shkin cats? Thash th' other. 'Good way shkin cats.' Very epi-epigig —very ep-igramash-ical. Wonder whash matter? Feel shea-shick. Ship mush be pitching. An' I shee two of you—two Finnegans. Thash funny."

"Shall I help you again, sir?" asked the still intact Finnegan.

"Yesh, if you pleash. Very good whishky. Not 'customed to it, but got duty to p'form—duty to my country an' to my bro'r offisher."

"Here ye are, sir."

The door is not locked. Let us leave this painful scene and hie us to the bridge, where Mr. Clarkson stands, with others, as nearly insane as a man may become with an outward semblance of sanity. With him are the captain, the navigating officer, and the gunnery and torpedo lieutenants. Aloft in the fighting-top an officer manipulates a range-finder and occasionally calls out results. The nearest ship of the opposing fleet is but seven miles away, and Mr. Clarkson knows by inspection of his watch that Finnegan has been closeted but twenty minutes with the chaplain. He has paced up and down, shuffled his feet, wiped his face, and made such inane and sometimes explosive comments on the situation that his manner and mood have become apparent to all. And the calm, grim, imperturbable captain, who has been observing him furtively for the last five minutes, at last speaks.

"You say that everything is ready below, Mr. Clarkson?"

"Y-y-yes, sir," answered the officer, paling at the lie which might ruin him.

"You seem strangely upset. Yet I have seen you under fire as steady as a rock. Anything the matter?"

"A jumping toothache, sir."

"Well, well—a toothache! Go down at once to the surgeon. No man may work and fight with a jumping toothache. Hurry, though, for, by all indications, we will commence firing within five minutes."

Mr. Clarkson hurried. He rushed down the bridge steps, at the risk of his neck; he raced aft on the main-deck and down to the gun-room, where he hurled himself bodily at the chaplain's door, hardly taking time to turn the knob. It opened, and a glance apprised the officer of the situation. Mr. Parmlee sat with his head bowed on the table, breathing heavily; the bottle was three-quarters empty, and Finnegan, in the act of putting down his glass as the officer entered, stood erect and saluted. The room reeked with the odor of whisky, but Finnegan was most certainly in a normal condition.

"Finnegan!" yelled the lieutenant in his ear. "Where did you put the keys—the keys you found on the superstructure-deck this morning—the keys that Mr. Parmlee lost?"

"I didn't have 'em, sir," answered Finnegan. "I only wanted to tell the chaplain 'bout 'em; but he didn't seem to care, and then you put me under arrest, sir."

"But what about them? Where are they?"

"They went down the ventilator, sir. He put 'em on the lower rim, 'longside the glasses, an' when he picked up the glasses he knocked 'em down."

" Which ventilator? "

" Last one aft on the port side, sir."

Mr. Clarkson shot out of the door. He was gone five minutes—long enough for an active man to visit the coal bunkers and the two magazines in the bowels of the ship, and not too long, perhaps, for a sufferer from toothache to obtain treatment in a crowded sick-bay. He returned with the face of a happy boy and assisted Finnegan in lifting Mr. Parmlee to his berth.

" I don't understand this at all, sir," Finnegan ventured to remark.

" Don't try," said Mr. Clarkson, seizing him by the two shoulders and looking him squarely in the face. " Don't try—and, Finnegan "—he gave the old fellow a vigorous shake—" say nothing about this, and I'll see that you have all you need of—of this stuff, that keeps you in good condition. Understand?—all you need. *But don't tell on the chaplain!* "

" Very good, sir—thank ye. I won't blab on him, sir. He's a good, kind man, but any one can see, sir, that he can't stand much of it."

" Go to your station, Finnegan."

Finnegan passed through the door, and Mr. Clarkson drank some of the whisky. Perhaps he needed it more than did Finnegan.

Through the fierce sea-fight that wound up that day—through the thunderous uproar of heavy guns and the rattling, ringing, and crashing of hostile shot and shell—the worthiest hero of that ship's company slept the sleep of the overtaxed and exhausted. He had done his utmost and had given his all.

For the apothecary's clerk betrayed him.

THE SUBCONSCIOUS FINNEGAN

THEY were on the after part of the superstructure-deck—the loafing-place of officers off duty —and they were discussing poor old Finnegan. Mr. Clarkson, the executive, was there; Mr. Felton, Mr. Parmlee, the chaplain; Dr. Bryce, the surgeon; and the chief engineer—a man skeptical of all things unproved by mathematics. Finnegan was down in the " brig "—the slatted ship's prison on the berth-deck—sleeping off the effects of the drink that had undone him; and so could take no part in a discussion affecting himself. But he had an able champion in the surgeon, who had just answered the chaplain's assertion that he was past redemption.

" Not at all," he had said. " All he needs is enough Dutch courage, and he is a better man than he ever could have been without it."

" But is not that an index of failure? " asked Mr. Parmlee. " God never created man in his image to then depend upon whisky."

" How do you know? If He made man, He made whisky."

" He's right, Mr. Parmlee," said Clarkson. " Of course he can get drunk if he drinks enough; but it takes an amount that would kill an ordinary man. And what would paralyze an ordinary man—say a quart—is just Finnegan's load. It wakes him up, and he's at his best."

" But isn't it funny," ventured young Mr. Felton, " that it should work so differently on Finnegan? Even granting his superior capacity, at no stage of intoxication is the ordinary man roused to his fullest mental activity."

"Yes, he is," quickly rejoined the surgeon. "Only he doesn't realize it. The mood passes too quickly. In Finnegan's case, seasoned as he is, he can make the most of this stage. In fact, he falls back upon his subconscious mind. And the subconscious mind, gentlemen, is almost supreme in its intelligence and knowledge."

"What do you mean by the subconscious mind?" asked the engineer. "Is it a real thing—an entity —or only a figure of speech?"

"An entity—the primordial brain; the intelligence that cares for drunkards and children, for sleepwalkers, blind men, homing pigeons, and exiled cats. It sees without eyes, hears without ears, and talks, or, at least, communicates with other minds in sympathy with itself. We call this telepathy. It is the language of brute creation."

"And where in the body is this primordial brain, doctor?" asked Mr. Felton. "In the head?"

"Right where you carry the brain of your Whitehead torpedoes, Mr. Felton—amidships—distributed along the spinal-cord and in the solar plexus."

"I know that a punch in the solar plexus is often fatal."

"Exactly—fatal as a bullet through the head. When that brain is disturbed, if only for a second or two, the heart stops beating for lack of orders to beat. That brain attends to all involuntary bodily functions."

"So Finnegan's brain is in his stomach," commented the engineer. "Always thought so."

"It's hardly a brain, though," said the surgeon. "The brain is merely the central station of the five senses, and what it knows it receives through them. This subconscious mind, as I said, is supreme. It knows the time without the help of the clock. You've often wakened at eight bells just before the bell strikes, haven't you? It is clairvoyant, telepathic, and absolute in memory. It remembers for life every face passed in a crowd, every word heard from babyhood to death. And the strange part of all this is that in spite of its wonderful powers it will believe what is told it, no matter how absurd."

" Is that why a hypnotist can make such a fool of a fellow? " asked Mr. Felton.

" Exactly. The subconscious, or subjective, mind believes itself a dog, and proceeds to bark—or a cat, horse, scrubwoman, or whatever is suggested to it. It lacks the power of criticism, and is innocent of suspicion."

" Do you think," said the executive, " that if Finnegan's subconscious mind were told that he didn't like whisky, it would believe it? "

" Not only would it believe, but would act upon it, and Finnegan would lose the taste for it."

" Then, in the name of all that is good, let us try," said the chaplain, enthusiastically.

" There are strong reasons why we should not," said the surgeon. " First, Finnegan is already in the subjective state when drunk, and bound by auto-suggestions in favor of whisky which might overcome any from an outside source that would conflict. When sober he is a nervous wreck, unable to be hypnotized, too irritable and antagonistic, you see. Second, he is better off under his present form of subjectiveness than he ever could be otherwise, either as a normal man or a continuous hypnotic subject. Third, it might kill him. Though the spirit might be willing, as Mr. Parmlee would say, the flesh is weak, and with his whole nervous system attuned to alcohol—every brain-cell charged with it—he could not survive the change."

"Well," said Mr. Clarkson, determinedly, "you could watch him, couldn't you, and, if things went wrong, straighten him up with whisky?"

"Yes, provided I could make things go wrong. I am not a hypnotist."

"What is a hypnotist?"

"Any person who is positive, for lack of a better term, compared with the subject's negative. Any person whom Finnegan fears, loves, or respects—in short, any one who has a commanding influence over him, can hypnotize him by the ordinary methods."

"I am all that," said Mr. Clarkson. "What are the methods?"

"The simplest is to induce the subject to look steadily at some bright object—such as a brass ball or button, a dancing spot of sunlight reflected from a mirror, a star in the sky, or anything that will fix the attention and slowly distract the objective mind—the brain—from the world. Then that brain will doze off, as in sleep, and the subjective brain will arise to the situation."

Mr. Clarkson stepped to the break of the superstructure, then looked back and said to the surgeon: "He's been in about four hours. Is that long enough to sober him up?"

"Plenty, if he has slept."

"Always does," said Mr. Clarkson. Then he called down to an orderly to direct the master-at-arms to release Finnegan from the brig and bring him up.

Finnegan soon appeared, in the custody of the master-at-arms, unkempt and unwashed, his gray

hair tousled over his wrinkled face, his eyes blinking
stupidly in the strong sunlight. " Just waked up,
sir," said the master-at-arms. " Hungry and on
very bad terms with himself. His language is very
disrespectful to the service, sir."

" Very well," said the executive officer. " We'll
attend to him."

The petty officer departed; Finnegan looked sourly
around on his investigators and saluted. They returned the scrutiny, and all answered the salute.

" Finnegan," said Mr. Clarkson, sternly, " fix
your eyes on that gilt ball of the flagstaff. Look at
it steadily and see if you can see anything wrong
with it."

" Got a twist in it, sir. The sheave-holes don't
lay 'thwartships. One's forrard and t'other aft.
But I'm an old man, sir; I can't climb like I—"

" Never mind. Look at it."

Finnegan looked. " Wants a new coat, sir," he
said at length.

" Yes, we know that. What else? Look steadily
at it."

" Flagstaff has a little list to port, sir. It got
warped in the gravin'-dock at Malta, when we lay
one way so long."

" That's all right. Look at it. Look hard."

Finnegan stared at the ball; the rest stared at him,
Mr. Parmlee with almost boyish eagerness in his face,
the engineer with grinning incredulity.

" Give him a drink," said the latter, as Finnegan's
eyes wandered from the gilt globe to their faces.
The old fellow's face brightened.

" Good idea," remarked the surgeon. " It'll steady
him a little."

He sent an order down to the sick-bay by the

orderly, and soon a stiff allowance—a full "second mate's drink"—arrived from below. Finnegan imbibed it gratefully.

"That reached his subconsciousness, I'll wager," said the engineer.

"Thanky, sir," said Finnegan, wiping his mouth and looking at the surgeon. "It's very good stuff, sir; but if I might make bold to say so, sir, Mr. Parmlee, askin' his pardon, has much better."

"Finnegan!" exclaimed the agitated chaplain, with his face aflame.

The surgeon and executive smiled, but the rest roared.

"Never mind that, Finnegan," said Mr. Clarkson. "Look at that ball."

Again the old man stared at the ball, and again his eyes wandered. The surgeon beckoned the first lieutenant aside. "Afraid it won't work, Clarkson," he said, softly. "Try pure mesmerism. Sit him down, make him look into your eyes, and pass your hands downward before his face. Command him mentally—that is, *will*—that he go to sleep. It is possible that you have projective force. There is such a thing distinct from the subjective power of the other."

"Sit down on that skylight," commanded Mr. Clarkson, approaching Finnegan.

"All right, sir, if you say so," whined the old man. "But you want ter square me wi' the master-at-arms, sir. Last time I sat down on a skylight he—"

"Never mind the master-at-arms. Sit down!"

Finnegan gingerly seated himself, looking around nervously. Mr. Clarkson faced him and said, sternly, "Look me right in the eyes."

Finnegan did so. Mr. Clarkson elevated his hands and brought them down with a sweeping gesture before the face of the victim. The victim looked curiously at him. Again the officer raised his hands and brought them down, while his face assumed a stern, almost fierce expression.

"Tell him he's sleepy," whispered the surgeon in his ear.

"You are sleepy," said the officer. "You are very sleepy. Go to sleep."

"I never could sleep on deck, sir," protested the old fellow. "Some men can calk off the whole watch in a coil o' rope, but I have to turn in, sir."

Mr. Clarkson continued the passes. "You are sleepy," he repeated. "Look me right in the eyes and go to sleep."

"I ain't sleepy a bit, sir."

"Look me in the eyes!" sternly commanded the lieutenant. Finnegan obeyed him, and the mesmeric passes continued.

"They do say, sir," said Finnegan, with a half-confident, half-deprecating smile—"the fellows on the fo'castle, I mean, sir—they say that at times—askin' yer pardon, I say—that sometimes yer not quite yerself, sir—that is, not quite right in yer head, sir."

A roar of laughter went up, and Mr. Clarkson desisted.

"That'll do," he said, angrily. "Go down below!"

The old man arose, saluted, and departed.

"Did he speak from his subconscious knowledge?" asked the engineer. "What do you think, doctor? Did Finnegan diagnose correctly?"

"Not at all," answered the surgeon, gravely.

" The experiment has failed because of contrary auto-suggestion, and because of the presence of skepticism. An incredulous engineer, whose soul never rises above grate-surface and coal supply, will spoil any psychic investigation. Clarkson, does Finnegan ever take the wheel? "

" No, he's not a quartermaster."

" Can you stretch a point and put him there to-night? "

" Why, yes; but what for? "

" This: I've talked with many sailors in my time, and they all agree that when at the wheel on a dark night with no stars to range by—so that they have to steer by compass alone—they get into a sleepy, half-comatose condition, in which they calculate their pay, dream of home, hear voices, talk to people a thousand miles away, and, in fact, give every evidence to me of being in the subjective state. Yet they steer a straight course. The compass, brightly illuminated, hypnotizes them. It might hypnotize Finnegan. But there must be no engineers around." He glanced meaningly at the culprit, who left the party with a grin on his face.

" Go ahead with your experiment," he said, over his shoulder. " I prefer sleep."

" Finnegan's a good helmsman," said Mr. Clarkson. " I'll try him in the first watch. It'll be a dark night."

It was more than a dark night. There was fog; and the big steel battle-ship charged through it with a dozen lookouts posted about the decks and up aloft. Mr. Felton, officer of the deck from eight to twelve, stood near the bridge binnacle, peering into the blanket of darkness ahead. On the other side of the binnacle stood his assistant, a sublieutenant, whose chief business on watch was to look at the compass and say nothing. Though not a watch officer, Mr. Clarkson was on the bridge, as were the surgeon and chaplain; and Finnegan was alone in the pilot-house —where he had gone grumblingly—while the rightful incumbent of the trick, a quartermaster, kept watch beside the door on the bridge with orders to " stand by " to relieve Finnegan at a second's notice.

" How long, doctor," asked the executive officer, as the four stood at the bridge rail, where Finnegan's face was easily visible through an opened window, " before he will be in condition? "

" Can't tell. Perhaps he won't be. But the experiment is worth trying. Mr. Parmlee is the man to work it. He has a soft, persuasive voice, and Finnegan wouldn't be too startled. You or I, Clarkson, would frighten him."

" What must I do? " asked the chaplain.

" Oh, after a while, when he has dimmed his eyes and brain by looking at the compass, sneak in and talk gently to him. Simply tell him that he doesn't like whisky—that he only thinks so, but is mistaken. Don't be too sudden; stand beside him for a while without speaking. Stand for half an hour, to throw him off his guard. Lecture him mildly but insistently."

" And you think," said the executive, " that such talk will pass the scrutiny of his brain and reach his subconsciousness? "

" Yes, provided that brain is off its guard. You must know that the only time that oral suggestion is possible is when one brain is going off duty and the other coming on. At this time they are in communication, and a statement delivered to one will be understood by the other. Auto-suggestion, too, is only available at this stage."

" What is auto-suggestion? " asked Mr. Felton.

" A suggestion made to yourself. You know that if you go to sleep humming a tune, you will wake up humming it in the morning."

" Yes," assented the young lieutenant. " And if I go to sleep desiring to waken at three, four, or five o'clock, I will invariably do so to the minute. Is it the same faculty? "

" The same. Any man can do it. And if Finnegan could determinedly say to himself just before going to sleep that he didn't like and didn't need whisky, he would wake in the morning with the thought—carried through the night by the subconscious mind—and be benefited while he slept by the reformatory work on the cells of the brain and nervous system of that believing subconsciousness."

" Then, why can't he be instructed and do it himself? " asked Mr. Clarkson.

" Because such an effort would require more will power than Finnegan possesses. With will power to suggest it to himself he would not need his subconscious help. He would simply quit. But Finnegan needs outside suggestion."

" Has this suggestion anything to do with mesmerism? " asked the chaplain.

" Yes and no. A mesmerist is always a hypnotist, but a hypnotist need not be a mesmerist. Mesmerism is still a mystery. A mesmerist is one possessing strong projective power, who exercises this power mainly by making passes before the face of the subject. It is as though a subtle emanation of some force left his finger-tips and affected the subject. A hypnotist is one who takes advantage of the voluntary surrender of the subject, and suggests, either by voice or strong mental effort. This last is the 'absent treatment' of Christian Science."

"Then there really is something in that," said Mr. Parmlee.

"Science, but no Christianity," answered the surgeon. "Absent treatment is merely telepathy—a suggestion delivered by the operator to his own inner self, which sends it during sleep to the inner self of the patient."

"Wouldn't that work on Finnegan?" asked Mr. Clarkson.

"Certainly, if you've the time and patience to keep it up, night after night. Have you? I haven't."

"I have," said the chaplain, eagerly.

"But, Mr. Parmlee," said the surgeon, gently, "the job is too big for one to tackle alone. If you were a mesmerist, or even a strong, masterful character of a man, you might succeed, with everything favorable, in about five years. As it is, the whole Christian Science Church couldn't touch Finnegan without hypnotizing him; and that is what we're trying to do to-night."

"How does he look?" asked the executive, peering in at the old man. "Is he getting there?"

Finnegan was standing motionless beside the small wheel which, as a mere lever, admitted steam to the steering-engine below. Now and then he twirled it back and forth, with his eyes fixed on the compass in the binnacle. The group slowly sidled up to the pilot-house, and one—Mr. Clarkson—took a hurried look into the bridge binnacle. "Dead on the course," he whispered as he joined them. As they listened and looked they heard Finnegan crooning

softly to himself, and suddenly the crooning became
articulate:

" In the hallway—all day—
   Mary Ann, me darter.
 She goes to slape in the childer's cot—
   Mary Ann Kehoe—Kehoe-o-o-o-oe—KEHO-O-O-O-O-OE!"

" No go," said the surgeon, stifling his laughter.
" Come away and give him a chance. He's doing
well."

They mustered again at the bridge-rail. An hour
had hardly gone by, and there was still plenty of time
for the experiment, provided that Finnegan would
do his part. He was doing his work well; silent
now, he stared steadily at the compass and steered
so straight that the sublieutenant was impressed to
the extent of speaking of it to Mr. Felton. But Mr.
Felton did not respond with any great enthusiasm.
He was officer of the deck; and when one is officer
of the deck on a ten-thousand-ton battle-ship rushing through thick fog at eighteen knots there are
things of more moment than the mere matter of a
straight course. He had strained his eyes until the
fog was yet mistier, and strained his ears for sounds
of whistles and horns until to him the deep-toned
hum of the engines was hardly audible. He had sent
repeated injunctions to the lookouts to listen carefully—to report anything that sounded like fisher-
men's horns or steamers' whistles, and had sternly
enjoined upon the bridge quartermaster to heave on
the whistle rope at intervals of two minutes. But
he had not slowed down; a collision is just as possible at half-speed as at full speed, and in spite of
sentiment and law there are officers and captains who
prefer to be on the ship that strikes the blow to

being on the ship that receives it. Both the captain and Mr. Felton so preferred, in spite of the fact that nothing afloat but icebergs and battle-ships as heavy as this big ship could safely oppose her. There is logic in the theory. A ten-thousand-ton battle-ship, with a ram like a meat-axe, will cut through a steamship at half-speed as a knife cuts through cheese, and a fishing-craft caught on her bows would be lifted and thrown aside in two pieces. Yet, should either be the assailant, the result might be as disastrous. So the *Argyll* charged over the Georges Banks on her way to Halifax at full speed, with Finnegan steering straight and Mr. Felton and his lookouts anxious only for the safety of others. But the three idlers on the bridge, with fair confidence in Mr. Felton, were only anxious over Finnegan.

"You must enlighten me, surgeon," said Mr. Parmlee, "a little further—as to what I am to do."

"Nothing," answered the surgeon, "for half an hour; then speak in a whisper. If he answers, wait longer, and try again. When he don't respond, begin your gentle lecture; but don't arouse him."

"I think I understand. Well, I will try. But tell me—would not this be the soul that I appeal to —Finnegan's immortal soul?"

"Some think so—some don't. I can't tell you. It is denied by those who call the ego the soul, for the ego is pure consciousness, and consciousness depends entirely upon the evidence of the senses."

"Altogether? Oh, no, doctor."

"Oh, yes, Mr. Parmlee. Just consider, now. Try and imagine yourself stone blind from birth—you never felt the sensation of light; stone deaf—you never heard a sound in your life; your sense of taste and smell entirely dead; also, your sensory nerves dead—so that you never felt anything that touched you—never felt heat and cold. You wouldn't know much, would you?"

"No, not a great deal."

"You would know nothing. You would not be conscious that you were alive. There would be no ego. But, unless you died from lack of exercise, you could live and grow fat provided that food was placed in your stomach; and if the motor nerves were not also dead you could move about under the care of the subjective mind. This mind is the *sixth sense* so often spoken of—that possessed by the totally deaf and blind, who *feel* the presence of solid objects and *feel* the impact of sound."

"Yes," said Mr. Clarkson, "we've all heard of almost miraculous divination by these stricken people. Blind men really do find their way around."

"And cats come back—carrier-pigeons, too, and migrating birds. They travel for miles and days over country never cognized by any of the five senses, but—better sneak in now, Mr. Parmlee. Don't speak for half an hour."

The chaplain entered the pilot-house, where, in the dim light from the binnacle, the watchers saw him take a position on the other side of the small steering-wheel. Finnegan made no sign of recognition, and those without conversed awhile, then relapsed into silence. The minutes passed; the sublieutenant performed his duty of occasionally peeping at the bridge compass; Mr. Felton stood braced against the bridge-rail more statue-like than Finnegan. At each end of the long bridge was a lookout, as intent and immovable as the officer. The fog grew thicker, and the rumble of the engines seemed louder in consequence, while the two-minute blasts of the whistle burst through the clogged air like thunder-claps.

Suddenly Mr. Parmlee shot out of the pilot-house and joined his coreformers. He was palpably agitated.

"I cannot perform my part," he said, brokenly. "I waited, as you directed, and then whispered his name. And what do you think? He answered, in a whisper: 'Hush, sir! Don't talk to the man at the wheel. I know what ye want, sir. Here y' are. Take a nip, sir. You were good to me once, Mr. Parmlee.' And he handed me a bottle. Here it is— almost empty. And there is whisky on his breath."

The surgeon chortled. "Well," he said at length, "toss it overboard, chaplain." Over went the bottle. "He's in good condition for good steering, so—best let him finish his trick. But he can't be hypnotized otherwise to-night. I'm going down."

He disappeared, followed by the chaplain; but the executive officer remained on the bridge, ab-sorbed in meditation of a more or less gloomy nature. He occasionally looked at the compass, only to find no fault in the steering; but this did not absolve Finnegan, for when four bells struck, and the bridge quartermaster moved toward the pilot-house, the of-ficer stopped him.

"For bringing whisky to the wheel," he said, sternly, through the opened window, "you shall steer two hours more."

"Very good, sir," whined the old fellow, submis-sively.

Mr. Clarkson resumed his position at the bridge-rail. The captain, with full confidence in his officers, was asleep; but his confidence was embodied solely in his executive officer, whose confidence in Finnegan's helmsmanship was not equaled by his confidence in Mr. Felton, who, though officer of the deck and a competent man, was young—very young to have charge on such a night. So Mr. Clarkson remained *ex-officio* in charge.

Five bells struck, then six and seven; and the last half-hour of the watch was drawing to an end when the sublieutenant peeped into the binnacle and startled them all with a yell.

" She's four points off her course!" he said, excitedly. " Starboard!—starboard hard! What's the matter with you? Are you asleep?"

Mr. Clarkson had been looking at Finnegan through the window a moment before. The old man had not changed his attitude. He still looked fixedly at the compass with eyes that were wide open, yet dead in the dimmed light. But now, as the sublieutenant's voice broke the silence, and the first lieutenant looked again, he saw Finnegan's face working convulsively, though his pose was as rigid as before and his eyes still dead in the dim light from the binnacle.

" Finnegan!" he shouted. " Wake up! Starboard your wheel and bring her back to the course! Jump in there, quartermaster, and take the wheel!"

" Yessir! yessir!" answered Finnegan, in the nervous tones of one suddenly awakened. Then the convulsions left his face and an anxious look came to it while he ground the wheel over. Then the quartermaster hurled him headlong against the door of the pilot-house and seized the spokes. " Coming back, sir!" he called, after a moment's scrutiny of the compass.

" Bring her back to the course!" said Mr. Clarkson, as he hovered over the bridge compass. But at the instant an uproar of shouts sounded from the various lookouts.

"Ship dead ahead, sir!" they called. "Port, sir! —she's crossing our bow to port!—hard over, sir!— right under the bow, sir!—a steamship dead ahead, sir!—port the wheel, sir—for God's sake!"

Mr. Clarkson took one look into the darkness and fog, then almost screamed the order to the quarter-master: "Steady as you go! Port!—hard a port! Hard over the wheel!" Then he jammed the engine-room telegraph to "Stop." The quartermaster spun the wheel, the rudder responded, and the ten thousand tons of steel shot past the stern of an equally large but flimsier ocean greyhound, from whose multitude of windows and deadlights shone the light of a thousand electric bulbs—from whose decks, even as she sank into the fog, came the shouts of startled men and the screams of women and children.

Mr. Clarkson moved the telegraph to "Full speed ahead," and again directed the quartermaster to re-turn to the course; then he called Finnegan from the pilot-house. The old fellow came out, in the attitude of a dog about to be whipped, and stood cowering before the mighty first lieutenant.

"You were asleep," said Mr. Clarkson, sternly. "You went to sleep at the wheel. What have you to say?"

"No, sir," answered Finnegan. "No, sir. I swear before God, Mr. Clarkson, I wasn't asleep. I knew she was swingin' off; I saw the lubber's-point a-movin' over to sta'board, but I couldn't move my hands, sir. So help me God, sir, I couldn't move my hands. I was a dead man. I knew, but I couldn't move. I'm an old man, sir—I'm not the man I was.

And you kept me four hours at the wheel, Mr. Clarkson, doing work that I don't get pay for. I'm not rated quartermaster, sir."

Mr. Felton was scanning the bridge compass, and apparently took no further interest in the case; but the sublieutenant, still younger, was much excited.

"There were fully two thousand human lives at stake," he said, excitedly. "And this man goes to sleep at the wheel. Oh, my God, what an escape. Hundreds would have been drowned."

"Yes," answered Mr. Clarkson. "If we had continued on our course, we would have rammed that steamship squarely amidships. And Finnegan goes to sleep at the wheel. Finnegan"—and the officer's tone was very gentle, considering the enormity of his offense—"go down, ask the main-deck corporal to awaken the surgeon and send him to my room. Then turn in."

"Very good, sir—thanky, sir." said Finnegan. "And I won't do it again, sir—indeed, I won't. But I'm an old man, sir."

"Go down, Finnegan."

Finnegan saluted and departed.

An hour later, at the end of a long conversation between the surgeon and first lieutenant, the former said: "There is no doubt in my mind, Clarkson, that Finnegan put himself into the subjective state, and that his subconscious self took charge of him—that is, his subconscious mind had clairvoyant knowledge of the position of that steamship, out of sight in the fog, and simply prevented his muscles from acting until you commanded him to 'wake up.' That command wakened him, and the ignorant and very much limited objective brain took charge, and he moved the wheel. The sublieutenant's language, though intelligible enough to a wakened brain, meant nothing to the subconscious. Your command to 'wake up' did the business. It was a suggestion."

"But," said Mr. Clarkson, " admitting this, what put him into this subjective and clairvoyant state? Was it whisky or long gazing at the compass?"

The surgeon reached for a cigar, lit it, and puffed vigorously before replying.

"I do not know," he said. "Neither, I believe, does any man on earth. The captain, as you know, says that there is the index of an inscrutable Providence in all of Finnegan's actions. Let it go at that. I shall experiment no further with Finnegan."

"And I shall see that he never lacks for his inspiration," said the executive, abandonedly but firmly.

"As a medical man and a student of science," said the surgeon, "I ratify that. But we can expect no approval from Mr. Parmlee."

"No," said the executive, gloomily, " nor any help, of action or advice, with a big steamship under the bow."

THE TORPEDO

MR. RYERSON was not concerned with international etiquette; it was not his business that his captain's action in sending him with a detail of men on board this Japanese torpedo-boat at three in the morning might involve England in the war, should Russia find it out. Russia might go hang—Japan, too, as far as he was concerned; he would instruct a Russian as quickly as he would a

Jap, or torpedo the ship of either without asking why, provided he was so ordered. Nor was it the nature of the work that had got upon his nerves this dark night. It was cold, of course—even for the month and latitude—and there was snow in the air, with a keen, penetrating wind from seaward that reached in through pilot-cloth and flannel; while the suspected proximity of Russian warships made it wisest, even as subjects of a neutral country, to work without lights. And the Japanese he had come to instruct—only the commander of whom understood English—seemed to be as stupid as they were eager to learn. These things of themselves could not disturb the trained and experienced torpedo lieutenant of H.M.S. *Argyll;* though it was because he was a trained and experienced officer, with a proper pride in his country, his ship, and himself, that he was disturbed. Finnegan—Old Man Finnegan—the only one of the whole ship's company privileged to drink with impunity, the most skilled and efficient seaman of them all when properly primed, the butt of all hands when thoroughly drunk, or thoroughly sober, had, as the work progressed, shown signs of elation and enthusiasm, due to nothing but unwise over-stimulation; and this, to the scandal of the British service, before the eyes of these critical, though untutored, Japanese, who knew nothing of Finnegan's peculiar privilege. While they were at work on the forward torpedo-tube, Mr. Ryerson had driven the old fellow away with unkind and indelicate comment on his condition, and it was a little later that the Japanese lieutenant in charge of the boat informed Mr. Ryerson that Finnegan had sneaked aft in the darkness and taken a long swig from a large, flat bottle. So, when the Whitehead torpedo had been driven home in the tube, the breech charged, primed, and closed, the tube swung around a few times, and the discharging mechanism explained to the Japs, Mr. Ryerson hunted for Finnegan, and found him " soldiering " under the lee of the after funnel.

" Where's that bottle? " demanded the irate officer.

" Got no bottle, shir," answered Finnegan, saluting unsteadily.

" Don't lie. You were seen. Where's that bottle? "

" Washn't much, Misher Ryerson, and I put it away, shir."

" I should think you had put it away," coughed the officer, backing off. " Heavens, what a breath! Keep to leeward of everybody. Go and hide yourself, Finnegan, and when we go back I'll report you for getting drunk before the heathen. Come aft here, men! " he called. " We'll try this other tube. Pick up a Whitehead on the way."

Whitehead torpedoes, be it known, are mechanical fish about sixteen feet long, carrying two hundred and twenty pounds of gun-cotton in their heads, which travel under water of their own volition to explode upon impact, but which are aimed and merely propelled from long, eighteen-inch tubes by the explosion of a small charge of powder which, compressing the air behind the torpedo, exerts a pressure just sufficient to overcome its inertia. The small Japanese craft, a recent acquisition from America, was equipped with a bow and a stern tube and four torpedoes, one of them already placed in the forward tube, the others stowed in brackets about the deck. As her commander had explained, it was his hurriedly drafted crew's inexperience that had induced him to steer up in the face of the *Argyll's* search-light and ask instructions of the English.

Torpedo methods having been explained at the forward tube, there was little to do on the other except to load, charge, and close it. So, while his men, followed by the eager Japanese, came aft with a torpedo, Mr. Ryerson opened the breech, and when they were ready he said: " In with it now, and let's get through. Finnegan, clear out! Go and hide yourself, I said."

Finnegan, who had untactfully stumbled in front of the blunt nose of the torpedo, held poised in air behind the tube, was pushed aside just as he was about to peep into the long, hollow cylinder, an inspection well performed by the lieutenant a moment before.

" I think that everything is all right, Finnegan," said Mr. Ryerson, ironically, bowing politely to the old man in the darkness. " Now go and hide yourself."

" Hide m'shelf," repeated Finnegan, softly and stupidly. " Very good, shir—hide m'shelf—m'shelf. Hide m'shelf."

He disappeared behind the group, and the torpedo was inserted in the tube. But it stuck when about half-way in, and all the strength of the men could not push it farther.

" Out with it," ordered the officer. " Let's see what's wrong. Put it back in its chocks or it'll take you overboard."

It was a wise order; the boat was rolling heavily, and the men, weighted by the torpedo, were unsteady on their legs. Mr. Ryerson struck a match within the tube, but as far as the glow reached saw nothing but shining steel. "All clear here," he said. " Something wrong with the Whitehead."

He went to the torpedo and felt all over it with his hands. " No wonder," he said, as he fingered the clutch, or T-iron on top, which, fitting into a traveler within the tube, held the weight of the torpedo while being ejected. " It's bent; but, still, not too much, I should think. Try it again, men, and I'll see if it enters the traveler."

The men stooped for the torpedo, but did not pick it up. There was a bumping noise alongside, a few muttered but intense expletives in Russian, and an uprush of large, active men who fell upon the Englishmen and Japanese alike with cutlass and pistol.

" Into the boat, our side," yelled Mr. Ryerson. " This isn't our fight. Away with you all."

And away they went, bowling over with fist or shoulder a few Russians in their path, to enter their boat in a manner not prescribed in the regulations —by flying leaps. Mr. Ryerson, however, was mindful of naval etiquette to the extent of being the last to leave, waiting at the rail with drawn pistol—the only arm in the party—while his men rushed by him.

" All down? " he called, when the hegira had ceased.

" All here, sir," they answered from the boat.

Then he jumped, first discharging his pistol into the face of an oncoming Russian with a cutlass.

In the white glare of the *Argyll's* search-light, unwisely turned upon them by the watchful battle-ship, and to the sound of Russian oaths and Japanese outcries, the Englishmen pulled on the oars, ducking their heads to dodge the fusillade of bullets with which the Russians answered Mr. Ryerson's shot. But soon the search-light lifted and covered the torpedo-boat, by which time the oaths and outcries were silenced; then they could see the boat, with empty hawse-pipe, drifting astern with the tide, while limp forms dropped from her rail.

"Hell!" shuddered the lieutenant. "Capture and massacre! They've got the boat, but I wonder if they can fix that torpedo. I'd like to have finished the job."

A trained and efficient torpedo lieutenant must have a mechanical soul; hence the remark. But, from association of ideas, the remark was followed by another, much louder.

"Is Finnegan here?" he called.

"Finnegan—Finnegan," the men replied. "Pass the word. No, sir. Not here. Finnegan's gone, sir."

A groan went up from them, and there was a perceptible lessening of vigor in their strokes, as though they waited for the order to turn back, unarmed though they were, to rescue the beloved old reprobate. It would have been hopeless, even with arms; the torpedo-boat, still illumined by the search-light, was now emitting black smoke from all three funnels, and was plainly under steam.

"Give way, men!" ordered the lieutenant, excitedly. "Nothing but the ship herself can stop her now."

But the ship did not, even though they found the crew at quarters when they boarded her. And when Mr. Ryerson had made his report to his superiors, mournfully mentioning the loss of Finnegan before he spoke of his unfinished job on the tube, the grave-faced captain seemed little concerned with either.

"I am sorry you fired your pistol, Mr. Ryerson,"

he said, " even in self-defense, with the situation so strained."

"Do you think complications may arise, sir?" asked the young officer, anxiously.

"Who knows? I trusted to your discretion, or—but let it go. We may hear by wireless at any moment that war has been declared, and then it will not matter. Still, in the absence of such news, I should rather that the Russians had struck first."

"They attacked the boat, captain. They've got one of our men."

"Some diplomats might argue that we had no business there," responded the captain, quickly, but with a smile. "However, we'll hope for the news."

"And Finnegan, captain?" inquired Mr. Clarkson, the executive officer. "Shall I send a shot after that boat, or shall we trust to Finnegan's luck?"

"Trust to his luck; it is all we can do. There is an inscrutable Providence behind Finnegan; he never yet got drunk but to a purpose—unknown to himself perhaps, but vital."

"Where did you see him last, Mr. Ryerson?" asked the executive.

"It was when we were loading the after tube. He was much in the way, and I told him to go and hide himself. I wonder if he did. I hope so—my God, yes. I hope he did, and escaped that butchery."

"Was he stupidly drunk—that is, ready to fall down?"

"Oh, no—he could navigate; and he said he'd drunk it all, or, in his words, 'put it away,' so he couldn't have got much worse."

"Put it away," repeated the first lieutenant, musingly. "Well, Ryerson, he's dead, no doubt; but wherever he hid himself, at your suggestion, he went where he had first hidden the bottle."

"Small comfort," remarked Mr. Ryerson, sadly. "They would kill everybody, drunk or sober. It was too dark to distinguish uniforms. Poor old devil; it's all my fault."

"No, Ryerson," replied Mr. Clarkson, gently. "Not your fault at all. Get it off your mind. Think of something else."

"You are not to blame, Mr. Ryerson," added the captain, fully as kindly. "Go and turn in now. Get what rest you can."

"Think of something else," said the executive. "Think of anything at all—some mechanical or mathematical problem."

Whereupon Mr. Ryerson, being, like all mechanical souls, largely amenable to suggestion, responded with a grateful look at their sympathetic faces, and went to his berth resolutely thinking of the only mechanical problem on his mind—that of the damaged torpedo; and, being young, went instantly to sleep, to waken at daylight with only a dumb regret for Finnegan, and his soul fully obsessed with the still unsolved problem: Could the Russians repair it?

All hands had breakfasted, and, bolting his hurriedly, he went on deck; there was excitement in the air. It was a clear, cold morning, and the wind had lulled to a gentle breeze that barely crisped the level waters of the bay. Inshore from the *Argyll*, and about a half-mile toward the southern point of the bay, swung at anchor a second-class Japanese battleship, and astern of her two armored cruisers, from whose protection had come the inquiring torpedo-boat of the night before—all riding at short cables, all flying battle-flags, and belching thick smoke from every funnel. The cause was apparent: lying off the northern point, about three miles away, were two uncouth Russian battle-ships and two cruisers, from which, doubtless, had come the cutting-out party; and dodging back and forth among them was the captured torpedo-boat. The four craft, battle-ships ahead, cruisers in the rear, were coming in column, and even as they came, while Mr. Ryerson was climbing the bridge-stairs to join his brother officers, a puff of smoke left the third ship, and a shell hissed over the water. It fell short of the Japanese fleet, but it was the signal of battle. The three ships answered with every gun that would bear, tripped their anchors, and steamed ahead.

"Hopelessly outclassed," said the captain, as he viewed the Japanese ships through his binoculars. "That little *Shikoku*, with her two ten-inch guns, and the *Hondo* and *Yesso*, with nothing bigger than six, against those four bruisers." He looked toward the Russian fleet. "Do you make them out, Mr. Clarkson?"

"Yes, sir," answered Mr. Clarkson, his glass to his eyes. "There are the two new battle-ships, if I'm not mistaken—the *Ladoga* and *Onega;* and there are the *Königsberg* and *Dünaburg*, armored cruisers, about the weight, I think, captain, of the *Hondo* and *Yesso*. The torpedo-boat is making tracks."

"And that is what we must do," rejoined the captain. "They're going to fight, and we are in the way—that is, unless war is on; and if that is the case we'll know very soon. Those ships are right out of Newchwang, and would have the news—by wireless even—long before we would. Lift the anchor, Mr. Clarkson. We'll move on."

The *Argyll* also was lying at a short cable and

belching thick smoke from her funnels. It was but five minutes' work to get under way, and she steamed seaward at full speed, aiming to avoid the line of fire. But even though her amicable intent was further indicated by the hoisting—long before eight bells, in view of the emergency—of a large and conspicuous British ensign, the intent was seemingly ignored by the Russians; for an eight-inch shell arrived from the largest cruiser—the flagship—struck the *Argyll's* stern, exploded, made a large and ragged cavity in that part of her, and lifted the ensign, flagstaff and all, overboard.

"Heavens!" gasped the captain, as he looked at the shattered deck and the prostrate forms of men— some writhing, others still—visible through the smoke. "Was that shot aimed? We are out of the line of fire."

"My fault—my fault," groaned Mr. Ryerson. "The torpedo-boat has told them."

"What of it?" demanded the executive officer, excitedly. "It's war—that's what it is. War *must* be declared, captain. They aimed that shot. They wouldn't dare to without authority from St. Petersburg. They have fired on her Majesty's ship."

"Yes—yes," rejoined the captain, pale of face and calm of speech. "But we must make no more mistakes "—he looked significantly at the unhappy Mr. Ryerson—"we have made enough. We will try to get the despatch-boat off Weihaiwei. There may be news for us."

He entered the chart-room abaft the pilot-house, and while the intermittent, rasping sound of wireless telegraphy arose above the humming of the engines, the officers watched the carrying-down of the dead and wounded, and excitedly discussed the reason of that single shot; for no more were fired at the *Argyll*.

"We cannot connect," said the captain, when the rasping had ceased, and he came among them. "Yet we all know that England's ultimatum is given, and that she cannot retreat. But if Russia *should* give in? What then—if we answer that shot? And if she does not, what of the *Argyll* with that shot unanswered?" He looked perplexed.

"It was not a chance shot, captain," said Mr. Clarkson.

"It might have been; they have not repeated it."

"They are busy, captain," said the navigating officer. "They have knocked a chip off England's shoulder, and are waiting for England's return blow. And in English history, captain, it has never been withheld." There was entreaty in the voice of the navigator, and a little of the perplexity left the face of the captain.

"They have shot away the ensign, captain, and have killed our men," said Mr. Clarkson. "There is no signal for apology. War *must* be on, sir. The despatch-boat is captured, surely, or we should have received orders."

"But the consequences, gentlemen?" said the wavering captain. "You are young and patriotic, but I am responsible. A false step at this juncture will involve England in the imbroglio. France must follow; then Turkey, Germany, and possibly the United States. In these days of wireless telegraphy we can afford to wait until sure."

"But the attack on the torpedo-boat was arranged with regard to us, captain," implored Mr. Clarkson. "They knew we were there. It was done under our guns. They fired on our men."

"Our men ought not to have been there, and a shot had been fired at them."

Though the captain's words were emphatic, there were doubt and hesitation in his utterance; and he did not look at Mr. Ryerson.

"And they've killed Finnegan," ventured this young officer.

"He was drunk," responded the captain, somewhat regretfully.

"Too drunk to take care of himself, captain," said Mr. Clarkson, earnestly. "You have said yourself, sir, that Providence was behind Finnegan—that he never gets drunk but to a purpose that is vital. Perhaps it is showing in this. He got drunk, sir; he delayed the boat-party in its work, and involved it in the friction with the Russians that has resulted in that shot—that insult to England—to the end that, in the absence of news that war is on, we may, by resenting the insult, act rightly and save England's prestige."

"Quarters, gentlemen!" answered the captain, promptly. "Strip ship for action! We'll take a hand in this."

And so was reached the decision that sent the *Argyll* into battle, that menaced the integrity of boundaries, the ownership of isthmian canals, the peace, the purpose, and the progress of the world for a hundred years—not because England's dignity was in danger, but because Old Man Finnegan got drunk.

There was confusion confounded in that ship for a few moments. Drum-calls, bugle-calls, whistles, and profanity troubled the air. Men scurried about, in and out of superstructure doors—up and down hatchways and ladders. Stanchions, gratings, all wooden deck-fittings went below the water-line; all boats, with the plugs out, went overboard, fastened together, with their oars for a sea-anchor; everything movable, or productive of splinters, was placed out of the way of shot and shell, except the signal-yard and halyards; and to this yard arose numerous combinations of small flags, each holding a message to the Japanese, while high overhead flew the white naval ensign of Britain—another chip to replace the one knocked off. Then order came out of chaos, and all was quiet but the voice of an officer aloft calling out ranges.

Rounding slowly to a port wheel the *Argyll* headed to cross the bows of the Russians and take a position at the rear of the Japanese column, this being the matter decided with the small flags. But long before she reached her place the eight- and thirteen-inch rifles in her turrets were speaking, and several tons of steel had reached the vicinity of the Russians.

Mr. Clarkson had gone to his station in the forward turret, and the other officers to various gun-positions scattered about the ship, where, subject to telephonic communication from the conning-tower, they oversaw the work of hurling steel through the air. But Mr. Ryerson's specialty was the launching of mechanical fish, useless at more than two thousand yards' range; so, after an inspection of his torpedoes and his men, he returned to the bridge as an aide to the captain and navigating officer.

No one cares to enter a conning-tower in action until driven in by gun-fire, and the captain and his officers remained without, where, though there was greater danger, there was more air and a clearer view. Leaving out the tale-bearing torpedo-boat, now far to the rear of the Russians, the two fleets were evenly matched in numbers, each consisting of two battle-ships and two cruisers; but the advantage in weight of armor and armament lay with the Russians; for the two heavier ships of the latter were equal to the *Argyll*, while the *Shikoku*, the Japanese battle-ship, was much smaller—hardly better, in fact, than an armored cruiser of a Western power. Her position in the van was her undoing. While the fleets were approaching she received the full fire of the *Ladoga* and the *Onega*, the two leading Russian ships, and armor-piercing shells, designed for heavier work, entered her citadel, exploded within, disabled her engines, and set her afire. She reeled drunkenly out of line and came to a stop. Smoke poured from hatches, ventilators, and gun-ports, but her heavy guns were speaking and sending their messengers while her crew could breathe in the turrets. The following ships came up and passed her, and as the *Argyll* brought her abreast it could be seen that she was sinking. But there is no stopping to save life in a sea-fight. The *Argyll* passed on.

Whatever the animus of that first eight-inch shell, there was no mistaking that of the horizontal hail that pounded the *Argyll* now. The *Hondo* and *Yesso*, ahead of her, received attention only from the *Königsberg* and *Dünaburg*, the two cruisers of the Russians, while the battle-ships, high-sided, heavily armored craft, sent their twelve- and seven-inch shot and shell directly at the *Argyll*. Soon the formation was broken, and the battle became a *mêlée*—the cruisers engaging in a four-cornered fight by themselves, the *Argyll* engaging the two battle-ships, steaming up between them in order to use all guns.

And from the heavier of these guns came *thirteen-* and *eight*-inch shot and shell.

Loosely speaking, a battle-ship's gun-positions are protected by armor equal in thickness to the caliber of the guns within, and it is accepted that pointed projectiles from these guns will, at short range, pierce such armor on an enemy's ship, but will shatter to pieces on the outer surface of armor that is slightly thicker. Thus the *Argyll*, though fighting two ships, each as heavy as herself in total weight, had the advantage of one inch in armor and calibers, and, had victory depended upon large-gun fire, this inch would have won it; but an important factor in naval warfare is the efficacy of the secondary battery of quick-fire guns, potent against gunners, gunsights, and torpedo-boats; and about the time that the captain and his aides were driven into the conning-tower this battery, scattered about the *Argyll's* deck, superstructure, and fighting-tops, began to disintegrate under the well-directed seven-inch shell-fire of the *Ladoga* and *Onega*.

Men died under that storm of steel and flame; shrieks and groans followed the rattle and roar of each exploding shell; smoke and gas came into the conning-tower, blinding and choking the inmates, and Mr. Ryerson, his ears ringing, his eyes streaming, striving to keep a lookout through a peep-hole to port while he attended to three telephones and a speaking-tube, had little time to think of unsolved mechanical problems, or even the fate of poor old Finnegan. Yet for one brief moment the troubles of the night flashed into his mind because of what he saw far away through his peep-hole—a high-crested wave moving over the sea, and behind it three stumpy funnels and a glimpse of low hull.

" The torpedo-boat, captain!" he called. " See her—over to port! She's making for the cruisers!"

"I see," answered the captain, withdrawing his pale face from the slit before him. "Bring every eight- and six-inch gun to bear upon her. We haven't a secondary gun left; but she *must* be stopped."

They could not stop her. A torpedo-boat at thirty knots is an elusive target, and though the sea about her was churned into foam by the fusillade from the *Argyll*, the *Yesso*, and the *Hondo*, she seemed uninjured and went on.

"Nothing but small calibers can touch her," exclaimed the captain, as he looked. "We have nothing, but perhaps the Japanese cruisers can do it. Protect them. Turn every gun possible on those Russian cruisers. Sink them quickly."

And by speaking-tube and telephone this order went to the turrets; but not before Mr. Clarkson in the forward turret had discharged the two thirteen-inch rifles in his care at the target aimed at—the *Ladoga*, the nearest and largest battle-ship. One after the other, two pointed cylinders, each over half a ton in weight, sailed through the air and struck nearly in the same place, at the water-line at the stern. There were two explosions, and when the yellow smoke had cleared they could see that the whole after part of the monster ship had disappeared, and that she was settling by the stern.

"Steering-gear gone, surely," remarked the captain. "Let her alone for a while. Attend to those cruisers."

They were attended to; and in five minutes—the *Königsberg* down by the head, the *Dünaberg* leaning heavily to port—they were making for the beach, their guns silenced and their crews swarming on deck. No cruiser may withstand the fire of a battle-ship.

In the integrity of that oncoming torpedo-boat now lay the palm of victory, and the Russian battle-ships profited by the lesson, turning their guns to the Japanese cruisers; but by this time they had demolished the last of the *Argyll's* small rifles, leaving nothing but the heavy eight- and thirteen-inch guns in the turrets—terrible weapons when they could touch a target, but useless for quick work. So, having the *Ladoga* at his mercy when he should have time to choose position, the *Argyll's* captain directed his fire at the *Onega*, hoping to disable her and trusting to the secondary guns of the cruisers to stop that menacing torpedo-boat.

She could not be stopped. The demoralizing fire of the Russians silenced the guns of the *Hondo* and *Yesso*, and the two cruisers, enveloped in steam and smoke, headed shoreward, struggling lamely to reach the beach, and still pounded by the pitiless fire of the battle-ships. But things were happening to these battle-ships. Little by little, as the *Argyll's* shells plunged into them and exploded, their softer parts changed shape and identity. Superstructures were reduced to scrap-heaps, and the seven-inch fire lessened as gun after gun was demolished. Funnels, boat-cranes, and ventilators became tangled masses of steel. Masts bent, tottered, and fell, one of them —on the smaller ship, the *Onega*—jamming the protruding guns of the forward turret and putting them out of action. Then an uprising of shattered metal amidships and a cloud of steam and yellow smoke told of exploded ammunition and punctured boilers; and but for an occasional belching from the still intact after turret this ship's work was done. She heeled to starboard, settled by the stern, and showed signs of sinking.

There was still the *Ladoga*, however, a floating pile of iron unable to steer, but with two intact turrets containing four twelve-inch rifles, and there was an onrushing torpedo-boat, now but half a mile away. Yet, aside from the presence in the fight of this torpedo-boat, the battle was with the *Argyll*, even though there was nothing left of her but her citadel, conning-tower, turrets, machinery, and the submarine part of her cellular hull that floated the whole; for it was but a matter of time when she could hammer the three remaining Russian turrets out of commission. But on came the torpedo-boat; and, there being nothing but an occasional twelve-inch shell coming their way now, the captain and officers stepped out of the conning-tower to watch her.

There was a mournful procession making for the beach—four smoking, reeling ships creeping along, the two in the van spitting at the two in the rear, these two spitting at the low, three-funneled craft rushing along between its two high waves. And over to the southward was a still more mournful sight—the sinking Japanese battle-ship, her deck crowded with men and her boats far away from her.

Neglecting the battle-ships, the captain gave steam to the *Argyll*, and she rushed ahead, her eight-inch guns barking at the one dangerous enemy; but nothing touched the small terror—more feared by naval men than the largest fighter—and she raced on, rapidly closing the distance between herself and the rearmost Japanese cruiser, the *Yesso*. In a storm of rattling small fire she crept up, passed out of sight behind the cruiser, and emerged ahead, her crew wheeling a torpedo from amidships to the smoking tube in the bow. Then a convulsion was seen in the cruiser; she rolled to starboard, rolled back, and out of all midship apertures came yellow smoke. She did not roll to starboard again; she settled as she lay—torpedoed.

On went the destroyer, her crew launching home the second torpedo. The officers on the *Argyll's* shattered bridge watched her through binoculars, the pallor of intense emotion showing through their grime-stained faces, and only the mechanical soul of Mr. Ryerson rising above the horror of the situation to inspire the remark between tightly drawn lips: "Bunglers—they handle it like a piece of beef—not torpedo-men."

The murderous craft disappeared behind the other Japanese cruiser, and again was the death-blow delivered. The *Hondo* rolled, smoked, and settled, like her sister, and out from behind her again emerged the torpedo-boat, turning slowly in a wide circle, her crew again wheeling a torpedo forward.

"Our turn next," said the captain, grimly, as he moved the steering-lever to port and gave full speed to the engines. "We'll meet her end on."

But the wide curve of the torpedo-boat became a straight line, and she rushed south toward the sinking *Shikoku*.

The two Russian battle-ships were still sending heavy shells into the soft parts of the *Argyll*—in view of this the deck seemed the safest place on board—and, while her own thirteen-inch guns were answering the Russian fire, her eight-inch fire was directed solely at the elusive torpedo-boat. Yet nothing hit her from this point. It was only when she drew near to the burning, sinking Japanese battle-ship that a storm of small projectiles from a still intact secondary battery met her and drove her back; in the froth of water raised by this hail of steel she turned swiftly on her keel, and, steering for a point ahead of the onrushing *Argyll*, raced along to meet her. She presented a moving target on this course, not only to the dwindling small fire of the *Shikoku*, but to the eight-inch fire of the *Argyll*, and she came on uninjured, only to again court real danger when she should turn for the final, end-on rush in the *Argyll's* track; and even then she could expect only one blast from the forward guns before she would be within their limit of depression. But when she had turned suddenly in the *Argyll's* path, and the two craft were approaching at the rate of their added speeds, it was fated that one eight-inch shell, sent from a hurriedly swung turret, should hit her squarely in the bow and explode. When the yellow smoke had cleared, it was seen that there was little left there of that bow, or of the torpedo-tube above it, or of the men near it; but, though perceptibly down by the head, she was still coming at a good rate of speed, and her balance of men were rushing aft to man the tube in the stern. Soon she was within the range of torpedo action, and a little later within the circle of gun depression; but still she came on, slower and slower as she settled, her remnant of crew, with sure death before them, waiting for close quarters before striking the last blow permitted them by fate.

"All hands on deck!" said the captain. "Every man for himself now! Hammocks, Mr. Ryerson!"

A man-of-war-man's hammock, if the mattress be half filled with cork, is an efficient life-preserver. The cry went through the depths, and seven hundred men swarmed up, black and grimy, more or less naked, each bearing his hammock and breathing deeply of the sweet, fresh air. They crowded to the side and looked at the coming death with more of relief in their faces than anxiety; they had been an hour in closed compartments.

But there was anxiety in the faces of those on the wrecked bridge; the human dread of death is keener to those who must watch and wait—who cannot move and work. Pale of face, with folded arms and tightly pressed lips, the officers looked at the crippled little craft with its handful of men dancing and shouting around the tube at the stern—doomed themselves, but bound to take with them to the bottom this strong and majestic battle-ship with her seven hundred souls. Only the executive officer was practical.

"Did they torpedo the *Shikoku?*" he asked, calmly, of Ryerson.

"I don't know—I didn't notice," answered the young officer, explosively. "Why, yes, they must. There's none on deck. They repaired the damaged one, after all, and put it in aft."

"Here she is, gentlemen," said the captain. "Good-by, everybody. Each man for himself, but —I shall go down with my ship. I thought too much of Finnegan's importance."

The supreme moment had arrived. The *Argyll* was steaming at eighteen knots, the torpedo-boat at about fifteen—a total rate of approach equal to thirty-three knots an hour. At this railroad speed the little craft, with her nose nearly buried and the tube trained athwartship, swung up alongside of the giant battle-ship, so close that the whites of the Russians' eyes were plainly visible. She came amidships, a puff of smoke arose from the breech of the tube, a cough of compressed air came to their ears, and there shot out of the tube—not a deadly Whitehead torpedo, but Old Man Finnegan, with a bottle tightly clinched in one outstretched hand, a frightened, sleepy, just-awakened expression on his face, and a yell of protest coming from his throat which the water cut short as he dived. A chorus of laughter and encouraging yells responded, and a hundred shipmates went overboard to his rescue.

"That was it!" hysterically gurgled the torpedo lieutenant, a little later. "The bottle was the obstruction in the tube, and he hid himself where he'd first hidden the bottle."

"And the Russians," said the practical Mr. Clarkson, gravely, "thought the tube was loaded, closed it, primed it, and fired him at us. But the captain was right, after all. Finnegan is an instrument of Providence."

THE SUBMARINE

BY wireless telegraphy, international code-signal, and despatch-boat gossip her existence was known to the allied fleets, but the world at large had learned of her, while yet in process of construction, through indiscreet official babbling at St. Petersburg and immediate publication of the news in the London *Times*. Later on, Japanese spies heard of her as far inland as Lake Baikal, coming along on a flat-car of the Siberian railroad, and so reported; but at Harbin all trace of her was lost—it was not known whether she would proceed farther east to Vladivostok, or whether she would turn south and take to the sea from Newchwang, Shanhaikwan, or Port Arthur. But, though her whereabouts was doubtful, her plans and specifications were known to every officer on every ship from Vladivostok to Shanghai; and to all lookouts, search-light men, and boat parties instructions were given to watch for an object resembling a green washtub floating upside-down.

This would be her conning-tower—all that would show when she had risen to the surface for a peep around. For the rest, according to specifications, she was sixty-three feet long, cigar-shaped, with five torpedoes and a tube in her nose, a gasoline engine for surface running and a reversible motor-dynamo, drawing power from a storage-battery charged by itself, for submarine work. With ballast-tanks empty she floated high, and could easily be seen; with these filled with water she sank to the awash condition, from which she could dive out of sight in a few seconds by the aid of her motion and horizontal rudders. But, with every tank full and her engine stopped, she still possessed a reserve buoyancy which would bring her slowly to the surface. She could travel awash four hundred miles; submerged, fifty. In this radius of action she could expend her five Whitehead torpedoes, and return to port again and again for more. Her torpedoes were miniature models of herself, with thirty-knot speed, automatic controlling-gear to replace the human intelligence within the mother-boat, and a two-hundred-and-twenty-pound charge of gun-cotton in their heads that exploded on impact. Her mission was secret and unseen; her blow, sudden and deadly; and even though she struck no blow, her presence in Eastern seas was of more injury to the *morale* of the crews than was the gun-fire of action, for she was conducive to neurasthenia; officers wore an anxious,

worried look, men lost their appetites and saved on
their mess-money, and Old Man Finnegan, of the
Argyll, stopped drinking. It was bad for his nerves
to stop so suddenly; and, as it was given him to be
the first one to see that inverted washtub, while out
at the end of the boat-boom, he promptly sang out
the news to the bridge, then fell overboard.

The ship was anchored in a deep and narrow
strait, with a swift but smooth tide running past.
Mr. Felton was officer of the deck; he saw Finnegan
fall, saw the circular steel object coming up on the
port quarter, and immediately ordered a boat cleared
away for the one and the secondary battery for the
other, while all hands rushed on deck and the captain
and other officers joined him on the bridge. But Finnegan needed no boat; he slid up sprawling on the
turtle-back of the oncoming submarine. And the
latter needed no immediate attention from the battery, for a circular hatch flew up from the top of the
conning-tower, and a keen-eyed, shrewd-faced man
popped his head out, yelled incomprehensible things
in a strange tongue at Finnegan, finished with a
profane request in good English to come amidships
and trim the boat—which Finnegan obeyed—and
steered the curious craft up under the boat-boom,
where he slowed down, by which time the cutter
lowered for Finnegan was in the water.

"On board the torpedo-boat!" shouted Mr. Felton through a megaphone. "What's your name and
nationality?"

"Thunder and blazes!" answered the man in the
conning-tower. "Are you English? I thought you
were Russian. Well, damn my fool soul!"

"Keep your hands up in sight," called the lieutenant. "Don't move a lever, or we'll sink you. This

is his Majesty's ship *Argyll*. Come aboard and give an account of yourself. Step into that cutter."

"Wait," interrupted the *Argyll's* captain. "Before you leave, empty your ballast-tanks. You are too low in the water—too elusive."

"Empty now, captain," answered the skipper of the lesser craft. "We've got the equivalent down aft in the bilges. The tail-shaft was badly packed, and the engine-room's nearly full of water. We've stopped the leak from within. Oh, I'm a damned fool."

"Then come on board."

"Yes, sir, I will, as the jig's up. But suppose I make fast to your boat-boom first. There'll be no strain on it. I'm steering with the diving-rudder hard down to trim her against that weight of water, and must keep her turning over, or she'll sit on her tail."

"Do so," answered Mr. Felton. "Finnegan, take that man's place at the wheel and steer after the boat-boom."

"Steer small," said the captain to Finnegan, as he climbed out of the hatch and stood knee-deep on the submerged deck. "It's an air-engine steering-gear. Don't touch anything but the wheel."

The old man, shaky with age and nerves, floundered into the conning-tower and took the wheel— the upper spokes of which were visible to those on the high bridge of the battle-ship—while the boat's commander waded forward on the round and unstable platform to where a ring-bolt showed through the water.

"Strikes me," he said, with a quizzical glance at Finnegan and at those above, "that there's no real necessity of a second man getting wet feet when the first is drenched through. But I'm not bossing this."

He was doomed to a worse wetting. He had fastened the end of a line thrown him from the boom to the ring-bolt, and was reaching for a hanging Jacob's ladder to climb to the boom, when those above saw him sink out of sight; then they saw the open conning-tower rush forward, settling as it came. Some saw Finnegan's face, with its look of pained amazement, others only heard his yell: " Leggo me legs—leggo! Lemme out!" Then Finnegan and the conning-tower went under, the rope snapped, and the water was smooth but for the ripples caused by the swimming captain and a line of large, irregular bubbles that stretched ahead for a hundred feet and stopped.

It happened so suddenly that not a shot was fired, though every gun in the port battery was trained and ready. Not a gunner on board would shoot at Finnegan unless ordered, and Mr. Felton had not given the word. But he ordered the boat, after it had picked up the swimmer, to pull ahead ready for Finnegan or any others who might have climbed out of that open hatch against the inrush of water; and in ten minutes, none appearing on the surface, he called it back. Drenched and dripping, the submarine boat's commander was brought into the presence of the captain and officers of the battle-ship.

" Well, sir," asked the big captain, sternly, " what explanation have you to offer of this trick? "

" No trick at all, sir," answered the pale and crestfallen man. " I suppose that my engineer and my quartermaster, who attends to the diving-gear, took a chance that I would not. If they die, I am merely a prisoner. If they live, I am disgraced."

"Disgraced? You, an Englishman, serving Russia, talk of disgrace?"

"An American, captain, who never saw England," answered the man, with dignity. "An officer of twenty years' service in the imperial navy. Lieutenant Bronsonsky, in command of the Russian torpedo-boat *Volga*—plain Jim Bronson back in Indiana."

"Um—humph! Different, of course. What happened to your boat?"

"None of my men understands English. Some one gave full speed to the motor, under which we were running. The diving-rudder was inclined; it balanced her at half-speed, but at full speed made her dive. If they succeeded in closing that hatch in time they may save their lives, but not the boat. Nothing but a wrecking outfit can raise her, even if found."

"Is the hatch easily closed?"

"A strong spring keeps it up, and also down, when pulled past a dead center. A man must reach up for it against the downpour of water. I doubt that it could be done."

"How about air? Is there enough?"

"Plenty of compressed air, and a reserve store of oxygen. If they escape drowning, they will starve before they will suffocate."

"But why," asked the captain, "were you alone in these seas without convoy? And why did you approach us so unwisely?"

"Now, captain," answered Bronson, with some hesitation, "you are scratching the hide of the bear. I do not know. Russian diplomacy, I suppose. I can tell this much, however. My orders were to conceal myself until I reported to the admiral of the outer squadron, except that in this strait I was to deliver verbal information to a battle-ship, which, alone of the Russian fleet, was ignorant of the news that I carried."

" And the news? "

" It is known to the world, and to you. The presence in Eastern seas of five English submarines."

The captain smiled and bowed. " Yes, known to the world, for we have been at pains to advertise it. It is demoralizing to an enemy to have him feel that at any moment a submarine may creep up unseen and torpedo him. We are now, thanks to your mistake, freed from this strain upon our nerves. How did you make such a mistake? "

" Why," said Bronson, coloring, " I simply took you for the Russian ship. She closely resembles you."

" Inferior in armor, armament, and marksmanship," said the captain, dryly. " She went to Weihaiwei yesterday as an English prize."

" But, captain," interposed Mr. Clarkson, in sudden alarm, " *are* we free from this strain upon the nerves? What is to prevent that boat from coming back and torpedoing us? They have Finnegan. They must know we are English."

" You need not fear," answered Bronson, serenely; " she is helpless, and when the tide has drifted her to three hundred feet depth, she will be crushed in by the pressure."

" Did you inform your men that you were captured? "

" No," said Bronson, knitting his brows. " They couldn't have known. I only told your man in English to steer small and to touch nothing but the wheel."

"Were you running under the motor?" asked the executive.

"Yes," answered Bronson. "It was the only precaution that I took."

"Was there a starting switch in the conning-tower?"

"Yes." Bronson's face lighted. "And your man—"

"Finnegan's luck, perhaps, captain!" interrupted Mr. Clarkson. "You know your theory."

"You think he started the motor?" asked the captain. "But why? Was he intoxicated?"

"There's the rub," answered the officer, doubtfully. "He was sober as the chaplain. Now, if he were drunk, I would swear that trouble was coming and that Finnegan would be in it—an instrument of Providence, as you call him. But he was sober—beastly sober."

"Yes, I know," said the captain; "but what trouble threatens us more than did that submarine—now on the bottom? We have command of these seas."

"I don't know. And Finnegan was dead sober. Had you any whisky, vodka, or other intoxicant in that boat, lieutenant?"

"Not a drop," answered Bronson. "Nor any alcohol, nor varnish."

"Well," said Mr. Clarkson, "if he was drunk, or *could* get drunk, I'd be ready for trouble. But he was sober, and of course, being sober, he didn't start the motor. He's done for, captain."

"I believe so," answered the captain. "In fact, I see no hope for any one who went down in that boat. You see, Lieutenant Bronson," he said to the puzzled prisoner of war, "our man Finnegan

occupies a peculiar position with regard to the ship's
company and the service regulations. Several times,
by being drunk and under control of his instincts,
he has been the means of saving this ship and our
lives. So, trusting that no harm will come to him
that is not already come, we permit him to drink all
he pleases. If he were drunk, and had started your
boat to the bottom, we might believe that he did
so for some purpose known only to God and his
own subliminal self; but he was sober, so our
theory is useless. Now, you are, of course, a prisoner, but on parole. You will be provided with
dry clothing. Make yourself at home among my
officers."

So Lieutenant Bronson, of the Russian navy, became for the time a supernumerary officer of his
Britannic Majesty's battle-ship *Argyll*, and, clad in
an undress uniform supplied by one of the English
officers, mounted to the forward upper fighting-top,
where, with the strongest binoculars on board—bor-
rowed from the captain—he was able to report unofficially, but decisively, on the character of a long,
low, destroyer-type of craft that crept around the
headland down-stream, hovered a few moments, and
then hurried seaward at thirty knots, followed by
about half a ton of steel from the *Argyll's* six-inch
and secondary guns. "Russian scout-boat," he remarked to the deck, then turned his glasses else-
where on the smooth waters of the strait—where
might appear some traces of his lost boat or his men.
Late in the afternoon, when the tide had turned and
gained its maximum strength, he called attention to
something that glistened in the sun, far over toward
the other shore, and soon after he pointed out another such object just behind it, then another,

farther out in the stream, then a fourth, far to the rear of them all.

" Torpedoes! " he called to the bridge beneath. " They've shot them out to lighten her. They float, you know, when their motion stops. There should be another somewhere."

He turned his glass around for a moment, then hailed again: " Man overboard! " and pointed dead ahead. Then a dozen lookouts repeated the call, and Bronson came down to the bridge.

The man could be seen with the naked eye; a swarthy, bearded fellow, who swam remarkably high out of water, even for a strong man. But Bronson, after another inspection through the glass from the end of the bridge, stopped the comment on this by the quiet remark: " He's not swimming at all; he's riding a torpedo. Look out for it, gentlemen, for you'll find the safety-gear unscrewed from the detonator. That's my engineer."

Whitehead torpedoes being standardized, are valuable to any craft carrying tubes, and boats were sent to bring them in, one of which brought, also, the bearded Russian engineer. Mr. Bronson translated his story.

" It was the quartermaster," he said, " who reached up and moved the starting-switch in the conning-tower. He easily surmised, by my talking in a language strange to him, that we were captured, and when he saw me relinquish the wheel to Finnegan he acted."

" But did anybody drown? " asked Mr. Clarkson, eagerly. " Where's Finnegan? How did that man get out? "

" Some must have drowned," went on Bronson, gravely. " The quartermaster got Finnegan out of

the way and closed the hatch; and then she was
bumping along the bottom, unable to rise even by
her own motion against the diving-rudder—hard up.
They shot out the torpedoes, but still she would not
rise; then they drew lots and ejected themselves, one
by one. The quartermaster swam to a torpedo and
was rescued by that scout-boat, but the rest must
have drowned, for the engineer did not see them."

"But who remained behind?" asked Mr. Clarkson.
"Who drew the fatal number?"

"Finnegan—he was treated fairly and instructed
in the method."

"Poor old Finnegan," groaned the executive officer. "Done for at last. He has saved thousands
of lives when drunk, and now must die, sober and
instructed, to save a half-dozen enemies."

The groan echoed, mentally, throughout the ship,
and men went to their sleep that night praying for
the soul of the gentle and ridiculous old man they
had loved.

But at daylight there were other things to think
of. Sharp but intermittent firing was heard, and
hardly had the crew got to quarters before there
staggered around the headland below a large mer-
chant-built steamer, with huge derricks fitted to each
mast, a few small, quick-fire guns mounted in high
places and barking as she came, the white naval ensign of Britain flying from each mast and gaff, and a
volume of smoke belching upward from amidships.
She was afire, and, as if this trouble were not enough,
she was perceptibly down by the head, proving that
at least one compartment was filled. She turned into
the strait and came toward the *Argyll*.

"The mother-ship, lieutenant," explained the captain, as Bronson appeared on the bridge. "She car-

ries our five submarines and a holdful of White-
heads. Your friends are after her."

"And after you, too, captain," answered Bronson.
"Look there." He pointed to the upper end of the
strait, where, far out over the gray sea, were two
grayer spots, from each of which, even as they looked,
came a twinkle of flame. "That scout-boat has reported you."

"And you, too, lieutenant," answered the captain,
grimly. "She rescued one of your men. What will
happen to you for losing that boat?"

"The salt-mines of Siberia for me," answered
Bronson. "I am pondering on the ethics of desertion."

The captain glanced inquiringly at him, then said,
"I will release you from parole, if you wish."

"Thank you, sir. I accept the release, officially;
but will always maintain it, personally, between you
and myself. But I am still pondering. I cannot
desert yet. Please put me in irons."

The captain smiled. "No," he said. "You cannot escape."

But, being a prisoner no longer under parole,
Bronson left the bridge; and by this time two foun-
tains of water had arisen on the smooth waters of
the strait perilously near to the *Argyll*, proving that
the men behind those twinkles of flame had the range.

Then two booming reports came over the sea;
but the *Argyll* remained at anchor and waited.

The gun-fire from behind the headland below had
not ceased, and soon appeared—three miles out, however—the scout-boat of the day before. She passed
slowly across the opening, firing at the mother-ship
but maintaining a safe distance. Then a three-
funneled, high-sided, armored cruiser appeared in

view, then a short, bulky battle-ship, and another smaller cruiser. All directed their fire at the reeling mother-ship, coming on in her smoke, her crew working at the heavy forward crane.

"Only three submarines on her deck," remarked the captain, as he viewed her through his glass. "She has left two of them somewhere. I wonder if they're near by?"

And now the two ships coming on from above—battle-ships, evidently—changed their fire from the *Argyll* to the other; and their range-finders were good and their aim was good, and the shells that they sent were heavy, and when one lifted a shower of water over the whole slanting deck of the mother-ship the *Argyll* acted. She was caught in a trap, but that unarmored, unprotected mother with her five small ducklings needed her care, and, lifting her anchor, she steamed out to meet her, the secondary battery silent the while, but the after-turret guns belching at the two ships at sea, the forward ones at the battle-ship, the two cruisers, and the scout. And her aim was good and her range-finding excellent, and the shells she sent so much heavier than those sent at her that with a little more time she might have saved that distracted mother, for the two cruisers and the scout withdrew from range as fast as their horse-power would admit. But the battle-ship remained broadside to the target—flame, smoke, and pointed steel coming from her turrets, and every fountain of water raised by these pointed steel shells closer to the fleeing mother-ship than the last, until finally one struck her in the stern and raked through her length. She separated into fragments.

It was not an instantaneous explosion; beginning at the stern she seemed to split in two, while a line of rising flame and smoke traveled forward. Then the two sides disintegrated and sank; the masts leaned—one forward, the other aft—and fell; a cigar-shaped submarine boat, swung high at the forward derrick, went higher in air, and fell into the turmoil beneath; while two others, lifted sidewise from the shattered halves of the hull, whirled end over end and fell into the sea. Up and out from this riot of destructive forces came a huge expanding cloud of black and yellow smoke, while over the sea, echoing and reverberating against the wooded shores of the strait, went a crashing continuity of sound as of a repeated drum-call of artillery. Every Whitehead in the hold had exploded separately, and when the cloud had thinned there was nothing left of the mother-ship but a few floating fragments of wood, and, showing for one instant before it sank, the round conning-tower of a single submarine.

And now the *Argyll* received the gun-fire of the three ships, one but a mile below her, the other two, breast to breast, coming down the strait. The cruisers and the scout-boat were still going; they seemed to be agitated, smoking hard from their funnels and flying numerous small flags in different combinations. But the battle-ship they had deserted, though weaker than the *Argyll*, steamed boldly into the strait, and, as she was already close enough, the latter stopped her engines and drifted with the tide; then the two ships above slowed down, and, the *Argyll* in the center, there ensued one of the hammer-and-tongs, give-and-take conflicts from which the big English battle-ship had ever emerged victorious—because no shell was made that could penetrate her eighteen-inch armor, and no armor that could withstand her thirteen-inch shells.

Bronson, gloomy of face, appeared in the conning-tower, where the imperturbable captain and his aides had taken refuge from the storm of steel. He waited until the captain had withdrawn his eyes from a peep-hole, then said:

"Your master-at-arms will not confine me, captain."

"Are you still pondering on the ethics of desertion?" asked the captain, again gluing his eye to a peep-hole.

"The problem is unsolvable," said Bronson. "By the laws of honor and of Russia I should be fighting against you; by the laws of nature and of blood, I should be with you. There are penalties for violation of law."

"What do you mean?" asked the captain, without looking around.

"I notice that your fighting-top batteries are silent."

The captain paid no more attention to him, and Bronson climbed the ladder that led up the mast to the lower top.

It is an axiom in the world's navies that no man may live through an action in a fighting-top, and Bronson, aloft with the dead, could not but have been impressed by the sight of the fall of the lower Russian ship's foremasts, tops, guns, dead men and living, and the small signal-yard to which, even as the mast crashed down, small flags were ascending. But the ship went on, a man now exposed on her forward bridge waving a wigwag back and forth until abreast of the *Argyll*. And now, though her heavy shells still came toward the big, invulnerable Englishman, it was noticeable that her whole secondary battery of quick-fire and machine guns was directed astern, at something which only Bronson, high in air with a pair of service binoculars, could make out.

"A submarine!" he called. "They're running away from it. Now it has dived."

Gun-fire on the upper ships suddenly ceased, and the *Argyll's* captain and aides came out of their refuge to see these two, with a furious turmoil of water at their sterns, backing and turning in their lengths. The wigwag had told the news.

"There it is again!" shouted Bronson, excitedly. "It's up for a peep around. Now it's under again."

Professional excitement and enthusiasm are excusable, even when aroused over the performances of an enemy. Bronson, who had gone aloft to die, had a new interest in life.

"The mother-boat must have dropped one somewhere," said the captain, "or else it's the one they had hoisted when she blew up. Just in time, too," he added calmly, as a crash sounded and a quiver went through the ship, while a cloud of smoke and splinters went up from the stern. A shell from the lower ship had struck.

"Steering-gear gone, sir!" called a quartermaster from within the conning-tower.

"Thought so," remarked the captain. "We're hit in our weak spot. We're helpless, but—praise God for that submarine. Look at them go."

The two backing and turning Russians had straightened around. The other, still waving the wigwag from her bridge, had passed them, and was leading the parade. Behind was an occasional glimpse of a small, circular conning-tower, which appeared for only an instant and then dived.

The big, helpless ship swung slowly around, steer-

ing, after a manner, with her twin screws, but helpless to maneuver. Yet her batteries were intact, and
she continued her hammering blows on the fleeing
ships; and these, as they gathered way, resumed their
response. Shot and shell again crashed into her soft
spots, but the officers did not again enter the conning-tower. They were too interested in that other
and smaller conning-tower. It appeared again and
again, each time remaining longer in sight, and at
last seemed to be approaching the *Argyll*, which had
swung end on to it. Then it dived again, and
Bronson, his new interest in life much stronger,
came down to the main-deck unperceived in the
confusion.

"She's coming," said the captain. "I wonder if
she fired a torpedo."

"Don't think she got near enough, sir," answered
one of his lieutenants. "But consider the moral
effect of these boats, captain. She frightened away
the scout-boat and the cruisers. They went away
signaling."

"Yes, one such boat is worth a whole fleet until
fighting begins. She has frightened them all away.
Here she is again."

The small conning-tower again arose, a hundred
yards ahead. This time it remained above water,
and they expected the hatch to open and her commander's head to appear, when their attention was
brought closer to themselves. A large shell had
struck the foremast just below the lower top, exploded, and sent the upper part of the mast whirling
overboard; the blast of flame and smoke and the
sudden compression and expansion of the surround-
ing cushion of air threw every man on the bridge
upon his back.

"Poor Bronson!" gasped the captain. "His problem in ethics is settled."

The men, little hurt, arose one by one and looked, some in time to see the hatch open in the approaching conning-tower, others when a man had clambered out.

"Ship ahoy!" yelled the man, standing knee-deep in the water ahead of the ship. "Why d'ye run away fur? Hey—ye brass-bound, murtherin' sons ov a codfish a-arishtocracy! Lemme out o' this contrapshion. D'ye hear me?—damn yer eyes!"

"Finnegan!" yelled a chorus of voices from gun-ports and apertures. And the beloved name went through the ship. Crews deserted their guns and crowded out for a look at him. He began dancing about in the water, shaking his fist and reviling his officers, profanely and unkindly, demanding that he be taken on board at once, and rebuking them for their heartlessness in running away. Those on the bridge were speechless at first, then the captain spoke.

"He's drunk," he said, an expression of awe and wonder on his smoke-stained countenance; "and still an instrument of Providence. But how did he raise that boat alone, and how did he get drunk?"

As the small submarine boat came abreast, men on the main-deck went over after Finnegan. Yelling and shouting joyously, they pulled the profane and abusive old man off into deep water, and held him up, finding him at last an inert and lifeless load on their hands; then a bowline was lowered, and he was pulled aboard. But in the confusion in the water no one had noticed that one man had climbed up the submerged deck of the submarine, floundered along to the tower, and entered it. It was only when the noise of the hatch snapping down came to their ears and they saw the small conning-tower disappear before their eyes that they suspected who had entered the boat.

But as to how Finnegan had raised the boat they did not learn from him; he knew nothing about it, he insisted, when the surgeon had revived him. Months later, the explanation came in a letter, part of which the captain read to his officers.

"I was released from parole, you remember," said the letter, "and took a chance that Finnegan had weathered—that's all. Five torpedoes going out did not lighten her enough; but five men—nearly a thousand pounds more—going out, did the business, and she must have floated up with Finnegan. He only had to start the motor, but the water awash in her destroyed her trim; that is why she dived so often. He turned on the oxygen, too, and I nearly suffocated before I got things straight."

"Oxygen," murmured the surgeon. "That's what made him drunk."

FIFTY FATHOMS DOWN

THE United States submarine torpedo-boat *Diver* had come to the surface to blow out, to recharge her storage-battery, and to restore her supply of compressed air to its working pressure of two thousand pounds to the square inch. The first two were accomplished, but, there being something wrong with the air-compressor motor, the last was delayed while a machinist and two electricians swore over it—or under it, for it was at arm's-length overhead—and the boat, in the awash or diving condition, ran along under her gasoline engine. Breen, temporary commander, raised his boyish face up through the conning-tower hatch, the hinged lid of which was held upright by a strong spring, and looked around at the night. It was pitch dark and starless, but, over to the east, the upper limb of a full moon was just appearing above the horizon. The hinged lid of the hatch prevented a view astern; the engine exhaust drowned the lesser sounds of the sea.

A curious, rushing sound mingled with the puffing of the exhaust, a voice high above and astern sang out, " Something under the bow, sir! " and a huge bulk of blacker darkness struck the small, semi-submerged craft a glancing blow from astern, heeled it a little, and bore it under. Breen was washed downward by the inrush of water, but held a grip on the conning-tower ladder, and found voice to call out: " Stop the engine! Shut off the gas! " Then, against that almost solid column of descending salt water, he fought his way upward until, face above the hatch again, but looking now into the blackness of the deep sea, he seized the hand-hold of the hatch-lid and pulled it down. It closed with a force that would have shivered anything but armor steel, and Breen, half drowned, fell to the floor of the handling-room. As he raised himself he could hear faintly, through the steel walls from the void without, the lessening pulsations of a steamer's screw.

" Run down! " he gasped, choking the water from his lungs and supporting himself by the ladder, for the boat was rolling twenty degrees. " Anything carried away? "

" Seems not, lieutenant, " answered the chief-electrician—" nothing but the auxiliary motor. I've burned it out—had my hand on the switch when the jar came. But we're sinking, sir."

"We've taken in more than the reserve buoyancy, surely," said Breen, looking at the depth-indicator, which already marked forty feet. The hand moved, as he looked, to fifty, sixty—and more.

"Blow out every tank!" he ordered.

The ballast and trimming tanks were emptied, and the scant store of compressed air was further lessened thereby; but, though the indicator hand moved more slowly, it moved as steadily and as surely. The boat was still sinking.

"Start the motor and connect up the pumps!" said Breen. "What am I thinking about—wasting time and air over tanks with all this water washing about?"

"Can't, sir," answered a machinist from the neighborhood of the engine. "The motor's soaked through. A lot came down the air-pipe 'fore I could close it, and all the rest has come aft, too."

Breen looked, and became thoughtful of face. The depressed engine compartment now held the water taken in, and the lower half of the armature was immersed. A sunken submarine, with main motor short-circuited by water and auxiliary motor burned out, without means to pump, to move, or to compress air for power, is in a serious plight. But Breen's face cleared in a moment.

"Man the hand-pump!" he said. "My God!" he added, in a semi-whisper as he glanced at the indicator. It marked one hundred!

As many men as could find room for their hands on the pump-brake put forth their strength, but could force very little water out against the pressure of the sea. They looked at Breen, doubt and anxiety showing in their faces.

" Out with the torpedoes! " he said, bravely and cheerfully. " We had a reserve buoyancy of three hundred, and we're carrying several thousand pounds of steel and gun-cotton that we won't need right away. Disconnect the levers and unscrew the detonator! "

Whitehead torpedoes—mechanical fish—are merely aimed and started by the craft that carries them. They propel themselves by their own motive power, steer themselves in the direction originally pointed, and—at an under-water depth automatically chosen —if they hit nothing within a practical radius, lock their engines and rise by a reserve buoyancy to float and be recovered. Breen's last order carried a meaning to these men that was reflected back in their pale faces as they removed the starting-levers and the small fan-wheel which, by the torpedo's motion, would bring the detonator into action. " Any port in a storm," muttered one. " They're good life-buoys on a pinch." They withdrew the Whitehead always carried in the tube, prepared it like the others, inserted it, and closed the breech; then, opening the bow port, they turned on the compressed air, and a cough, a thud, and an inrush of water testified that the torpedo was out. They blew out the tube, closed the port, opened the breech, and hauled forward another torpedo, while Breen studied the depth-indicator.

" One hundred and ten," he called, " and still sinking! Out with them all, quickly! "

The sinking boat was now slightly " by the stern " from the expenditure of the water that had replaced the torpedo, which water is, under normal conditions, retained in a tank and shifted aft to others as torpedoes are hauled forward, in order to maintain the horizontal trim of the boat; but they were expending weights now, and it mattered not if the boat stood on her tail for a time, provided she floated. She did give promise of the erect attitude, reaching an angle of ten degrees with the release of the third torpedo; but at this moment there was a shock and a shudder through the steel hull, then a bumping, scraping sound.

"Good!" exclaimed Breen. "We've reached the bottom, one hundred and twenty feet down. Three hundred and fifty's the crushing-point."

"But we're scraping along with the tide, sir," answered one of the men, "and we may go deeper."

"Then we'll find the torpedoes right above us," said Breen, promptly. "Out with the other two."

Out they went, one after the other, and after them the water in the tube. The boat lifted her bow to an angle of twenty-five degrees, but the scraping and bumping of the propeller-guard on the bottom continued, and the depth-indicator told them that she was now one hundred and thirty feet below the surface, and dragging down-hill. The men at the handpump quit the fruitless labor and joined them. They looked into one another's pale faces. Only Breen's showed decision.

"Draw lots," he said, bringing forth a box of matches from his pocket, "as to who goes first."

"You mean last, sir, don't you?" asked the engineer. "It makes no difference who goes first on the chance of swimming up over a hundred feet to find a torpedo at night; but some one must remain to fire out the last man, sir."

"I remain," said Breen. "No arguments about

this. I am the commander, and should have kept a better lookout."

"But, lieutenant," said the other engineer, "can't we shoot the boat up on a slant by the engine? The sparkers are out of water."

"The conning-tower hatch would still be under water, and we would be far away from the torpedoes. They are now right above us. We know that much. Who goes first, now?"

"I will," said one of the trimming-tank men. "But, lieutenant," he added, "we can swim up in two minutes, I should think, and I've held my breath three; but how'll we know which way to swim? It's night up there. We can't see."

"If your head and stomach don't tell you, let your knife hang loose by the lanyard. It'll hang down. Swim parallel. Hold on. Keep your shoes on"— the man was shedding them—"take all weights out that you can. Put your coats on, all of you. It's a cold night up above. You'll need your coats riding a torpedo."

"Good-by, sir. Good-by, boys—all 'round. No time to shake hands. If I find a Whitehead, I'll keep singin' out."

He threw open the breech of the tube and crawled in. A man stood with his hand on the compressed-air valve; another stood by the bow-port lever; Breen himself was at the breech.

"Take a good breath when you hear the breech closed," he called in, and was answered. Then he slammed to the swinging breech-door, locked it, and waved his hand to his men. They knew the drill. Water was admitted at once, the bow port was lifted, compressed air was turned on, there was the usual cough and thud and inrush of water, and a man under a pressure of four atmospheres was swimming, somewhere, through water black as night, guided only by his knife lanyard or the *feel* of his head and stomach.

The tube was blown out and another man said good-by and crawled in. He was ejected. Then the performance was repeated again and again, while Breen watched the dials that told of depth and inclination, and listened for a cessation of the scraping sound of the propeller-guard. There was none, and both inclination and depth registers showed increase.

He himself ejected the last man, and stood up, alone, in a boat one hundred and forty feet beneath the surface of the sea, her bow lifted to an angle of thirty degrees from the horizontal, her main motor drowned and her auxiliary motor burned. There was one chance in a million that he would be rescued; but, as he stood on the slanting floor of the handling-room, the hope of this one chance came to him, for the scraping and bumping had ceased.

He looked at the depth-indicator and waited. No; she was not rising from the expenditure of weights, as he had hoped for a moment; the propeller-guard must have caught on some projection on the bottom, and was holding her from drifting farther with the tide. This was proved to him by a new and faint sound coming through the steel walls of his coffin— the sound of rustling water passing by. But it soon gave way to the bumping and scraping; and when, two hours later, this grew fainter and finally ceased, and he again looked at the depth-indicator, he saw a reading of three hundred. He was fifty fathoms below the surface.

Breen's emotions for the next few hours need not be recorded. They were mainly concerned with that one chance in a million, and ended in prayer; but following the prayer came the much used and abused, homely but practical, reflection that the Lord helps those who help themselves, and he arose from the floor where he had thrown himself and looked around —first, at the air-pressure indicators. All but two registered at zero; he had two tanks at two thousand pounds pressure, and he could have blown out a few more torpedoes, or men, or tanks of water, but not that water washing about aft. He thought of the storage-battery beneath the flooring—ninety large jars of sulphuric acid, in danger from contact with that washing salt water—and, removing the hatch, inspected it. He found that the last jars aft lifted six inches above the water-level, and, knowing that they were designed for an inclination of forty-five degrees, was reassured on this point. Salt water and sulphuric acid are a bad combination in a closed compartment; and his air was already bad enough from the fumes of smoking insulation and the leakage of gasoline from the engine.

He looked at the burned-out motor overhead in the handling-room. It worked the air-compressor and one of the bilge-pumps, the other being connected to the main motor, under water and equally useless. He had a naval officer's knowledge of electricity and motors, acquired at Annapolis, and this told him that it would be hopeless, even for an expert mechanic, to attempt rewinding that small motor with the dried-out wires of the other. He studied the main motor, nearly buried in water. When dry it worked with seventy horse-power. It would pump out, against the pressure of the sea, the water that kept the boat down. If clear of this water it would dry out—in time. In what time? Breen had fifteen

days' supply of food and water for a crew of eight
—one hundred and twenty days' supply for himself.
His air-supply was short, but—suffocation is a long
death.

The lower part of the armature and fully half the
height of the field magnets were still immersed. He
needed more weight forward or less aft; and as his
eye roved about the maze of fixtures—pipes, valves,
and machinery—it rested upon the useless gasoline-
engine—a two-thousand-pound weight. Removing
his coat, he first made sure that the gas-feed valve
was screwed tight, then, delving for wrenches, span-
ners, and hammers in the engineer's locker, attacked
the engine. He was working for life, and such work
is exhilarating for a time. Breen sang while he
worked.

Two weeks later he was not singing. His clothing
a greasy envelope of rags and shreds, his face haggard, his eyes sunken from too close looking into the
eyes of death, he dragged forward with bleeding
hands the connecting-rod of the after-cylinder, and
piled up a scrap-heap of similar fragments beside the
torpedo-tube in the bow. The engine was stripped
to the supporting column that bore the weight of
the motor and the pump, and the boat was not yet
on an even keel; but the last lower coil of the field-
magnet was lifted from the water by the shifting of
the weight, and when he had cleared the storage-
battery wires from all contact with water he re-
warded himself with a few deep inhalations from his
nearly exhausted compressed-air supply, and sat
down to wait—until the insulation was dry.

Being a government officer, not yet relieved from
duty, he had kept the log, and knew the flight of
time by this and the clock; and in another week he

realized with sinking heart that the motor was *not
drying out.* A little reflection told him why: in the
sealed-up hull the atmosphere was saturated with
moisture, and no more evaporation could take place.
In a fit of utter and suicidal desperation he turned
on the last few pounds of his air-supply and lay down,
weary of work, weary of thought, hoping now, if
death would not come speedily, that unconsciousness
would—that he might at least be relieved of the
torture of headache that now afflicted him. And unconsciousness came, in the form of sweet, refresh-
ing sleep, brought on by the suicidal extravagance in
air. And when he wakened there was a thought, or
the remnant of one, a lingering survival of something he had dreamed—a phrase repeating itself, and
dwindling away, as the details of valve and piping
took form before his eyes. It was of gases, this
thought—of a drying agent for gases—something he
had studied years ago at school. A drying agent
for gases? What was it? Then it came to him out
of the forgotten chemistry in his subconscious mind:
" Sulphuric acid."

He had ninety jars of it under his feet. He had
lead and copper piping in his scrap-heap forward.
He had two electric fans used for ventilation on the
surface, and a blower, fixed in the air-pipe, but
available on a pinch—all four wired and ready,
with a thirty-six-hundred-ampere-hour battery to
drive them. Wild with hope, he sprang to his feet
and went to work. In three hours he had constructed
from the back of his coat a cone-shaped funnel that
stretched around the wire guard of a fan-wheel;
and this he fitted onto the end of a length of lead
pipe, the other end of which was all but immersed in
the acid of a battery jar in the hold. With the fan

buzzing and blowing into this funnel, and a stream of air ruffling the surface of the acid, he yet went on contriving; and with another fan, unscrewed from its shelf and rewired to a new location, he caught this dried air as it rose and drove it aft over the motor. Smiling like a child with a toy, Breen sat down and watched it, his mind intent upon chemistry, that he once had hated, that he had so completely forgotten.

The air was again very bad; his head was aching as it had ached before, and he needed no clear recollection of the forgotten science to know that the dominant irritant was the carbonic-acid gas from his lungs. How to purify the air he did not know. This boat was not equipped with the apparatus for such purpose that he had read of in plans and specifications, and all the chemistry that would come to him was the old, familiar class-room test for carbonic-acid gas, or—as he liked to call it now, with his mind on chemistry—carbon dioxide. This testing reagent was lime-water, but the chemical term for it was beyond him. He went to sleep at last, thinking of lime-water—lime-water, and the chemical name for it.

As he slept, fitfully, with intervals of half-waking thought, chemical terms, long forgotten and bearing no seeming relation to lime-water, ran jumblingly through his head—potassium chlorate, manganese dioxide, chloride of sodium, chlorhydric acid. These persisted through the jumble, and remained when he had wakened. He repeated and remembered them. But what had they to do with lime-water? Nothing, that he could remember. Chloride of sodium was common salt, he knew, and he had plenty of it, dissolved in water—more than he wanted. Chlorhydric acid—hydrochloric acid—muriatic acid —an acid containing no oxygen, the one gas that he

needed so badly—formed of hydrogen and chloric—
chloride, chlorine gas. Good, so far. Chlorine—also
a constituent of the salt in his bilge-water. But what
of it? It was oxygen that he wanted. Potassium
chlorate—chlorate of potassium. This contained
chlorine. Manganese dioxide contained oxygen; but
what did it mean? Why should these elements and
compounds come to his mind? He had something
of blind faith in the relevancy of thought, but he
wanted to know only of lime-water, with which he
could catch the carbon dioxide in the air and free
the oxygen. This last thought was an advance, but
he could go no further in this direction. His mind
returned to chlorhydric acid, to hydrogen, to
chlorine. How were they made? They were all there
—in his sea-water. But why these persisting
thoughts? His waking thought of sulphuric acid as
a drying agent meant something. Did it mean more?
Sulphuric acid, one of the most powerful chemical
reagents known—the most powerful electrolyte—
electro—electrolysis—" Hurrah! "

He bounded to his feet. He had it. Electrolysis
of water yielded oxygen and hydrogen. But why
had manganese dioxide and potassium chlorate so
persisted in his mind? And lime-water—what had
that to do with his problem, now solved by electrolysis?

Slowly the memory of school-day lessons learned
by rote filtered up from the past—of the test-tube
manufactured of oxygen by the union of these chem-
icals in the presence of heat. And lime-water, with
its affinity for carbon dioxide? There was no lime
on board, hence no lime-water. But there was water
—too much. Where was the affinity? It was slower
in coming, but it came—the old lessons learned by

rote and forgotten. "Carbon dioxide is soluble in water, volume for volume." "Oxygen is but slightly soluble in water—about three parts in a hundred."

"I see how it is," he said, with the infantile smile that had come to his boy's face in this trouble. "It's the subliminal self that remembers everything; and when you've guessed all around the subject it pops out and hits you when you've touched it."

He found some spare insulated wire among the stores, and rigged two lengths from the poles of the battery, scraping the ends and immersing them in the salt water. A few bubbles arose, then ceased.

"Funny how things come back when you need them," he said, as he pulled up the wires. "I want platinum electrodes and solder and soldering fluid— chloride of zinc—zinc cut by hydrochloric acid. Wonder if I'll have to make my acid?"

He did not. He found a soldering outfit in the locker, then rummaged his scrap-heap forward for platinum sparkers, and, finding very little of the precious metal, ruthlessly smashed all but three of the electric bulbs that lighted his prison, robbing them of the platinum wires that led the current into the carbons.

Clumsily—for he was but a theoretical mechanic —he soldered the ends of the platinum wires and fragments to the copper ends of his terminals, about half to each, making brush-like electrodes of the largest possible surface-exposure. Then he immersed them, and was gratified at the result. Bubbles arose in generous quantity.

"Now, which is which?" he said, as he leaned over them. "Let's think. Water—hydrogen and oxygen—H_2O—two parts hydrogen to one of oxygen. But the bubbles seem about the same size."

He stopped and inhaled deeply of the air over one column of bursting bubbles; a little of this brought on a curious feeling of faintness, with a desire to draw a longer breath.

" Hydrogen, surely," he said. " Now the other."

A half-inhalation over the other bubbles sent him back, coughing and choking, with a bitter, astringent taste in his throat.

" No," he said, as he pulled up the wire. " That is not oxygen. It's some other gas. I must separate them, somehow."

He racked his brains for the rest of the day—until his clock told him that sleeping-time had arrived—but could not remember more of his chemistry. He could only fix in his mind a few chemical facts not forgotten: that he was using up the existing oxygen by combining it, in his lungs, with carbon to form carbon dioxide, ten per cent. of which, in the air, might be fatal; that the hydrogen which he would make, with his oxygen, was non-poisonous, like the nitrogen of the air, but that, there being less of it as a diluent, he might suffer from a preponderance of oxygen; and that this astringent gas that would also evolve from the salt water was a deadly poison to be got rid of. But how? Was it carbon dioxide? He did not need to sleep on the problem; he had already slept upon and solved it. It came to him suddenly in the formulated sentences of the morning. Water would absorb carbon dioxide, volume for volume, while oxygen would only give up three parts to a hundred.

" What a fool I am!" he muttered. " I can simply blow the whole mixture back into the water again and again, and get rid of everything but the oxygen and hydrogen."

The motor was dryer to the touch, but still much too damp for use; so, for the present, he left his air-drying apparatus intact, and constructed a supplementary pneumatic feed system that would have scandalized a mechanical or electrical engineer, but was a triumph of driven genius to poor Breen, dying of headache at the bottom of the sea.

First, he reversed the polarity of the fixed blower in the air-pipe overhead, so that it worked downward; then he propped up and secured a section of gas feed-piping that would catch the mixed bubbles as they burst, and deliver the mixture to this blower. Below this fan he suspended a fairly air-tight funnel formed of the seat and one leg of his trousers, and to the funnel secured another length of copper piping, the lower end of which he hammered flat, so that it would spread the flow of gases to a fan-shaped stream conducive to a large number of smaller bubbles. This end he immersed in the deepest part of the flooded engine-room, sacrificed his shirt to form a hood over the bubbles that would rise, and under this hood arranged his original funnel and fan that drove air through the lead pipe to the sulphuric acid. He had contrived an apparatus to manufacture two volumes of hydrogen to one volume of oxygen, with an unknown quantity of poisonous gas—that would suck into itself the foul air of the closed hull and drive it, with the mixed gases, in a divided stream into the purifying water—and that would force the oxygen which arose onto the drying sulphuric acid, to be then sent back over the damp motor. Arranging his battery wires in the water, he turned on all the fans and tested the result by his sense of smell. There was but the slightest bad odor in the blast from the last fan—not enough to distress him; and,

utterly tired out, Breen went to sleep as happy as
a man may be on the cold sea-bottom without shirt
or trousers and barely reprieved from lingering
death.

When he awakened, his fans still buzzed merrily,
his headache was gone, and the motor much dryer
to the touch. His problem seemed to have been
solved, for there were no more chemical terms or
" guesses " remaining from his sleep. Yet, as he felt
of the damp motor and noticed the hydrogen bubbles rising and escaping into the air without going
through the drying process, he felt, and obeyed, a
strong impulse to turn them into the pipe that caught
the others.

" Can't do any harm to dry the hydrogen," he
mused ; " and it would mix with the oxygen later, in
any case, while the water won't absorb it—only the
carbon dioxide."

A few moments later he noticed an utter absence
of the bad odor in the blast from the acid to the
motor, and felt only a slight increment of gratifica-
tion. It was long after, with a larger experience of
and dependence upon the infallibility of subliminal
promptings that he realized that it was *not to dry*
the hydrogen that he had turned it into his pipes.

From this on his problems were mechanical; he
was interested in the rapidly drying motor and its
potencies when he dared turn the current into it.
He realized these potencies—he knew that the seventy-horse-power motor could pump out the water
and bring her to the surface; but knowing, too, that
under the coils moisture would remain long after the
surface windings were dry, and that a short-circuit-
ing of coils might rack the insulation to pieces by
the formation of steam, he waited a full week after

the last dampness had apparently gone; then, uncoupling the motor from the shaft and turning on the switch, he carefully moved the controller and gave it momentary contact. A thin cloud arose from the motor and the armature moved an inch. He inspected the cloud; it seemed to be steam, not smoke, and he tried it again with longer contact. The armature moved farther, and again he shut off the current, assured himself that there was no burning, and turned it on. This time he left it on, and stood over the motor, watching the steaming armature slowly turn at about the rate of a steamboat's paddle-wheel, while the commutator brushes threw out sparkings six inches long. His theoretical knowledge of electricity told him that these sparks indicated a waste of current; and he noticed that when his body interposed between the motor and the blast of dried air from the last fan in his system the sparks were reduced to minute points, hardly visible. With nothing to do now until his motor gained power enough to pump, he busied himself in constructing a hood that would enclose the commutator and brushes, using his undershirt for material and singing as he worked. A man may be joyful at the bottom of the sea, shivering with cold in one garment, provided he is hopeful. And Breen was hopeful; his hood was a success; it stopped the extravagant sparking, but did not save enough current to work the pump, which fact he learned by connecting it. The armature moved faster, but stopped short against the small resistance of the inert water in the induction-pipe. So he turned off the current, overhauled and lubricated the pump, and waited.

He was very happy now, singing and talking to himself, while his heart beat a thumping accompaniment to the music, and the steel walls of his sunken prison rang with his words, delivered in shouts. He was not in the least cast down when two of his lights burned out, and he danced forward in rag-time step, secured the remaining bulb, and danced aft with it, adjusting it just forward of the motor, where it would illumine his system of buzzing fans and bursting bubbles.

He did not enter up the log this day, nor keep further track of the passage of time, being too lofty of soul to concern himself with such trifles; nor did he go to sleep when the time for it came around. Who would sleep with a seventy-horse-power motor dying out and needing attention, with a beautiful plant manufacturing, purifying, and drying air— sweet, cool air, to be breathed by himself, and no other? How pleasant it felt to his burning face and tingling fingers when he placed himself in its way! The world above, with its millions of men, had mil-lions of cubic miles of air to breathe no better than his, that he had made for himself. This thought so pleased him that he put it to rhyme, and sang it to the steel walls in the voice of a boatswain's mate in bad weather. Louder he sang, and louder, until the music went out of his voice and left it a screech.

There were a few hours of this, when he fell down near the motor and lay there.

Years later, as it seemed, he awakened in pitch-black darkness, with an irritating, pungent odor in his nostrils, a burning sensation in his throat, a clattering, rushing, roaring sound in his ears, and a pain in his head such as he had never felt before. Only one sensation could he place—the odor in his nostrils, the astringent action that he knew so well. Then his position and plight came back to him by degrees. His last light had burned out. His air-plant was still working, but the poisonous gas was escaping. How and why?

He reached out, felt the supporting column of the engine, and located himself; then he crawled to the different parts of his pipe-and-fan system, inspecting them by the sense of touch. Everything was as he had left it—the wires still fed bubbles into the pipe to the upper fan, the last fan still caught the air as it rose from the acid and sent it over the motor. Perhaps the motor would now work the pump. He found the switch and controller in the darkness, turned on the current, and felt his way back. The armature was turning—just a little faster than before. Shutting off the current, he coupled on the pump, and again gave power to the motor, only to find that the pump stopped it. The solid, inert, incompressible water in the induction-pipe could not be stirred. Yet there was power in the motor; he had tried to stop the armature with his hands, but could not. Two men could not—nor three, by the way it felt. If he could multiply that power? If he could give it purchase? If the water were more yielding—compressible—so that the motor, once started, would go on? Compressible, like air?

Air—compressible air. He had too much air—bad air, too. It gave him the pain in his head and the roaring in his ears. Crawling forward as far as he could go, he found a sweeter atmosphere, and thought it out. There was little logic or coherency in his thoughts; he only wanted to devise means to get rid of that poisonous flow of gas, which came from he knew not what defect in his apparatus, but which he could only stop by stopping the supply of oxygen. The air-compressor motor was burned out, otherwise he could pump air into any of the tanks, and outboard when the pressure was great enough. Could he turn that rotary bilge-pump into an air pump? Could he make an aperture in the induction-pipe above the water? Crawling aft into the stifling atmosphere near the motor, he found an elbow in the induction-pipe made up of a T-joint and a plug. Securing a wrench that fitted, he removed the plug and laid it on the motor-bed. Then he turned on the current, assured himself that the motor was turning over, and crawled forward out of the fumes. Here he remained, and after a long time, when a new sound as of the clapping of an outlet valve came to his burdened ears over the uproar, he shouted approval, and again was happy. He was pumping bad air out of the boat, and all was well with him. He was not even hungry nor thirsty; but, after a time, when the clapping of that valve in the outlet pipe had become a familiar sound, and his head had stopped aching, he felt somewhat sleepy; and, as the pile of machinery on which he lay was a hard bed, he crawled aft a little, where the greasy oilcloth flooring was softer. He went to sleep here, face upward, directly beneath the conning-tower hatch.

Years, generations, centuries passed while he lay there, and he wakened once or twice in a decade, listened to a far-away, roaring sound punctuated by the clapping of a valve, and went to sleep again. He wasted no energy in thinking about these sounds; they were the only sounds in the universe, and beyond his care and control. But at last a new sensation came to him, one that affected not his ears nor his organs of taste or smell; these were dead, killed long ago by that terrible, blistering gas. The sense of touch was lost in the all-pervading pain that saturated his whole body. The sense of light was but a memory, lost in the darkness that had engulfed him with the burning-out of the last bulb. But now, as he lay there on his back, the sense of light and sight seemed returning. Through his half-closed eyelids a dim glimmer of yellow and gray came into his brain. He opened them wide, and took in the details of the conning-tower ladder, the circular tower just above, and an occasional flickering image of the starboard deadlight moving up and down, back and forth, on the port inner surface of the tower. Light! Where did it come from? He arose painfully to his feet, and fell down. The boat was in motion, pitching somewhat, and rolling—ever so slowly—while water still washed around among the battery jars. He arose again, supporting himself by the ladder. The motor, dimly showing in the gray light, was spinning rapidly, the fans were still buzzing, the outlet valve still clapping at regular and more frequent intervals. The boat was afloat. He slowly climbed the ladder, found the hatch unscrewed—unconfined from within—exactly as he had left it ages before when he had fallen, half-drowned, from the ladder. Exerting all his strength, he pushed upward, but could not budge it. The outlook was gray through the deadlights, and only as the craft rolled did the occasional glimmer of yellow light come in from the starboard. She was on the surface, but with the top of her conning-tower awash—all below it buried. Even had he succeeded in opening the hatch against the slight weight of water sliding over it, he would only have swamped the boat and gone down again to another eternity. He looked at the motor, buzzing noisily and working a rotary pump that pumped—air.

Weakly and painfully he descended and crawled
aft into the blistering fumes to where he had left the
T-joint plug and the wrench; and without waiting to
stop the motor he turned that air-pump back into a
bilge-pump, heard the gurgling sound of water in the
pipe that accompanied the last few heaves he gave
to the wrench, and crawled forward to where the air
burned and choked him—just a little—less. Here
he waited, listening to the new cadence and slower
rhythm of that clapping outlet valve and the blessed
sound of gurgling water in the pipe, while the light
above grew stronger and the growing hope of life
in his heaving breast strove vainly to formulate itself
into words of prayer to pass his cracked and bleeding
lips. Then the buzzing of fans and motor softened,
the rhythmic cadence of the clapping valve lessened
and lowered, the gurgling sound of water ceased,
and, though the fans still whirled slowly, the pumping came to an end. The thirty-six-hundred-
ampere-hour battery was exhausted, but the work
was done.

Breen again climbed the ladder and pushed upward on the hatch. It yielded, and when the lifting
spring was past the center it flew upright. Raising
his head and shoulders through the opening, he
looked across a dark, heaving sea at a full moon
hanging above the horizon. He had seen it last a
month before.

And the air that he took into his poisoned lungs
cut like myriad knives of ice.

Three members of the Board of Inquiry, that later
exonerated Breen from misuse of government property, met at the Army and Navy Club long before
he was able to answer questions, and unofficially discussed him. One was a captain, another a surgeon,

and a third an engineer who was also a naval constructor and an electrical expert.

"One thing we'll have to find, surely," said the captain; "that is, that the course in chemistry at Annapolis is not thorough. I passed in the subject; but what did I know? What do I know now? Who but a specialist like Breen could save the boat and his life in that manner—if he did save his life. How about that, doctor?"

"He'll pull through," said the doctor. "His hair will turn dark again, and the wrinkles will go in time. Lord, how he looked!—sixty years old, gray-haired, and emaciated. Shows what an excess of oxygen will do, even diluted with all those poisonous gases. His lungs and throat are just so much raw meat."

"But it's funny," said the engineer. "No one can deny Breen's knowledge of chemistry—that's understood. Yet—he was in my class, you know—Breen just pulled through his exams by the skin of his teeth. Chemical symbols were worse than Greek to him, and chemical equations a deep, dark mystery. And yet, down there in the dark, at the bottom, he took a chance that nothing but utter desperation would induce me to take, and made a discovery in chemical reactions not down in any text-book and never announced by any one that I know of."

"What chance? What discovery?"

"Well, this. Electrolysis of water is easy, as we all know, and the product is oxygen and hydrogen, which can be breathed for a time; but it is an explosive mixture that would have blown him to eternity had enough of it touched a spark from either of those three fans."

"But he had enclosed the commutators."

"Yes, but that was his chance, nevertheless. Here

is another: He turned both wires into the pipe leading into his fan system. He was evolving large quan-
tities of chlorine gas from the salt in the water, and
this is equally explosive when in contact with hydrogen, not only from sparks, but from strong light.
Now, he was in pitch darkness, of course, and every
pipe feed led directly in front of the next fan, so
that the mixed gases did not touch the sparks and
explode. But what he risked was the poisoning effect
of that free chlorine before he made his discovery."

"And it did poison him," said the surgeon.
"Ripped his mucous membrane to shreds and
smithereens. But what did he discover?"

"That hydrogen and chlorine gas, mixed in utter
darkness and violently agitated, will combine without
explosion into hydrochloric-acid gas. Water takes
up four hundred and fifty volumes of this gas, but
only two and a half volumes of free chlorine, and
less of hydrogen. His discovery saved his life."

"But," said the captain, dryly, "he made a much
greater practical demonstration. He has proved that
men may safely be ejected from torpedo tubes, that
a Whitehead will support two men in the water, and
that the man left to die can turn into gas and expel
by the bilge-pumps the weight of water that holds
down the boat. How much—in this case? Did you
figure it out?"

"About a pint," said the engineer; "I must ask
Breen, though, about the new reaction. It's not quite
clear."

But Breen did not enlighten him.

THE ENEMIES

HE was a young man—not over twenty-four—when I first met him. He came down the dock dressed in nondescript rags which, to the uninitiated, might stamp him as tramp or dock-rat; but to me, taken with his keen glance aloft at our rigging and his sure-footed jump from the stringpiece to the fore-shrouds, they bespoke the deep-water sailor. He dropped to the deck, came straight to the galley door, and looked in.

"Cook," he said, in the deep, raspy voice of strongly fibered men, "I'm hungry. Will you gi' me a bite? I'll saw wood, or peel taters, or—anything at all."

I had but a scant supply of kindling and a sprained wrist; so I set him at work. Later, as he ate his breakfast in the galley, I had a chance to study his face. It was a particularly ill-favored face —not vicious at all, but ill-adjusted by nature—disproportionate. Nothing was in harmony: his ears, though well shaped, stood straight out from his head; his mouth, neither large nor small, was made up of two very thick lips, between which showed two irregular rows of strong, yellow teeth. His eyes were dark and steadfast, deep-sunken in cavities topped by thick eyebrows that met over the nose; and his nose was the nose of a fighter, short, broad, and aquiline. But, as though to atone for her niggardly treatment of his face, Mother Nature had given him the figure and grace of an Apollo. Clearly this was not a man to be satisfied with beggary, and when he had finished his meal and thanked me I asked:

"What's the matter? Have you no boarding-house?"

"Well, yes," he answered, looking me squarely in the eyes; "but I cleared out 'fore I got in debt. I'm through wi' deep water—that is, I'll try starving awhile 'fore I ship again to be thumped and damned like a dog. Ever been deep-water?"

"Yes. One voyage."

"I've made three—three too many. And I went against my will each time. Shanghaied each time, and I skipped at every chance, and tried to get work ashore, but—you know how boarding-masters own us, and how the police are with them, always."

"Yes, I know," I answered; "and I blame no man for trying to escape the life; but can't you get a job on the docks?"

"No; I don't belong to the union, and, as for laboring work, there are ten men waiting for each job, all known to the boss. I hope to slip into something soon, but meanwhile I have to eat."

"What work are you best at?" I asked, idly, for I saw little hope for him. A sailor ashore cannot compete with Italian laborers.

"I have no trade," he answered. "I was a night-watchman in a Brooklyn lumber-yard when they first shanghaied me; and I was studying medicine nights by a dark-lantern and attending lectures in the afternoon. You may not think so, but I'm a high-school graduate. But that's all past now; I can't go home in these clothes, and I'm too old to take up study again, anyhow. No, I'm fixed."

"Why not go coasting until you save some money?" I asked, more interested now.

"Oh, I've tried to," he said, his dark eyes lighting. "They treat men decently on the coast, I hear, and that's a strong point wi' me. I wasn't born to be hammered, and I always hit back, and get the worst of it. But there's a union here, too; and I can't join it without a little money for dues and initiation."

" Ever command men? "

" Been bosun. I'm an able seaman, all right."

" Well, I'll tell you. Clear out now, and come back this afternoon. The skipper wants a second-mate in this schooner, and you might do. I'll sound him at dinner-time. The mate and crew are aboard, and we sail in the morning."

" Thank you, cook. I can't navigate, but second-mates don't have to, as I understand. Yes, I could do the work, I know. And, of course, the skipper won't expect a well-groomed man out of a deep-water fo'c's'le. I'll get clothes the first chance."

The upshot was that John Waverlie sailed with us as second mate, with an outfit of clothing paid for with money loaned by myself. I had asked few favors of Captain Samson in the five years I had signed with him, and this, with my offer to anticipate possible advance-money, won me my point; for I was thoroughly impressed with Waverlie. He fell into his place easily, mastering the slight difference between square and schooner rig seamanship before we had finished the passage to Cedar Keys, where we took an assorted cargo. Here he showed himself a master-hand at rigging purchases to discharge this cargo, which comprised the stock of a dozen country stores; and in stowing lumber for the return trip his natural intelligence served him well in lieu of ex-perience at cargo work—which a deep-water man does not get. By the time we reached Boston he was sure of his berth and his future, should he care to remain in the coasting trade.

At Boston he paid me the money loaned, packed his belongings, and left to visit his home, where, he said, he had not been since leaving school. I supposed I had seen the last of him, and was rather surprised when he appeared in less than a week and asked the skipper for his second-mate's berth. He was taken on, and we sailed for Aspinwall.

Since the visit home his manner had changed—his earnest, dogged cheerfulness giving way to a half-surly indifference to the presence of others which was somewhat repellent. But he never overstepped the line—he was invariably civil, and in his attitude toward the crew he was all that sailors desire in an officer. He invited no freedom nor familiarity, but abstained religiously from ever raising his hand or voice in anger—a hard rule to follow, considering that even coasters occasionally ship a fo'c's'le lawyer who yields to nothing but a knock-down.

" I've seen enough of it," I heard him say to the captain, " and I know its futility. I've been hammered senseless more than once just to keep me at work; and it wasn't necessary. Nine men out o' ten will do as they're told; the tenth may wait; but he'll do it."

There was something on Waverlie's mind—something too deep and heavy for confidence. Often during the last dog-watch, when work was done and he stood in his favorite spot near the weather-poop steps, gazing steadily over the sea, I could hear, as I passed him, his heavy breathing, hoarse and throaty, which in a smaller, weaker man would have been a succession of groans. But in time, as we passed up and down the coast, these moods left him, though his silent self-absorption remained.

He bought himself a quadrant, an epitome, and a

nautical almanac, and, against the ill-concealed ridicule of the first mate, studied navigation, asking no instruction from either him or the captain. And he did not appear on deck with his quadrant until, one night six months later, he brought it up to take a lunar—to the wonder of the skipper—and followed the feat by taking a meridian observation next day which tallied closely with that of his superiors. He was a navigator, and did not hesitate so to proclaim himself. His boyhood schooling had made it easy for him.

But it did not lessen the growing gulf between himself and the jealous first mate; and one day at Charleston, when there was a little friction with the overworked and exhausted crew, the angry first mate twitted the mild-spoken Waverlie with cowardice in not treating the men as men deserved to be treated by competent second mates. Waverlie coolly invited him over the side to the dock, and there he thrashed him into half-consciousness, to the result that the disgruntled and humiliated mate quit the schooner. Waverlie took his berth, and a second mate was shipped in his place.

As first mate he gave satisfaction, and after a few more trips there came a second and unexpected promotion. Captain Samson sickened and died at Rio Janeiro, and Waverlie took the schooner home. Then, after an interview with the owner, he was formally installed in command. In three years from the time I had fed him, a hungry waif looking for work, John Waverlie had become captain of a well-equipped three-mast schooner, and I was proud of my judgment.

But Waverlie did not stop. Satisfied with himself, with more leisure, he studied and read, and gradually, as the months passed, he lost the little mannerisms, the small crudities of the seafaring man, relapsing, perhaps, into the refinement of his youth. His face and voice softened; the dogged stare left his deep-sunken eyes, showing now only under stress of weather or work. And he scrupulously held to his rule of discipline. He would discharge a refractory sailor on occasions, but on no account would he allow one of his mates to strike, threaten, or even curse a man of his crew. He smoked inveterately, but did not chew tobacco nor drink; and it gradually dawned upon me that he was more than a strong, self-made man—he was a gentleman.

He studied deeper into navigation than would most captains, and his knowledge of winds, tides, currents, and the geography of the sea gave him an advantage that is generally named as good luck; he was a " lucky captain "—he made fast passages with little damage to spars, sails, or rigging. This impressed the owner, who put him in command of a fine bark of the employ, engaged in the South American trade. He took his whole crew with him, and, as the bark carried a steward as well as a cook, he gave me the berth, and installed me in charge of the cabin.

And now occurred a series of happenings which led me to think that Captain Waverlie had reached his limitations. Success had been so easy for him after his escape from the thrall of the crimps that I did not wonder at his ordering fashionable clothing from the best tailors in New York, and stopping at the best hotels when in port. Nor did the quality of his evening enjoyments surprise me. In caring for his clothing I often found programmes of vaude-ville shows and music-halls, with literature pertain-ing to footlight favorites; for many a man of good

instincts but no social position will take his entertainment where he can. But I was more than surprised and greatly saddened when he called me from
my room one midnight in New York and thickly
ordered me to assist him to bed. He was palpably
drunk, and slept far into the morning. Then he
went ashore, and remained until the bark was nearly
ready to sail, when he came in a cab, in company
with a woman, whom he assisted up the gangway
and into the cabin. Later came an expressman with
a trunk, and later in the day a clergyman. Then the
first mate and myself were called into the after cabin,
where Captain John Waverlie, sober, erect, and
proud, gave his name to this faded woman, whose
breath, even as she uttered the marriage vows,
tainted the air of the cabin with the odor of whisky.
Her age could not be told from her face, but I judged
that she was younger than the captain. She was
of the blond type, with a splendid head of hair, and
fine blue eyes dimmed by illness; her face and form
were emaciated, and her features twitched continually from nervous trouble, brought on, perhaps, by
excessive use of stimulants. Or it may be that the
immediate cause was the rather sudden stoppage of
their use, as Captain Waverlie, after the first day's
license, placed the ship's liquor in my charge, with
orders to keep her from getting any. This I did,
though she often begged plaintively for a bracer. As
for the captain, he never, to my knowledge, drank
again.

We sailed to Montevideo and Rio that voyage, and
back to New York; and Captain Waverlie—neglecting no duty, however—spent his time in her company,
and grew younger in the dimmed light of those faded
blue eyes. That he loved her was beyond question;

and as the voyage progressed she grew more lovable. Regular meals, pure air, and the absence of liquor rounded her form, smoothed the lines in her face, steadied her nerves, and put music into her laugh. And there was little doubt that she loved Captain Waverlie.

But she did not like the sea, and at New York induced him to install her in an uptown apartment while he made the next voyage, and promised then to join him on the third. So, with tears in her eyes, she thanked me earnestly for my hardness of heart in refusing her the whisky that was killing her, and went ashore with her husband. We sailed without her, and Captain Waverlie nearly dismasted the bark on several occasions that voyage, " cracking on " to make a quick passage; for he missed her. I missed her too, unsentimental old man though I am.

We docked at New York late in the afternoon, and he hurried ashore. When he returned, on the evening of the next day, he came alone; he stumbled heavily down the gangway steps, and walked unsteadily about the decks for a few minutes before entering the cabin, where I was watching him from the forward door. He was not drunk, though when I saw his face in the lamplight I wished that he was. He looked twenty years older.

" Dead, steward, dead! " he groaned, hoarsely and brokenly—" dead by her own hand. She couldn't hold up—she couldn't hold up without me. It's my fault—all mine. I ought not to have left her."

It is awful to hear a strong man weep. He buried his head in his arms on the table and gave way to it, his choking sobs seeming to shake the framework of the cabin. I could do nothing—say nothing; but my own tears fell as I stood stupidly by and waited. At last he grew quieter, his paroxysms dwindled to the heavy, hoarse breathing which I had noticed years before, and then he lifted his head from his arms, with a look on his face that no sane man should wear.

" Buried in Potter's Field, steward," he said, " and I could not find her grave. Even that was denied me."

" I'm very sorry, captain," I stammered. " What can I do? Shall I get you something to drink—to steady you? "

" No, no! " he yelled. " I dare not. Don't give it to me if I ask for it. If I drink, I will murder. And it must not be that—not murder."

He stood up and paced the cabin floor in hurried, jerky turns. The exercise seemed to calm him, for he faced me with a strained smile on his haggard face, and said:

" Never drink when you're in trouble, steward. It makes things worse. I'll come around all right."

" Try to, sir. Try and forget it for your own sake."

" Yes," he answered, slowly and wearily. " I'll try and forget her "—he turned to pass through the after-cabin door—" but not—"

I did not hear the rest. He closed the door and I turned into my berth—but not to sleep.

There was no more of it. He " came around," as he had said, and we made another voyage, uneventful until within a day's sail of Sandy Hook, when he met with an accident. It came of his never-failing consideration of his crew's comfort; he forebore calling the watch below to wear ship in a wind and sea which made it a hard task for the watch on deck; but, with myself at the wheel so that the sailor could help at the braces, and the captain assisting as well, the bark came around and the yards were swung. But in jibing the spanker as she swung up on the other tack the weather-sheet or guy-tackle parted, the spanker crashed over, and the broken rope, unreeving like a whip-lash, struck the captain on the left side of his face, and tore his right ear downward, half severing it from his head. I bandaged it in place, but, as it gave small sign of healing, he went ashore at New York for surgical treatment. When he returned, both ears were bandaged, and he explained, with rather a grim smile.

" I struck a place up-town," he said, " where they can shorten your nose or lengthen it, trim your ears into shape, straighten your teeth, or beautify your mouth. Surgical dermatology, they call it; and they wanted to give me the whole treatment. Well, I let them try on my stunsail ears, and they say they've made a good job of it, though I won't know until they're healed."

They *had* made a good job of it. His ears, which had stood out like wings, lay straight against his head when the bandages came off, and there was not even a sign of the operation, the slight scar left by the knife being hidden.

Aside from the strict habits of cleanliness and good taste in dress common to all successful and self-respecting men, Captain Waverlie had heretofore displayed nothing of personal vanity; but the straightening of his ears seemed to bring it into play. He stocked his cabin with works on anatomy and surgery, and all of the next voyage was a diligent student of these and of the advertising circulars given him by the institute which had operated on his ears. I often surprised him in front of his mirror, studying his misshapen features with an interest hardly to be expected in a strong, level-headed shipmaster. He had always shaved smooth, but on the run down the coast he grew a mustache, and on the return trip a pointed beard. Apparently neither suited him—his thick lips could not be hidden, and his broad nose spoiled the effect; so he shaved again. And at New York I found a reason for this new-born interest in his personal appearance. Our plutocratic owner, who seldom soiled his shoe-leather on the decks of his ships, brought his daughter, whom Waverlie had once spoken of, aboard the bark on a visit; and as I noticed the admiration in Waverlie's eyes I was glad, remembering the other.

She was a beautiful girl—of a beauty hard to describe, being due to her charm of manner as much as to her face and figure. She was about twenty-five, of the fair-haired, brown-eyed type so rare among women, and she possessed all the accomplishments which a rich man's daughter may acquire. Hardly the girl to take to a self-made ship captain, I thought; yet she would distract him from his memories. But I did not then know Waverlie—even after eight years of service with him. And a piece of news given out by the owner as he was departing seemed to lessen somewhat the difference between them. A new ship was thought of, to be launched in about a year—a four-masted ship for the China trade. And Captain Waverlie, the man of fast passages, was to command her.

"So, steward," he said at supper that evening, with one of his rare smiles, "I'm fated for deepwater, after all. No escape for me."

"But you go as master now, sir," I responded.

"Yes"—the smile gave way to the frightful look

his face had worn when he wept for the woman he loved—" yes, steward, master of a big ship—master of the lives and liberties of twenty or thirty human beings, a pet of the law and public sentiment. What a vengeance I could wreak on the men who misused me if I got them in my forecastle! "

" But you wouldn't, captain," I answered. " You're not that kind of a man."

" Well, perhaps not—perhaps not," he said, slowly. " We'll see what kind of man I may become with power of life and death. Men change as they grow older. And, by-the-way, steward, express no surprise at any change you may see in my countenance. I mean to take the treatment I spoke of, one feature at a time. You will be the only one to know of it. I want no gossip. Understand? "

I understood. Miss Irene was a prize worth a little suffering for; yet when he came on board on the evening before we sailed, with his nose bandaged, and walked the cabin floor all the night, wheezing with pain, I marveled at his fortitude. He explained next morning to his inquiring first mate that he had been assaulted, and the officer believed him. So he breathed through his mouth for three weeks at sea, and when the bandage came off there came with it a murderous steel clamp that had pressed his wide nostrils together and permanently shaped them. But it was not this which had reduced the arching profile to a straight line and given him a nose as correctly chiseled as that of a statue; an incision had been made on the bridge and some of the bony cartilage removed. Before the bark docked at New York the thin, red line of scar was gone.

Again he visited the surgeons, and again he went to sea with a tale of assault, mumbled between

swollen lips almost covered with strips of adhesive
plaster. These strips he removed continuously as
they loosened from the moisture of his mouth, and
for a few days he wrote his orders to the mate on the
log-slate and almost starved from the difficulty in
eating. Small muscles had been removed, he explained to me when able to speak, and the incisions
made inside of the lips, where they would not show.
The operation gave him a well-shaped mouth, which
harmonized with the nose above, but did not har-
monize with the bushy line of eyebrow higher up.
The last was a small matter, however, which, he said,
could be remedied with an electric needle. It was
his teeth which would trouble him most, and that
trouble he meant to bear on the next voyage.

What the crew, most of whom had signed with
him for years, thought of his changed appearance
found expression only in the casual remark of the
mate, that " if he got slugged a few more times it
would make a good-looking man of him." But on
this voyage he allowed his beard and mustache to
grow again, and when the owner and his daughter
again visited the bark at New York their joking
comments on his improved appearance were confined
to the hirsute growth. His lips were almost hidden,
and their good-breeding prevented reference to his
nose.

What progress he was making in Miss Irene's good
favor I could not guess; but she seemed very friendly
toward him, and I knew that he was a welcome caller
at her home. I hoped for the best, and as I wit-
nessed his excruciating agony on the next run to the
southward, I felt that he deserved it. They had
forcibly wrenched his teeth into line, wedged them,
and clamped them with steel. A drill of bad

weather off Hatteras brought on facial neuralgia, for which there was no remedy in the medicine-chest; but he held to those clamps and wedges until, on the run back from Rio, the warmth of the tropics brought relief; then he displayed as fine a set of teeth as may be imagined. And a lesser embellishment came of the improvement in his eyebrows; the thick growth was thinned and the junction over the nose was cleared away. John Waverlie had become a handsome man.

But with his change of appearance came a change in disposition, regrettably for the worse. He had one more voyage to make in the bark before the big ship building in a Maine ship-yard would need his supervision, and this voyage he made with a new crew, refusing to sign a single one of the men who had sailed so long with him. The mates were discharged with recommendations to the owner, and he would have discharged me had I permitted it. It took two days of argument and a downright refusal to quit to bring a reluctant change in his mind.

"But you must take what comes," he said. "I can't take a home crew out deep-water in a big ship with as many more strange men. There'd be trouble all the time. So I'm getting used to new conditions."

I could not admit his logic, but did not argue any more; and we sailed with two heavy-fisted brutes as mates, and a crew seemingly picked for their stupidity and incompetence, whom these two brutes kicked and cursed to their hearts' content. Captain Waverlie permitted it, and even silenced my mild protest against it. All the voyage, too, he displayed an irritability and a half-peevishness entirely foreign to his past attitude; but I credited this to chagrin he must have suffered at New York when the owner and his daughter had come aboard with a third visitor—a fashionably dressed, handsome man of about his own age, whose elegant bearing and brilliant conversation seemed strongly to impress Miss Irene. As the two stood apart for a few comments I heard the owner describe him to Waverlie as one of the ablest lawyers of the metropolitan bar. When they went ashore, Waverlie's dark eyes glowed like smoldering coals, but beyond a muttered curse—not meant for my ear—he said nothing.

Although he had discharged his old mates without cause, he rather inconsistently hunted them up when we returned, and the owner installed them as captain and first mate of the bark. Then he took me, under pay, up to the Maine ship-yard, where he was to oversee the finishing touches in the big ship's construction, and I was to cook for him, as the galley and cabin were now in readiness. On the day of the launching it was my province to provide the usual luncheon for the large party of guests which the owner brought on board. Miss Irene was there, of course; and much in evidence among them was Mr. Sargent, the lawyer, who seemed to be more than ever in the good graces of the young lady. He was at her side, supporting her as she stood in the knight-heads and smashed the bottle of wine on the stem; he monopolized her society through the day, and at luncheon they sat alone on the cabin skylight. While serving them here I overheard a portion of their conversation.

" It is fitting and apropos," Mr. Sargent was saying, " that the ship bears your first name only. For the last name doesn't become you at all, and you will change—"

" Mr. Sargent," she answered, laughing as she spoke, " what reason have you for that opinion? I am very well satisfied with my last name."

At this moment I was forced to go, and I heard no more; but I wondered how it would affect Waverlie. He bore himself well through the day; he was dignified, calm, and courteous to all, and only at intervals did I notice the devils in his eyes. But the strain was undoubtedly hard upon him, and toward the last he yielded. Mr. Sargent thanked him gracefully at the gangway for the day's entertainment, and hoped that the ship would not sail before a certain coming event, when he would be proud to entertain him. Waverlie responded with cold congratulations, and ignored the extended hand of the lawyer, who thereupon went down the gangplank flushed and embarrassed. That night the captain walked his cabin floor in a silent fury, until, his footfalls keeping me awake, I intruded upon him and asked if I could do anything for him. He was pale and haggard, but graciously thanked me and declined my ministrations. Then, in a sincere effort to ease his mind, I retailed to him the conversation between the two that I had heard as they lunched on the skylight. But I was at once made aware that I had not pleased him.

" Steward," he said, sternly, " your powers of observation are good, but you are valuable to me mainly as an efficient steward who knows my ways. Unless you can make up your mind to see nothing, hear nothing, and know nothing of what happens aboard this ship, you must go. I will get one who is discreet."

I protested, apologized, and promised; then he went to bed, and I followed suit in an unenviable frame of mind. It is not pleasant to be disciplined when gray-headed by one you love as a son. And I soon learned the futility of my gossip. When we were fitted out and towed to New York to load for Hong Kong, the owner came aboard and casually mentioned the coming marriage of his daughter to Mr. Sargent. But Waverlie displayed no emotion; it required the presence of his rival to excite him.

In due time we were ready for sea, and the captain shipped three mates, all bigger, noisier, more profane and foul-mouthed than the two he had taken on his last voyage; then he negotiated with Glasgow Mike, boarding-house keeper and shipping-master— the worst scoundrel and blackguard on South Street —for twenty-four able and six ordinary seamen. After the first interview in the cabin, Mike appeared no more in the matter, the details being left to two runners in his employ. These two worthies brought the crew and their dunnage down to the dock in express wagons early in the morning of our sailing-day, fully half of them unable to move from drink or drugs. They were lifted aboard, and the runners, indicating each unconscious man in his turn, answered to their names as the mate read the list from the articles.

" Only twenty-eight, all told," he said, running his eye down the column of names. " Where's George Smithers and John Carruthers? "

" Skipped out," answered one of the runners. " But we know where they are, and 'll have 'em here 'fore you leave the dock. That's all right."

They went ashore, and the mates bundled the unkempt lot of wretches into the forecastles. They were the usual type of sailors who man American deep-water ships—mostly foreigners, undersized, stupid, and ragged, enslaved at sea by the law, and robbed ashore by the crimps, who feed them for a few days, that they may enter an inflated claim against their " allotment " of wages when they sign again.

In an hour the two runners returned in a closed carriage with two more unconscious men. I stood in the galley door as they were lifted aboard, but could hear the captain, waiting at the gangway, ask the runners:

" Are these my men? Did they sign the articles? "

" It's all right, cap'n," said one, with a grin. " Signed an' got their allotment notes. This is George Smithers "—he kicked one quiet figure on the deck, then the other—" and this is John Carruthers. Good men when they're sober, too."

The runners went into the cabin with the captain, and the mates ordered the newcomers carried to the forecastle. As they passed me at the galley door I looked at their faces. George Smithers was Mr. Sargent, dressed in filthy canvas rags, and John Carruthers was Glasgow Mike.

I had promised to see nothing, hear nothing, and know nothing; so I said nothing, and the expression of Captain Waverlie's face at breakfast told me that it was the safest thing to do. A man who dared shanghai Glasgow Mike and a man in Mr. Sargent's position was not to be trifled with. But I thought and wondered sadly. The mate's comment on the shortage of men told me that thirty was the ship's complement. Whether or not Glasgow Mike had arranged the abduction of Mr. Sargent as the twenty-third able seaman, he himself, it seemed, was to fill the place of the twenty-fourth—drugged and shipped by his own runners. I thought, too, of that fair young girl robbed of her lover.

The runners went ashore, and we towed down the bay, made sail with the aid of the men awake, dropped the tug and pilot off Sandy Hook Lightship, and with a fresh westerly wind sank the land before noon. Then the sleepers were awakened. I was in the cabin waiting upon the captain and chief mate at dinner at this time, and it was loud and bad language on deck which apprised us that Glasgow Mike was asserting himself. "Go forrard," I heard the second mate roar at him, "an' if you want to see the skipper wait 'til he's done dinner."

The first officer chuckled between mouthfuls at this; then said: "Know who you've got forrard, sir? Glasgow himself."

"Who is Glasgow? What do you mean?" asked the captain.

"Glasgow Mike, the boardin'-master. Don't know how it came about, sir, but his runners put him aboard as a shipped man. I knew him, but there's no use in delayin' the ship an' one man's as good as another." The officer laughed heartily.

"I know nothing whatever about it," said the captain, with annoyance in his face. "I don't know one of those thieves from another, but I was forced to apply to one of them for a crew."

"And you've got the man you applied to, sir," answered the mate, with a grin. "It's funny—damn funny."

"I know nothing about it," repeated Waverlie. "I wouldn't remember the features of the man I bargained with. He put my case in the hands of his runners. I would remember them, I think."

They finished the meal and went on deck, the

second and third mates coming down when relieved
by the first. Second and third mates require little
waiting upon, and I placed myself in the forward
companionway, where I could see and hear. Forward were the newly awakened men, clustered about
the galley door. The workers were at dinner in
one of the forecastles. At the mizzen-hatch was Mr.
Sargent, pale and hollow-eyed, and on the weather-
poop steps, his head and torso showing over the
break of the poop, was Glasgow Mike. He was in a
furious rage.

"Now look here, skipper," he stormed, as he
climbed up. "What t'ell's this for, anyhow? What
am I here for in yer damned fo'castle? "

"As I understand matters," answered the captain,
stepping up to him, "you are here as one of my
crew, signed for the voyage to Hong Kong and back
to an American port of discharge."

"What!" yelled Mike. "Don't ye know me? I
shipped yer crew for ye. What t'ell's the matter wi'
ye, skipper? "

"I don't know you. I never saw you before. I
paid for a crew, and the men who brought you
aboard drunk gave your name as John Carruthers,
able seaman. I find that name is on my articles,
with three months' allotment of wages charged
against it, payable to Michael McSorley."

"That's me, all right—not John Carruthers. I'm
Michael McSorley, and I want ye to put me 'board
the first inbound craft. If ye don't, there'll be
trouble ahead for you. Ye'll never get a crew on this
coast again. Damn ye, don't ye know me? "

"That's enough. Mr. Mitchell," said the captain,
turning to the first mate, "turn this man to and
take the starch out of him."

The starch was thoroughly extracted from Mike in the next five minutes. He was knocked off the poop by a fist-blow, and, though he fought bravely during his jerky passage forward, he was not a match for the giant first mate. He was actually knocked, thrown, and kicked from the poop to the forecastle door, and here, with eyes closed and blood streaming from his face, he subsided.

Captain Waverlie watched calmly from the poop, and Mr. Sargent, with doubt and anxiety in his face, from the hatch below; then, as the flushed and victorious Mr. Mitchell swaggered aft the lawyer preceded him up the poop steps and faced the captain.

" I have grasped the situation, Captain Waverlie," he said, slowly, " in all but its latest aspect—as to why the man, your paid tool evidently, who assaulted me, chloroformed me, and threw me into a cab at my own door is now in the same predicament as myself. This is probably not my business, but may I ask your intentions in my own case? "

" My intentions, damn you! " roared Waverlie— " my intentions in your case? I have none, except to make you earn your pay. What cock-and-bull yarn have you got to tell? Out with it."

The lawyer was silent for a moment while he calmly studied the captain's face; then he said: " I have no yarn to tell. I will merely remind you that I am William Sargent, a friend of your owner's and the affianced of his daughter; that I have power over the machinery of the law far beyond your grasp; that I am fully aware of your motive in removing me from your path; and I also say that unless you kill me on this passage I will send you to state's prison. And if you do kill me, understand that a man of my position cannot disappear without inquiry and investigation."

"Damn your impudence!" answered Waverlie, as he seized him by the collar. "You—Mr. Sargent" —he shook him vigorously. "Why, I know the man as well as I know myself. You're George Smithers, signed on my articles as able seaman. If you're not what you've signed for, you'll wish yourself dead. Get off my poop-deck!"

"And do you deny my identity?" demanded the angry lawyer, struggling in his strong grasp. "I warn you—"

The captain released him, but drove his fist with all his strength into his face, stopping the speech and sending him crashing against the monkey-rail.

"Get forward where you belong!" he thundered. "Mr. Mitchell, turn the man to."

The mate, who had climbed the steps, turned him to. The process was not so painful to witness as in the case of Glasgow Mike, for the lawyer made no resistance, and, after being pushed down the steps and struck a few times, went forward hurriedly. Captain Waverlie, with a face almost black with passion, started below and met me in the companion. Something in my own face must have appealed to him, for he halted and laid his hand on my shoulder.

"Steady, old man!" he said, half kindly, while his features softened. "No doubt this has a bad look to you, but you'll justify it when you know what's behind. Remember what you promised me."

He went down, and I went forward to the galley, not because my work required it at the time, but to get away from the captain's vicinity and gain time to think. Mr. Mitchell—two bells having struck—was calling the men out of the forecastles. There was

much work to be done to get the ship ready for the
voyage—the long tow-line must be coiled upon the
forward house, the anchors rigged inboard and
lashed, the chain sent below and the fish-tackle un-
rove, chafing-gear seized on the rigging aloft, and
the decks cleared of fenders, planks, and dunnage.
Glasgow Mike, subdued and disfigured, having given
signs of efficiency, or, possibly, from being known to
the mate, was sent aloft on the fore with a marline-
spike, ball of spun-yarn, and a bundle of chafing-
mats. He cursed volubly, but softly, as he passed
me at the galley door, and mounted the rail to the
rigging. But Mike's trouble was short-lived. As
he stood on the rail preparatory to ascent, Mr. Sargent came around the corner of the house and halted
before me.

" I shall expect, steward," he said, " that you will
keep cognizant of what happens to me on this ship.
I shall demand that you testify in my behalf."

Before I could reply, Mike, above us on the rail,
burst out with a volley of billingsgate directed at the
lawyer.

" It's on your damned account," he said, in conclusion, " that I'm here like a shanghaied Dutchman." Then he let fly the marline-spike, which
glanced from Mr. Sargent's head and buried its point
a full inch in the side of the house. The lawyer
reeled, but recovered his balance, and with a furious
exclamation wrenched out the implement and returned
it. His aim was better. It was a pointed piece of
iron about a foot long and an inch in diameter at
its base. This heavy end struck Mike squarely in
the middle of the forehead, and without a sound from
his lips he stiffened his arms and fell backward into
the sea.

"Man overboard!" I shouted, and instantly the whole ship was in confusion, with the mate's loud orders, supplemented by those of the second and third officers, now up from dinner; the green and still stupefied crew rushing about aimlessly, and the canvas rattling aloft, for the wheel had been put down. But over the uproar came the stentorian tones of the captain on the after house, countermanding all orders. The wheel was put up, the half-swung main-yards hauled back, and men climbed down from the boats on the house.

"No use, Mr. Mitchell," he called to the mate amidships. "I saw that. He was dead before he struck the water. Bring the murderer aft and put him in irons."

In the presence of the whole crew, Mr. William Sargent, a leading member of the New York bar, was ironed and led below to the lazarette, and under the name of George Smithers, with myself as witness, entered in the captain's official log for the murder of a shipmate—John Carruthers. He was put upon a diet of bread and water, and every fifth day given the full allowance of the crew, according to law.

My feelings have nothing to do with this story, and I will intrude them no more. At the end of two months, pale and emaciated—half starved on his prisoner's fare—Mr. Sargent begged piteously to be allowed to work with the rest; for the darkness and solitude were killing him. His request was granted; Captain Waverlie released him and handed him over to the mercy of his mates, who, finding him utterly ignorant of seamanship, tortured him according to their lights. He was struck, kicked, and cursed on all occasions. Almost useless on a rope or in any heavy dragging requiring physical strength, yet occupying an able man's place, he was an offense to his watch-mates, and in the watch below they added to his punishment. He cleaned up the forecastle, carried their meals from the galley, cleared up the remnants, and often washed out a shirt at the behest of a big-shouldered " Dutchman " or " Sou'egian," who would call him a " tam farmer." As he could not steer, the mate in whose watch he belonged decreed that he should stand lookout all night.

Unable to eat much of the food fed to the men, and deprived of sleep in the afternoon watch—which left him but three hours out of the twenty-four—he became weaker and weaker, until, one day when the ship was beating up toward the China Sea, the end came. He was collared by the irate third officer for some petty fault and hurled along the deck. Unable to recover his balance, he fell heavily on the sharp corner of the main-hatch, and lay still.

I assisted in lifting him to the hatch. He groaned painfully, and could speak and tell his injury, but could not move a muscle below the small of the back, where the sharp corner had impinged. Captain Waverlie came forward and examined him.

" Take him down in the after cabin," he said. " His back is broken."

We carried him down and laid him on a transom, and when the sailors who had helped were gone the captain directed me to call the three mates and the boatswain. I did so, and they came, standing sheepishly in the forward door.

" I simply say to you, once for all," said Waverlie, " that I want no more of this. I've carried the same crew for years, and never needed to strike or ill-treat a man. If any one of you ever again lifts his hand to one of my crew, or even curses him, I'll disrate that one on the spot, if I don't put him in irons. That's all."

Out they went, but I remained, with tears starting in my eyes.

"God bless you for that, captain," I stammered. He turned to me.

"Hush, you poor old fool!" he said, slowly and yet gently. "Sit down in a chair and listen."

As I obeyed him, the injured man spoke.

"You are satisfied now, I presume," he said, between groans. "Now that you have seen me fatally injured, you stop the torture of the rest."

"Right, Mr. Sargent," answered Waverlie, as he seated himself before him. "Now that your end has come, it is no longer needed."

"You fiend! And do you hope to escape? Let me tell you that you will not. My murder will be fastened upon you, as sure as there is a God of vengeance."

"It will not. But there is a God of vengeance, and that is why you were delivered to me. Think a little. How will it be done? You have removed the man who abducted you. Had you not, I should have arranged it myself, for I shanghaied Glasgow Mike to get rid of him. The driver of the cab, who did not see you and whom you do not know, was one of the two that drugged Mike and brought him aboard. Mike had powerful friends, and New York will ever remain unhealthy to that man. Mr. Sargent, you have disappeared from the face of the earth."

"Murder will out—murder will out. Oh, you devil of hate! Could you not take your chance with a woman, like another man? Do you think you can win her now—you, my murderer? You cannot.

God will prevent it. Oh, my God! Irene! Irene! I was to be married in a month."

"She will not miss you," said Waverlie, calmly. "She never loved you. She accepted you to please her father, and because I made no overtures in that line."

"You lie!" shrieked Sargent.

"I do not. As far as a modest woman can, she told me of her love for me—in such little ways as tears in the eyes, involuntary speeches, certain little embarrassments. As an honorable man who did not reciprocate, I could do nothing but let you step in. But I saw that you stepped out. Yet, if the time comes when I can find room in my heart for a living woman, and I find that Irene has waited, I shall ask her to be my wife."

"Curse you! Not wanting her yourself, you prevented my getting her."

"I did. I determined on this course long before you first came aboard my old bark—before either of us knew Irene. I changed my features while waiting for my opportunity; I schooled myself in brutality, and when I took charge of this big ship I signed a crew that would be glad to scatter in a foreign port. I signed mates able to scatter them. Most of this crew will not see New York again. You will die, shortly, but you must not die in the hope of my punishment. I stood that punishment years ago, Bill Sargent."

The injured man's eyes opened wide at the nickname, and the captain, his voice taking on a high-pitched, trembling intonation, said to me:

"Steward, go into my room and bring me the photograph on my desk."

I did so. It was a large one of Miss Irene.

He handed it to Sargent, who held it with shaky hands, and stared at the beautiful face with a look I never want to see again, so full was it of dumb, hungry misery.

"Study it well," said Waverlie, sternly. "Look on the face of the girl you love, who does not love you, whom you do not deserve—whose sacrifice to you would be a black crime."

"Oh, God! Why do you hate me so? Who are you?"

"Steward, bring me those two pictures above you."

I stood erect and looked. On a small shelf against the forward bulkhead were two photographs which I had never seen before. The moment's glance I allowed myself showed me a picture of a sweet-faced, laughing girl of the blond type, and one of a well-dressed boy, with broad nose, thick lips, prominent ears, and earnest, honest expression of face. They were taken in the youth of John Waverlie and the woman we had taken to sea.

Waverlie took them from me and held the one of the girl before the eyes of the dying man.

"Do you know her?" he almost hissed. "Do you know her, Bill?"

"Minnie!" It came forth in a kind of gasp.

"Yes—Minnie, the girl we went to school with, Bill."

"In God's name, who are you?" screamed Sargent, rolling his head from side to side.

"I am all that's left of the boy who was once your friend—who dared love and win the girl you had cast eyes upon. The rest of that boy lies in a grave in Potter's Field with Minnie. And you are the scoundrel who poisoned her mind against me when I had

come to New York to study, who followed me and
employed Glasgow Mike to shanghai me—had you
forgotten his face and voice? I had not—who won
and cast off the girl I was to make my wife. And
were this all, Bill Sargent, I might have spared you.
But when, after years of searching, I found her,
married her, and nursed back her health and beauty,
you came again. You entered her nest—it was you;
the janitor you sent for whisky described you well—
and for that she killed herself. And because she
killed herself I have killed you. Yes, I take it all
upon my soul, though beyond the one knock-down I
granted myself I have not laid hands upon you. I
have killed you, Bill Sargent, by merely taking advantage of the sacred inviolability of ship-masters;
for, after you entered my forecastle, my attitude,
active or passive, will bear the test of legal investigation. I am backed up by the law."

The face of Sargent, pale and ghastly, had taken
on an expression of horror and fright. He said
nothing—merely staring at Waverlie piling up some
books on the transom at his feet. Against these
books Waverlie leaned the three pictures; then he
propped up Sargent's head with pillows.

" There! " he said, as he stood back. " There is
the face of the woman you love, the face of the
woman you killed, and the face of the man you
wronged. Look on them while you die."

Then he motioned me out of the cabin, and followed me.

I did not enter the after cabin again until Sargent
had been carried out for sea burial, three days later.
I found the pictures still in place against the books.

THE VITALITY OF DENNIS

THE crew of the *Wilmerdine* came down to the dock in two express-wagons, with their dunnage, and climbed, or were lifted, over the rail; then, while the six boarding-house runners who had delivered them stood guard on the dock, and the shipping-master who had sold them went below with the captain for his money, the chief mate inspected them from the poop.

An unkempt muster it was. Three lay helpless on the deck, others leaned for support against the rail or propped themselves against their clothes-bags—of which there were eight among the twenty. Not a chest was there; but one man guarded closely a pair of new carpet slippers; one held tightly under his arm a flannel shirt; others had other single articles—sou'westers, oil-skin coats without pants, oil-skin pants without coats, dungaree overalls, mateless boots, stockings, and mittens; and one of them, the raggedest and drunkenest man erect, defied Fate and Cape Horn with an empty, three-by-two pasteboard trunk such as little girls receive at Christmas for dolls' clothing. Two only seemed to know why they were there—clean, neatly dressed fellows, who took the initiative in shouldering their bags and heading for the forecastle. They were called back to assist the three helpless ones forward, and while they were doing so the captain and shipping-master appeared.

"What d'ye think of the crew, Mr. Saltup?" asked the latter.

The mate glowered into the hard face of the shipping-master and said, contemptuously: "It'll take me a month to lick 'em into shape. I never saw a good crew shipped out o' Frisco yet."

"And ye never will in an American ship while ye treat men like wild animals," said the other, who, with his money in his pocket, felt independent and virtuous. "Ye feed them on condemned navy stores, keep them up in their watch below, and hammer them with pump-brakes; then ye expect good men to ship deep-water. All the good men are in the coasters. None o' yer crew signed articles willingly, or knew where they were goin', but two; and ye couldn't ha' got them without a cash advance 'stead of a note—ye know that, cappen."

"I know it—blast their hides. I had to have two able seamen, at least. But they'll earn their money twice over this passage. I expect you to watch that they don't jump her."

"I'll watch, but don't ye fear, cappen. Sandy and Dennis want to get home. They bought drafts with their advance and mailed them ahead to their families. If they didn't want to ride with ye they wouldn't be here now."

The crew, those who could work, were called out; mooring-chains and fenders taken in, a line passed to a tug alongside, and the *Wilmerdine* towed to good holding-ground, where the anchor was dropped, and the bending of sails and the " licking into shape " of the crew were begun. No clubs were needed for the latter. The hammer-like fists of the two mates —both large men—answered every purpose; and when a man failed to answer " Sir " when roared at, or did not jump quickly enough to a task, he felt the weight of one—sometimes two at once—of these fists, and, if not rendered unconscious, was further punished by boot-heels. By noon half the crew were unable to go aloft, and the forecastle bunks contained three more unconscious men. The two men spoken of had escaped physical contact with their superiors, but had received their full share of the cursings and billingsgate applied; for they were of the crew and must be impressed.

"I do be thinkin', Sandy," said one of them as they passed a head-earing on the fore topgallant yard, "that this'll be a hot ship to thravel home in."

"Aye, mun, that ut weel," answered the other. "But beggars maunna be choosers, an' thirty shillin' a week is muckle money t' pay oot t' a bardin'-hoose. We've seened articles, an' we're oot in t' stream, Dennis."

"An' it's sorry I be thot I signed; fur I don't like the color o' the mate's hair."

The royal above them was bent and furled, and when they and the men with them had finished the topgallant-sail, they came down to the lower yard, the topsails having been disposed of by another gang. The chief mate, looking up from the forecastle deck, took especial note of the seamanlike way in which Sandy and Dennis handled themselves, and when the foresail was finished, and the men were laying in to descend, he sang out to the two to remain on the yard, and he would send up the quarter-blocks—in this case a pair of triangular iron plates, containing two sheaves, through which the chain topsail sheets would pass to the bitts below, after reeving through the sheave-holes in the ends of the yard. They were to bolt this iron triangle to the underside of the sling band at the middle of the yard, then shackle on and reeve off the sheets, which were coiled in the fore-top.

They comprehended and answered respectfully.

The mate fastened the quarter-blocks, with a hammer and wrench, to the bight of a buntline; they hauled them up, and proceeded with the job, while the rest of the men were driven aft to begin work on the mizzen, and the carpenter, whose duty it was to bolt on these fixtures, personally directed the job from below until finished and then resumed the work he was engaged upon—calking the fore-hatch. The mate on the poop, looking forward occasionally, saw that the two were reeving the sheets, and sang out to "bear a hand and lay aft."

A few minutes later a frightful cry rang out from forward, followed by shouts from Sandy, who was seen frantically descending the fore rigging, and from the carpenter, who appeared round the corner of the forward house, white of face, and holding his right arm tightly.

"Man fallen from aloft, sir," he called, and groaned with his own pain. Forward they tumbled —the two mates and the men on deck—and looked on a horrid sight. Dennis lay sprawled on the deck, one leg on the fore-hatch, the other doubled under him, while his neck was twisted so that he looked over his shoulder. His face was covered with blood, and he breathed in short, jerky gasps, which spoke of nothing but punctured lungs.

"Put him in his bunk," said the mate, as he viewed the sufferer.

They attempted to raise him, but the gasps were merged in a hoarse, rattling groan, and they desisted.

"Let him be," said the mate; "get his mattress out and lay him on it. Rig a whip to the fore-yard, some o' you; this is a hospital job."

And while Sandy bent over him and enjoined him by all that was dear in their memory and friendship to speak to him and not to die, the whip was rigged, the mattress brought, and poor Dennis tenderly lifted to a softer bed. A passing tug was hailed, whose captain willingly agreed to land the injured man; a broad plank was slipped under the mattress, to which the whip was bridled, and Dennis—now still and quiet—mattress, dunnage, and all, was lifted out of the ship he regretted signing in, and sent ashore in charge of the second mate and Sandy, who begged, with a face of misery, to be allowed to accompany his friend to the hospital. "For, sir, we've been sheepmuts an' freends seeven year the noo, an' if Dennis is to dee, I maun be wi' him," he said, and the mate in consenting proved that somewhere in his salt-seasoned anatomy he had a remnant of a heart. But he cautioned the second mate to watch the Scotchman and bring him back.

This officer returned alone an hour later, and reported to the captain and mate a wondrous thing, and a shameful thing—that no sooner was the dying man lifted to the dock, with his dunnage, by the tug men, than he sprang to his feet, shouldered his bag, uttered an Irish whoop, and, accompanied by his sorrowful friend Sandy, raced up the wharf and entered the short streets close by. He had pursued, but lost them around the first corner, and, after notifying a policeman, had come back for instructions.

But, in spite of instructions and actions on the part of the furious captain and the police, Dennis and Sandy were not found, and the ship sailed for Liverpool without them, with her carpenter nursing a black-and-blue shoulder for two idle weeks. For Dennis had come down hard.

At Liverpool, where, of course, the crew deserted,

the mystery was explained. The carpenter went ashore one evening, and, passing an eating-saloon, was accosted by a man in the doorway, whom he knew. It was Sandy.

"Come awa', Cheeps," he said. "Come; Dennis'll be vera glad t' see ye. He swears ye ware t' savin' o' him."

The carpenter shook hands with the Scot and was drawn within, where, seated at a table, behind a huge mug of ale, was Dennis, bright-eyed and wholesome. "An', Cheeps," went on Sandy, after the greetings and an order for more ale, "could ye inform me aboot ma clothes? I had a boony ootfit—brawn-new. Wha got them?"

"Who got 'em? Why, the men, of course. If it wasn't for that bag of yours they'd ha' frozen off the Horn. Your shirts never got cold nor your oil-skins dry till we struck the trades this side. What did you come around in?"

"We shipped in the *Harley Castle* a fortnight on, Cheeps," said Sandy, abstractedly. "Weel, weel, an' I've lost my clothes. But it's a' for t' best. I'm sawtisfied."

"Satisfied! You ought to be, with sixty dollars advance that you never earned. But what I want to know is, how this Irishman can break himself to pieces and then run like a scared jackass."

"Dead aisy, Chips," grinned Dennis. "Up on the yard we seed they were all aft an' clus inboard, an' cudent see us in the slings. An' you were beneath us, engaged with your corkin'-mallet, unsuspicious like; and Sandy here, at my request, slugged me on the nose—wance, twiste—murder! but it hurt; an' I smeared the blood from me nose all over me face, an' shuk hands wid Sandy—fur I didn't know

how he'd make it—and shlid down the topsa'l sheets
till I was six feet above ye, Chips. By the powers,
ye looked temptin'! An' then I jumped—"

"And came down boots first on my neck, and
yelled blue murder, and stretched out and died,"
interrupted the carpenter. "I've heard that a Jew
can't make a living in Scotland and Ireland. Now
I know why." But a grin of forgiveness overspread
the carpenter's face as he added: "It looks as
though the drinks were on me, boys—something
stronger than ale, too. What'll it be?"

THE HELIX

"WE can get up a jury mainmast, easy enough,"
said Captain Swarth, as he glanced around
at his shattered deck; "but how'll we keep it up?
Both main channels shot away, and not a ring-bolt,
cleat, bitt, or cavil left abaft the mainmast. What
d'ye make of it, Yank?"

Yank Tate, the carpenter, an expert in makeshifts,
and the most valuable man in that pirate crew, answered, slowly:

"I've been thinkin', capt'n—thinkin' hard. If I
had tools I could work, for we have the material;
but a big round shot's gone clean through my tool-
chest, and I can't find anything but the broad-axe
and the saw. We'll have to stay the mainmast aft
by a cat-stay, and forward by two to the 'midship
moorin' bitts; then rig a leg-o'-mutton on the main,
for we can't sling a gaff."

"But what'll we set up the cat-stay to?" asked
Angel Todd, the mate, his long and solemn face
more solemn than usual at the problem. "There's

nothing intact but the wheel and binnacle, and they won't stand the strain."

"Pass a rope around under the stern," answered Yank, "long enough to clear the wheel and binnacle and set it up to that."

"Right," said the captain. "Yank, you're a genius. Get to work, Angel."

"How'll we splice wire rope?" asked the mate. "She's wire-rigged everywhere. I never spliced it— never saw it before."

"Nor I," said Swarth, "nor heard of it; but it *can* be spliced; it's got to be."

They were taking stock after the running fight. Five miles to the north, rolling heavily in the trough with all canvas furled, lay the English war-brig that had chased them. It had been a stern chase and a long one, dead before the wind, during which Swarth, unwilling to luff and lose headway, had held his fire but for an occasional shot from a small stern gun, and had watched his craft being slowly disintegrated by the well-aimed fire of the Englishman. The after part had suffered most; the taffrail and the quarter rails to nearly amidships were ripped and shattered, while the cabin resembled nothing so much as a pile of kindling-wood; the main channels were gone, and with no support from the rigging a solid shot imbedded in the mainmast just above the deck had been enough to send it crashing down forward, springing the fore lower and topsail yards as it met them, and breaking squarely in two just below the crosstrees as it struck the rail. Then, when the submerging canvas pulled the two fragments overboard, Swarth might have given up. But the pursuing war-craft did not bear away after firing this shot; on the contrary, she luffed still farther, and as she rolled in the trough of the sea her shaking canvas began to come in, while smoke arose from amidships. So, surmising that she was suffering from internal disorder, he went on, dragging the fallen spars in his wake.

She was a brigantine, acquired by Swarth in the usual manner, and, as Angel had said, wire-rigged everywhere—one of the experiments that ship-builders are ever ready to turn out with each new invention. Not only were shrouds, stays, and back-stays of this newly devised wire rope, but also the running-gear—halyards, braces, lifts, sheets, and tacks—in all its turnings and doublings down to the last part for hauling and belaying, was of the re-fractory material; and not only was it wire rope, but steel-wire rope that, when slackened, curled into the spiral of the original coil. In all her maze of cordage there was not a piece of hemp or manila larger than a halter, nor longer than twenty-five fathoms—about the length of the fore brace.

Splicing wire—like chemistry and *materia medica* —is an experimental science. As Swarth had de-clared, it *can* be done by men who have spliced soft rope; but not at the first attempt. Those very able able-seamen of that crew got the heavy wreck of the mainmast aboard with but little trouble, trimmed it, and disconnected the topmast. They sent down the fore royal-yard, sawed it lengthwise into battens to mend the damaged lower and topsail yards, and used up most of the soft royal running-gear in the lashing thereof. With the lighter main topmast for a derrick, they up-ended the shortened mainmast, and lashed the new heel to the stump with more of the hemp and manila; then, with the urgent neces-sity of properly securing this jury mainmast, they found themselves confronted with the problem of wire-splicing.

They avoided it in setting up the two mainstays. Seamanship, which to a seaman is the will of Providence, decrees that masts shall first be secured from forward; and they found that two still intact and opposing legs of the main rigging would just reach from the masthead to the mooring-bitts amidships. and these they tautened in the ordinary way with lanyards through the dead-eyes; but the rest of the main rigging was broken or stranded, too short to reach anywhere; and to steady the mast from aft they had only the main topmast backstays, the fore royal backstays, and the fore royal-stay—five long pieces of steel-wire rope about the size of clothes-line, equal in tensile strength to six-inch hemp or manila, but, in the judgment of these old-school seamen, very weak to hold the strain of a heavy lower mast. They would need to double it many times.

So they would first splice a collar, or loop, in one end to slip over the masthead and rest on the cleat that Yank Tate had placed there for the purpose; and they tried it, one man after another. It looked simple—just the tucking of six ends under six strands, and tucking again, and once more. But, oh, the bloodshed and suffering, the groans and maledictions attending that job! Men who, a few hours before, had calmly faced gun-fire, who had seen some of their number shattered and dismembered by solid shot, who were accustomed to hand-to-hand combats with knife or cutlass, winced and complained as the refractory ends of steel sliced their hands and wrists.

But at last the splice was done—looking much like a bundle of fagots—and the collar sent aloft to slip

over the masthead. But now, in view of the pleni-
tude of wire rope and its uncompromising stiffness,
Swarth decided, first, that it would only be practica-
ble to set up the kinky cat-stay through pulley
blocks, one for each doubling; next, that with the
small number of strong blocks still serviceable—the
upper peak and throat halyard blocks, six sheaves
in all—it would be advisable to conserve these up
aloft and pass the lower turns around under the
stern. This obviated the long rope suggested by
Yank, but involved the splicing, end to end, of all
the rope, with *long* splices.

Painfully the blood-weary cutthroats went at it,
and it required the moral suasion of Swarth, Angel,
and Yank, each equipped with an iron belaying-pin,
to keep them at it. And when it is known that a
long splice in a steel-wire rope represents the acme of
modern seamanship, it can be imagined what a task
it was for these sore-fingered tyros to join the five
pieces into one long rope with junctures small enough
to travel through the blocks. Long before it was
done Yank Tate had slung these blocks to the masthead just below the collar, and, by means of a staging rigged under the stern, had nailed a succession of
cleats to the counter to keep each turn of the rope
in place, clear of its neighbors. It was a wet job
for Yank, as the craft was still charging along
through a lumpy sea, and every now and then he
went under as the stern sank. But not being
troubled with the sores and sorrows of the others,
he did not repine—even remaining to grease the
cleats and planking.

Nor did he repine when, at mid-day of the third
day of work, the wind having died away coincident
with the finishing of the splices, the craft rolled both

rails under and made his place on the staging a place of danger. His task now was to straighten out those kinky coils of steel wire and lay each turn in its bed between the cleats as those on deck passed it around; but Yank had the born mechanic's love of a good job.

The final setting-up of that cat-stay was easy; a tackle clapped onto each part, as it led downward from its block above, tautened it, and a spun-yarn racking held it while they shifted the tackle to the next part. A fathom or two of end remained when the job was done, and this, after nailing the part to the side, they allowed to trail overboard, as Yank emphatically and consistently had refused to cut steel wire with his broad-axe. There was a curious resemblance to shrouds without ratlines in the six parts of wire rope leading up from each side; and this, in fact, was just about what they were.

A little sail-making reduced the torn mainsail to a three-cornered " mutton-leg," and they hoisted it at once. Swarth would now have gone further, and sent up the topmast, to which they could have set a jib, upside-down; but the inflamed condition of his men's hands made such a step unwise at present; their hands hurt them more than did the impact on their heads of belaying-pins, and under stress their line of least resistance would be mutiny. So he waited, while the hot afternoon wore on, and whistled for a wind to blow them on their way—due south to their island retreat, where they could properly refit and recuperate.

They had dropped the smoking English war-brig below the horizon late in the first day of flight, and now calculated that, unless she had conquered the fire and resumed the chase, there were fully one hundred and fifty miles between them when the wind had failed.

The brigantine, with canvas flapping as she rolled, swung slowly around the compass, heading any way that she was thrown by the varying heave of an ugly cross sea, the dominant motion of which seemed to be, not from the direction the wind had last come from, but out of the west. And a filmy mist arising on the western horizon at about four o'clock indicated to Swarth that wind would follow the sea from here.

He ceased his whistling, ordered the flying-jib taken in, and the men obeyed him painfully, grumbling over their sores and making hard work of an easy job. There must have been some kind of poison from the wire, for their hands were swelling.

The filmy mist spread rapidly toward them, blotting out the western sun and eventually the eastern sky. Yet it presented a curious seeming of transparency—the horizon on all sides was distinct, and the sky above still looked blue. But it was an unnatural blue, and there was a closeness to the air that made breathing difficult.

The men lounged and shuffled nervously about the deck. Angel and Yank conversed in low tones near the poop steps, and the captain often consulted a new-fangled instrument called a barometer, which, though it showed a very low reading, gave him little light.

It suddenly grew darker. Overhead the blue had become gray, and a condensation of the filmy mist was forming a cloud. It became smaller and blacker, with tints of purple in the creases and a glistening rim on its western edge. It hovered directly over the rolling craft and descended until it seemed that the fore royal pole had almost punctured it. Here it remained, and a puff of hot wind filled the sails, then died away.

" How are you heading now? " asked Swarth, quietly, to the helmsman.

" South an' by east, sir," answered the man.

" Bring her due south when the wind comes. It's our course, but the Lord knows where it'll hit us from. Angel," he called, " haul down the jib and clew up the foresail and fore topgallant-sail."

As he spoke a white light blinded them, and a deafening report shook the whole fabric of hull, spar, and cordage. For a time not a man aboard could see or hear, though they could feel a warm deluge of rain and a furious blast of wind which seemingly came from all directions. Angel Todd groped his way to the jib and fore topgallant halyards, casting them off; then he called to the men to man clew-lines and down-haul, and a few, who heard faintly before their sight returned, responded in the darkness. But they knew by the feel of the ropes they pulled that the jib was in ribbons and the topgallant-sail aback. Then, as the darkness and dullness cleared from eyes and ears, they saw that the craft had sternway and heard their captain's thundering roar coming to them against the wind:

" Lay aft here two hands to the wheel! Swanson's struck dead."

Two came and found Swarth at the wheel, with a prostrate figure at his feet. There was a curious, pungent odor in the air, which lasted but a moment, then was blown away. The lightning had dodged the taller foremast and sought the best conductor— the wire that led overboard.

" Wheel's hard aport," said Swarth, releasing it

to them. "Due south when the canvas fills. This wind's out o' the north, and it's dead fair again." Then he called forward to furl the topgallant-sail, but to leave the foresail as it was.

Slowly the craft backed around, and, as the forward canvas flapped and filled, forged ahead and settled down to the course Swarth had given. The squall was pressing the seas to a flat surface of suds, but it was much lighter now, as though the lightning stroke had cleared the air; yet the sun was still hidden.

The jury mainmast had stood the pressure well; but as the mutton-leg made steering before that furious wind too difficult for safety, Swarth took it in—an awful job for those puffed and lacerated hands—and the craft sped on under her foresail, topsail, and fore topmast staysail. Then they lifted the dead man forward, but had not got him off the shattered poop before he wriggled and spoke, and they laid him down and questioned him. He knew nothing of the lightning stroke, he said, but complained of a prickly sensation all through him. Soon he could walk, and, later on, work.

The squall steadied to a gray gale, and mountain seas pursued the crippled vessel; but she rode them well, her only danger being the risk of broaching-to from the almost helpless condition of the helmsman; but, as night came down, Yank and Angel stationed themselves, ready to help should their hands give out, and thus equipped they steered on through the darkness by the compass alone, there being neither star nor cloud to range by. With a sore-handed man to hold the reel, Swarth hove and hauled in the log every two hours until daylight. Ten knots even she had made, he said, all through the night, and before that good fair gale died out they would be many hundred miles away from their enemy, even should she still be afloat.

The two men who came to the wheel at six that morning made such bad work of it that Swarth profanely rebuked them and called for two others; but there was no improvement in the steering, and he examined the hands of his crew. They were swollen out of all proportion, painful to the extreme, and they were unable to close their fingers around spokes or ropes. So he placed Angel and Yank at the wheel and sent them forward with poultices. In half an hour they all looked as though they had donned boxing-gloves; and, conscious of their utter uselessness at working ship, they essayed the next best thing —they climbed to the forecastle deck to keep lookout. Soon one of them called out:

" Sail ho!" and Swarth, looking where he pointed, observed a craft hove to on the starboard bow, not a mile away, and heading across their course. Her yards were braced nearly in the line of sight, which had prevented their seeing her before.

Swarth reached for his glasses, but as he brought them to bear another shout came from forward, followed by cries of amazement, and he looked where they now pointed. There on the starboard beam, just above the horizon, glowing faintly through the storm-cloud, was the sun—*rising in the west.*

There was no mistaking it for the moon, even though the moon had been full at the time and could rise at seven in the morning; nothing but the sun could penetrate that thick sky. Swarth involuntarily looked at the compass, but it told him nothing; the brigantine was heading south.

The men came running aft, and tremulously asked

questions which neither Swarth, Angel, nor Yank could answer. While they watched the luminary it rose higher—unmistakably so. It was the sun, rising in the west; but why?

What human mind can remain tranquil before such a violation of the laws of nature? Wonder and perplexity grew to terror. They clutched one another, and crouched down, with elbows raised, as though to ward off a blow. Swarth, pale and silent, stared at the rising orb; Yank Tate's face was a picture of childish fright as he helped Angel steer; Angel, doughty ex-missionary, steered a seamanly course, but cast the burden upon the Lord. With his eyes on the compass, his lips moved in prayer.

A hail came from over to starboard.

"Shorten down and round to, or I'll sink you!"

Not two lengths away was a black brig squaring away to a parallel course. She was under whole topsails, but the fore topgallant-sail was going up and her port battery was manned—the crews in position and the black muzzles protruding from the open ports. There was no escape. They had left that brig three hundred miles to the north. How could she have pursued them, missed them, and waited for them here? It meant a détour and twenty knots of speed, which is beyond the power of sailing craft. It was a mystery equal to that of the western sun.

"I've got you under my guns, Swarth!" roared an officer through a trumpet. "Heave to or I'll give you a broadside!"

"My men are all crippled," answered the pale but self-contained Swarth, "and we cannot handle sail. If I round to the spars will go."

"Round to and let them go!"

"Down with the wheel, Angel!" said Swarth. "The game's up!"

Swarth was but partly right. The craft rolled her fore topmast out in three rolls, but the well-stayed jury mast remained in place.

Three hours later, moored to stanchions in the man-of-war's 'tween-deck by leg-irons, Swarth and his crew received a visit from the captain. He was a blunt and candid soul, and greeted Swarth pleasantly.

"I've called you all kinds of a damned scoundrel, Swarth," he said, "since I've hunted you; but I never called you a damned fool. What did you come back for? Did you think I couldn't put out the fire in the galley and mend my steering-gear?"

"Come back?" queried the pirate. "I don't know—how did you get ahead of us?"

"I didn't," chuckled the captain. "If you'd only known you could have sunk me. I'm bound to port now to get more powder and get you hanged. The fire threatened the magazine and we doused it. By the way, your wheel and binnacle are just what I need to replace mine, that you knocked endways with the same shot that hit the galley stove. So I took them out before scuttling your old tub. But where did you get that compass? The needle points south."

"It does?" queried Swarth. "It never did with me—wait, yes, by Gawd. We steered due south by it, and fetched back here. That's why the sun rose in the west. But what—why, the lightning! It must have changed it—somehow!"

"Somehow, yes," repeated the captain, with a grin. "We figured it out before we scuttled her. That was a fine jury main rigging you put up—a coil of wire insulated by wood, around a magnet, with one end up above the coils and the other over the side. A little science is a dangerous thing, Swarth."

THE SHARK

THERE was a startled yell from aloft, and Green, the ordinary seaman of the port watch, was seen clinging tightly to the jackstay of the cro'-jack yard, and peering downward. He had dropped his marline-spike, which, turning slowly over as it fell, struck the water, point first.

"My God, sir," he sang out to the mate below him on the poop, "d'you see that shark? He's long as the jib-boom, sir."

Mr. Good stepped to the taffrail and peered over, just in time to see the tip of a dorsal fin disappearing from view, and a long, dark-green, shadowy form that merged, as he looked, into the deep blue of the quiet sea. The ripples, splashed by the marline-spike, obstructed his vision; but Green, higher in the air, could see farther.

"He's swallowed the spike, sir!" he called, as he stared down with wide-open eyes. "He swam down and caught it! He gi' me such a turn, sir, when I first seen him, that I dropped it."

"Look out you don't drop yourself!" growled the mate, good-humoredly. "Come down and get another."

Green started in along the foot-rope, and as Mr. Good resumed his scrutiny of the smooth, heaving swell he was joined by the helmsman, old Munson, the patriarch of the crew and a privileged character, who, there being no wind, dared leave the wheel. As they looked a long patch of dark green appeared, then the indistinct outlines of a man-eating shark— not so long as the jib-boom, but fully fifteen feet in length. He " rose " his dorsal fin and lay quiet, just beneath the surface and six feet abaft the rudder. Old Munson groaned a weary oath and said:

" He's come for one of us, sir. He'll follow along for seven days, and then he'll get one of us. Every seven days a man goes with a shark in the wake, sir. In my last ship—"

" Never mind your last ship, old man," interrupted the mate. " Take the wheel again; and don't stir the men up with shark yarns. I'll fix that gentleman."

He went forward and returned with a harpoon; and, having met Green on his way for a marline-spike, brought him along, and had him get out from the lazarette a coil of small rope, the end of which he fastened to the harpoon.

" It's a dead-easy shot," he said, as he mounted the taffrail. " Stand by to pay out lively when I hit him," he added to Green, " and be ready to catch a turn."

Holding on with his left hand to the bail of the spanker-boom, he poised the harpoon a moment, then, softly repeating, " Dead easy," hurled it downward. There was a scarcely perceptible flirt of the shark's tail, a back push of his fins, a flurry of the surface water, and the shark had moved about a foot to starboard. The harpoon was seeking the bottom.

" Haul in!" yelled the mate—for Green was dutifully paying out. " Hell!—how'd I miss?"

He looked down at the quiescent brute, and saw, or thought he saw, one wicked little eye close in a wink.

"All right, my joker!" he said, angrily. "We'll try again."

He tried again and again—and many times, to no avail. The shark was quicker of eye and movement than he, and at last he gave it up.

"Get to your work!" he said, sourly, to Green. "Finish seizin' off those gaskets."

"Please, Mr. Good," said Green, earnestly, "put me at somethin' else. I'll fall, sir. I know I'll fall, with him a-lookin' up at me."

"Get up on the cro'-jack yard!" roared the incensed officer. "Nice state of affairs, this is! Afraid to go aloft! What's the matter wi' you, hey? Up wi' you!"

Pale of face, Green went forward for another marline-spike. Mr. Good, fuming, and uttering profane comments on the situation, began coiling the wet rope on the top of the house to dry.

"He's right, sir," ventured old Munson at the wheel. "Shouldn't wonder if he went first."

"Will you dry up?" said Mr. Good, softly but intensely, in Munson's ear. "I'll get that shark yet, but if I hear any more croaking from you I'll have you aloft night and day."

Munson subsided, and the irritated Mr. Good gave over his coiling job and went forward again, bringing back this time a shark-hook and chain, with a large piece of fat pork for bait. Also did he bring Green, who had secured a spike, but had not reached the rigging.

"Now," said the mate, as he fastened the rope to the chain, "you stand by with the end of the spanker sheet, and, if he takes the hook, make a runnin' bowline—a slip-noose, you know—around the line, so as to slip it down over his head and bring him up by the tail. Understand?"

Green did, and, dropping his spike, cleared away the rope named, while Mr. Good gently lowered the baited hook to the water. The shark backed away from it a foot or two as it floated astern, then, cautiously approaching it, nosed it a little, and nibbled the pork from the hook.

"Well, blast your heart and soul!" exclaimed the mate, in amazement. Then he hurled Green's marline-spike at him, but missed.

"What's going on here?" said a voice behind him, and Mr. Good turned to face the captain, a man the antithesis of himself in manner and appearance. The mate was old, bearded, bluff, and profane; the captain, young, smooth of face, voice, and outline; the mate, tall, thin, and angular, but with an ever-present rough good-humor; the captain, short, fat, solemn, sour, and religious. "Your language is painful to listen to, Mr. Good," he continued. "What are you doing?"

"Trying to catch that hell-fired shark, cappen; and look at what he did—ate the pork and left the hook. Who'd think he knew enough?"

"Why not, sir?" said old Munson, in his raspy voice, turning and looking earnestly at the mate. "Everybody knows that sharks are inhabited by the souls of wicked skippers and mates who were hung for murdering sailors. I may have sailed with that same—"

"Will you shut up?" then roared the mate. "If you don't, I may be a shark myself some day."

"You might find something better to do with your time, Mr. Good," said the captain, peering over the taffrail. "That is one of God's creatures. Why should you wish to kill it?"

"Why? Because it's a damned shark, cappen. A murdering, man-eating shark."

"It has done you no harm, Mr. Good." The captain looked aloft. "I see the wind is hauling, and your yards will bear a little attention."

Caught in a dereliction, the mate went forward, muttering further and intense profanity, while the captain went below and Green aloft. Green moved slowly and carefully up to the yard, then slowly and carefully down and forward for the spike he had pretended to forget, by which time eight bells struck, and he remained there.

His sporting blood temporarily chilled, Mr. Good let the shark alone for the rest of that day; but at daylight next morning, it being his watch on deck, he looked over at the monster and was moved to try again. He tried, and lost more pork. Then he tried the harpoon, and lost his temper. Cursing furiously, he ran to his room and returned with a revolver, which he emptied at the shark; but, though his aim was good, the water stopped the bullets, and not one hit the big fish with force enough to disturb him. In a final outburst of rage and profanity, Mr. Good hurled the pistol at the big brute, and then, realizing what he had done, turned his profanity inward, and rebuked himself for a fool. Then the captain, aroused by the shots, appeared at his side and joined him in the rebuke.

"Why will you indulge your cruel instincts in this manner?" he asked, mildly.

"Well, cappen," growled the mate, "he's a cruel swine himself, and he's got the best o' me. I've lost my gun—'spect he's swallowed it. He eats marline-spikes. 'Twas a good gun, too. Cost me two pound ten in Liverpool."

"All you had, too," exclaimed the captain, seriously. "And you dropped it while fooling with that poor creature?"

"Wrong, cappen. I flung it at him after firin' six bullets at him."

"Oh, you miserable fool! And it was all the gun you had. I've heard you say so. Now, what'll—"

"Steady, cappen!" interrupted the mate, his face darkening. "Don't abuse me before the man at the wheel, sir. I won't stand it. Come forward a bit, if you please, and we'll talk."

The man at the wheel put on the abstracted look peculiar to all unwilling listeners, and the captain followed the mate to the weather-alley, near the poop steps.

"I know what's in your mind, cappen," said the mate. "You've no gun yourself, and depended upon me for any shootin' if the crew made trouble. Now, this is a good crew, and I don't need a gun to handle 'em; but I do need to keep 'em tranquil. And nothing upsets a crew like a shark in the wake. Besides, they wouldn't know it was my only gun if you hadn't declared yourself 'fore the man at the wheel."

"That's all right," answered the captain, peevishly. "I merely object to cruelty to dumb creatures."

"Well, I'll tell you, cappen, if you don't let me get rid of that shark you'll have to be cruel to sailors. I know sailors; I've been longer 'fore the mast than you, sir."

Few captains like such comparisons, especially if they be young and sons of owners. This one was very properly incensed.

"I care nothing for that, Mr. Good," he said, sharply. "I forbid you to torture that poor fish any more. You are setting an infamous example to those ignorant men forward, whose souls, in a measure, I feel accountable for."

"Well, I'll be damned!" said the mate, almost in a whisper.

"You certainly will be, if you persist in your evil ways," answered the captain, turning away.

"But what'll we do about that shark, cappen? He'll follow till he gets a man."

"Feed him," said the captain, turning half around. "Feed him until he is glutted, and he will leave us."

"Which man'll I chuck over first, cappen? Green? He's young and fat."

The captain turned squarely around.

"Feed him pork," he said, angrily. "Strike out a barrel of that fat Frisco pork in the 'tween-deck, and feed him until he is satisfied."

"It's down under three tiers o' lime-barrels, sir. It'll take the whole watch half a day to get at it. Won't live chickens from the coop suit him better? I've plenty other work for the men."

"Do as I tell you, Mr. Good," said the captain, sternly.

"Aye, aye, sir!" loudly answered Mr. Good. "I can do that, cappen."

As the mate had predicted, it took a half-day to get out a barrel of pork; and before the work was finished three men had contributed various articles to the omnivorous maw of the man-eater. They were of the second-mate's watch, for Mr. Good's crowd slept from breakfast until noon. Big Bill, a six-foot "Sou'wegian," too big to be handy in the contracted 'tween-deck, was sent out on the jib-boom at a tarring-down job, while his watch-mates wrestled with barrels under the second mate. Ordinarily Bill was as sure of foot and hand as a monkey, but on this occasion he had trouble with himself. Mr. Good, who, too angry and upset to sleep, was watching the ship while the second-mate was below, observed Bill flounder down from the jib foot-rope, and a moment later climb inboard and get out of sight.

Then Mr. Good, standing near the quarter-rail, noticed a tobacco-pouch float by, heard the swish of a dorsal fin, and saw the upturned white belly of the shark as he rushed at the prize. Then, unable to resist the impulse, he seized an iron belaying-pin from the rail and hurled it at the shark—but missed, as before. He also gave vent to the bad language which he thought fitting to the occasion, and then heard the captain's voice through a window:

"Mr. Good, those belaying-pins are the owner's property. You would not like it if I deducted their cost from your pay, would you?"

"Oh, damn!" growled the mate, as he moved away from the window.

As the second mate had given him his job, Mr. Good did not investigate Bill, who "soldiered" until four bells, when he came aft to take the wheel. But here he questioned him mildly.

"I dunno, sir," said Bill. "I loose my tobax-bag, und mine foot slip on der foot-rope. Den I think of dot feller under the stern, und next I know I fetch up on der martingale, sir. I yoost hold on, by golly."

"The shark got your tobacco," said the mate. "I saw him grab it."

"By golly. I bet it make him sick, sir. It make

me sick, to think of him waitin' for me. Ah-ah-ah!" Bill finished with a shiver.

The man Bill relieved—a German named Swanson, nearly as old a man as Munson—was told by Mr. Good to fox off the lanyards of the weather mizzen rigging, recently set up—a job requiring tarred rope yarns, a marline-spike, and a knife. Swanson procured his material and went to work, and when he first found occasion to use his knife twirled it out of its sheath with the usual flourish. But it left his hand with the momentum given it, whirled over his shoulder, and landed on the monkey-rail; here it rattled and slid about, as though imbued with life, then fell overboard. There was the now familiar swish of the dorsal fin as the shark dove for the morsel, and Mr. Good remarked:

"If he takes that, he'll get the belly-ache. Get another knife, Swanson." But Swanson was unnerved.

"It wass a sign—a sign," he stuttered. "A sign dot I go, sir. Und Green, he go, und you—you go, sir. You loose your pistol und Bill—we all go, sir. It wass a sign."

"More of a sign that we won't go, Swanson," said the mate, in rough kindness. "Go get a knife."

Shaking his head, Swanson went forward and remained there. As it was an English ship, Mr. Good was not impelled to follow and club him aft.

Limerick, an Irishman of the second mate's watch, had gone below with rubber boots on. These had distressed him in the hot 'tween-deck, and he had removed them; and to save his socks from wear he also removed them. The result was that his feet, moist with perspiration, slaked the loose lime scattered around from the leaky barrels, and soon became so painful that he pulled the boots on for protection. But the lime still ate into his skin, and he was forced to come up on deck, where he not only rinsed his feet in salt water, but rinsed out his boots with fresh. Then, after he had donned suitable footgear, he hung his boots on the jib guys to dry, and in doing so one went overboard. The shark got the boot; there was no doubt of it. For, though Limerick, peering aft from the cat-head, could not see, Mr. Good, on the quarter, called the news forward.

"It wass a sign, Limerick," whined old Swanson from the fore-hatch. "We all go by der shark."

"Sign be dommed, ye old bag o' bad news!" said Limerick, coming down the forecastle steps. "I'm thinkin' o' the cost of a new pair o' gum boots from the slop-chest. If the mate 'ud let me aft I'd like nothin' better than to give the murderin' thief the other boot on the head—bad luck to him!"

The barrel of pork was brought up, and broached alongside the fore-hatch; then, when Mr. Good had eaten his dinner with the captain—at which function neither spoke to the other—he procured the fattest chunk of pork in sight and brought it aft. The captain found it convenient to be there, and, as Mr. Good dropped the pork over the taffrail, looked down with the keenest interest. The shark, as though appreciative of the effort in his behalf, made more ceremony over this contribution. Instead of a greedy rush straight for the gift, he backed away, circled around, and then headed dead-on. The pork seemed to melt into the white glimmer of the shark's upturned belly.

"That's what he likes," exclaimed the captain, enthusiastically. "Give him some more, Mr. Good."

"Aye, aye, sir!" snorted the mate. "But he

doesn't like it so much as marline-spikes, pistols, baccy, and belayin'-pins, cappen; and he likes sailors' legs and arms better than all."

The captain raised his hand, and mildly said:

" Give him some more."

The mate funneled his hands and sent a mighty roar forward:

" One up—and bear a hand. An order of pork in a hell of a rush. And, say, cappen, I'm not much of a hash-slinger, but a mighty good head-waiter. Would he like some beans with his pork? "

The captain made no reply. Mr. Good was an expert seaman, and a valuable aid to one whose father owned the ship. An American named Thompson understood the order, and filled it.

" You'll get no tips in this hash-house," snarled the mate, as he took the pork from the grinning sailor. " Go for'ard and stand by for orders." Thompson departed, and Mr. Good tossed the pork to the shark. It was bolted with the same ceremony, but not so greedily.

" Will ye have some more, cappen? " asked the mate, with mock deference. " Or would he like some dessert? "

" As I said, give him all he can eat," responded the captain, with what dignity he could command.

" Once more on the rare and the greasy! " yelled the mate; and Thompson came aft with another portion of pork.

" No question about it," said Mr. Good, as he took the pork and dropped it. " That fish can never look a hog in the face again, and he'll never get a front seat in the synagogue. Holy smoke, cappen, he won't touch it."

The shark had nosed the morsel, backed away from

it, and, as it floated astern, resumed his position just abaft the rudder.

"Shall I give him the latitude and longitude," asked the mate, with fine sarcasm in his voice, "so he can find it again?"

"Give him all that he can eat," answered the captain. "Surfeit him, so that he will leave us." Then he descended to his cabin.

But Mr. Good fed no more pork to the shark that day. Instead, inspired by Limerick's strong language when he limped aft to the wheel at eight bells, he did a wonderful amount of thinking, as little compatible with his duties as chief mate as was feeding pork to a shark. Limerick was in agony, he informed Mr. Good. His feet felt as though he had stepped on a hot stove. The irascible but kindhearted old fellow called the next man to the wheel, and sent Limerick forward, following himself with appliances from the medicine-chest.

While among the men Mr. Good did his utmost, by admonition and ridicule, to counteract the influence of the two superstitious old croakers, Swanson and Munson, but with little success, even though backed by the lurid irreverence of Limerick, who was willing, he averred, to go down in a bosun's-chair and kill the shark with his one rubber boot.

Green made no secret of his terror, and whimpered unrebuked among men who, as a class, regard cowardice as the unpardonable sin. Swanson openly voiced his determination not to leave the deck while the shark was in the wake, saying he preferred going in irons to the chance of death after the "sign" given him. Big Bill was non-committal; but it was apparent that he had not recovered from the shock to his nerves. And old man Munson told yarn after yarn of the turpitude of sharks. The others of both watches shared more or less evenly the sentiments of these four. Luckily, it was fine weather, and nothing but routine work demanded that men mount the rail, but a gale of wind with a demoralized crew would be a serious proposition; and though the mate mirthfully forgave the two old croakers, he pitilessly berated Green, and drove all hands, even the crippled Limerick, up the weather main rigging to the topmast head and down the lee side before allowing them to go to supper. But the moral effect of the experiment was lost by a happening in the last dog-watch.

Though English, she was a wooden ship, and needed the daily pumping-out. When the watch was called to the pumps at seven, or, by English reckoning, three bells, a man readily mounted the rail amidships to draw a bucket of water. It was Thompson, a peculiarly efficient man, steady of head and hand— one who, under ordinary circumstances, would not indulge in horseplay or bravado; but a shark under the stern is bad for nerves, and Thompson yielded. He lowered the draw-bucket with a flourish, tilted it to fill it, hove upward with all his strength, and actually pulled himself overboard. As he fell with a splash, a cry of horror went up from the men amidships; they sprang to the rail, and threw over every rope's end in reach, then, their anxiety over Thompson dominating their fears, they swarmed to the top of the rail, ready to assist. But Thompson needed no help. There was small way upon the ship, and he arose close to the main chains. The ship was rolling heavily in the trough of a short swell, and, though this may have contributed to his loss of balance, it was his salvation now. Barely catching one iron bar with one hand, he was lifted out of water by the ship's roll, and as she plunged him back, he caught with the other hand and swung his right leg over the lower channel board. Here he rested a moment, as the ship again lifted him; but something brushed his dangling left foot, and he frantically finished his climb. As he appeared, pale and dripping, among his shipmates on the rail, a crunching sound was heard and a man sang out: "Great God, he's taken the draw-bucket, rope and all!"

Mr. Good wisely ordered the wash-deck pump rigged to prime the main pumps, and the job was finished, Thompson assisting as though nothing had happened.

Next morning Mr. Good turned out at four bells, fully an hour and a half before breakfast-time. He paid no attention to the ship, to the wind and weather, or to the washing-down of the deck, which, under the second mate, was proceeding in the customary manner. He went directly to the " bosun's-locker," and equipped himself with palm, needle, and twine, which he secreted in his pocket. Next, Chips being asleep, he sneaked into the carpenter-shop and secured a hatchet, which he tucked into his trousers. Then, hardly noticed by the busy second mate and his watch, he burrowed into the pork barrel and brought out the largest piece of greasy abomination that it contained. With this he descended the fore-hatch, and remained below until seven bells, when he emerged, carrying the pork, which had increased in size, and bore a line of big-twine stitching on one side. Passing the carpenter-shop, he again sneaked in and deposited the hatchet, then went aft, placed the pork, stitched side down, upon a bit of old canvas under the wheel-box grating, and peered over the stern. The sinister brute was still there, bluish-green in the morning light, inert but menacing. He flirted his tail and moved forward a foot; then—of course it was due to refraction—Mr. Good received a wink. Mr. Good returned it, solemnly.

"Not yet, you blooming son of a ship-owner!" he said, softly. "Not yet. Wait till your friend is up." Then he washed his hands and went to breakfast with the captain.

They were not yet on speaking terms, and the meal passed off in silence; but as the mate rose he said:

"Going to feed the baby, now. Will you be up, sir?"

The captain, his eyes on his breakfast, made no answer.

"He don't look well at all this morning, sir," continued the mate, edging toward the door. "He overate himself yesterday. I don't think pork is really good for sharks, sir."

"Mr. Good," sputtered the captain, "I object to your tone. I demand that you treat me with respect. I demand that you obey my reasonable and humane wishes in regard to that shark. I order you to feed him—to surfeit him, so that he will leave us."

"Yes, sir—yes, sir," answered the mate, meekly. "But I'm a humane man myself, sir. I wouldn't give a poor shark what is not good for him, any more than I would a baby, sir. Do you think draw-buckets are bad for sharks, cappen? Marline-spikes and belayin'-pins seem to agree with him, but it might be the draw-bucket, after all—not the pork. Come up, and see for yourself, sir."

Partly mollified by his mildness, the captain rose and followed him. As they reached the taffrail eight bells sounded, the watch-below tumbled out of the forecastle, and the second mate climbed the poop steps to report to his superior the happenings of the morning watch and be officially relieved. For the moment all hands were on deck. Perhaps the mild and humane Mr. Good knew they would be.

There was little wind, and little way upon the ship. The long, bluish-green thing of horror was clearly visible in the smooth sea beneath, and, as the captain and mate looked over, moved ahead expectantly, his white belly partly showing as he canted himself, his wicked and wide-open eyes watching upward. As they looked, a pilot-fish—the usual consort of a shark—darted up to his nose from to starboard, hovered a moment, and darted back. There was a streak of shade in the water, a wave of ripples left by the dorsal fin, and in a second the shark was on the starboard quarter, gingerly devouring some scraps of the men's breakfast that had drifted aft. Mr. Good shivered, and picked up the pork.

" He seems to be hungry," said the captain.

" Well," grunted the mate, " if he's hungry, why, he ought to be fed "—he tossed over the pork— " but, as I said, cappen, I don't think pork agrees with him."

The shark, as the greasy white lump struck the water, backed away a short distance; then the pilot-fish was seen, inspecting the find, apparently with approval, for he immediately shot over to the nose of his big friend to report. The shark backed a little farther, then reversed his engines and went ahead, turning to the right. He made two complete circles around the morsel before heading straight on, but then he made for it with the speed of a torpedo-boat, turning on his side as he drew near and shooting half out of the water with the momentum after his cavernous mouth had enclosed it. Then he quietly sculled up to his post just abaft the rudder, ready for further favors.

"Give him more," said the captain.

"Very well, sir," said the mate, resignedly, "if you think pork is good for him. But I think it makes him sick." Then, funneling his hands, he sent a roar forward. "Bring that pork-barrel aft on the poop!"

It took most of the watch to get the pork-barrel aft, and the rest of the men, interested in the proceedings, climbed the rail to observe. But by the time the barrel was deposited alongside the wheel-box the shark seemed to have lost interest himself. He was moving uneasily from side to side, backing and going ahead, as though in quest of something. The pilot-fish could be seen occasionally, darting to and fro, as though sharing the mood of the shark, but never approaching too close.

"I told you, cappen," said the mate, solemnly, "that pork didn't agree with him. You can see for yourself, sir, that it's made him sick."

"Nonsense!" said the captain. "Give him another piece."

Mr. Good tossed over another lump, but it received attention only from the pilot-fish, who drifted astern with it. The big fish seemed more agitated than ever. His movements were quicker and his excursions to the right and left longer. Suddenly he stopped, elevated his nose, and belched in air a quantity of what looked like soapsuds. Then he sank and shot away to port, only to return as quickly.

"Sick," murmured the mate, "very sick. I knew

it. He ought to have had some beans with his pork, or some belayin'-pins or hardware."

The captain watched with serious face. The second mate was beside him, equally observant. To one side, held to the poop by the spectacle, were the men who had brought the pork barrel aft, and scattered along the rail amidships were the rest of the crew. The shark seemed to appreciate his audience, for he was performing feats of agility now unusual to sharks; he was throwing somersaults in the air and occasionally standing on his head.

"What is the matter with him?" asked the captain, in mild wonder.

"I tell you, cappen," answered the mate, virtuously, "that you've made him sick. Pork's a rich diet. I wouldn't be so cruel to a poor ignorant brute, but *you* will, I see. Now you've got this on your conscience, sir, but my conscience is clear. I didn't want to torture the poor thing."

"Give him another piece," said the captain, doggedly.

Mr. Good fished out a succulent portion and flung it with all his strength at the shark, but missed.

Again the shark stopped, elevated his nose, and belched forth a deluge of white froth of a thick, creamy consistency. Then he backed away, raced furiously around in a circle, and repeated the performance. A black object whirled upward and sank.

"By the holy powers!" yelled Limerick, from the mizzen rigging, "if that ain't me boot I'm a Dutchman!"

Another violent outpouring brought momentarily to light several small black objects which might be belaying-pins, pistols, or marline-spikes. But when a rope whirled, snake-like, high in the air, they recognized the bucket-rope.

The sea around the shark was becoming milk-white and opaque, so that when he dived he was out of sight. But he did not remain long under water. He seemed to be seeking air, and would suddenly appear, shooting upward twice his length, to fall with a splash and resume his circlings and rushings. Then, after a wild and furious rush far to starboard and back to port, he sculled quietly up to the rudder, turned on his side, and lay still.

"Why, he's dead," said the captain, as the carcass floated astern. "Who would think that pork would kill a shark?"

"Who, indeed, cappen?" answered the mate, severely. "But care killed the cat, sir."

"Well, well, I don't understand." The captain went down the companionway, and the men began moving forward.

"I understand," said Limerick, wisely, as he lowered himself from the rigging. "I sh'udn't wonder, begob, if the son uv a thief's insides felt somethin' like me feet. They do say that quicklime be a powerful counter-ir-rytant. Maybe he got some lime wid his pork."

"Will you shut your jaw?" said Mr. Good, fiercely. Then, drawing near to the man, the last of the crew on the poop, he said in his ear: "Go down forrard with a broom and sweep up all that lime scattered around. I didn't have time. And keep your damn mouth shut, d'you hear?"

"Aye, aye, sir!" answered Limerick, cheerfully, as he turned away. "But d'ye know, Mr. Good, I feel powerful sorry fur the shark. I know just how he felt, sir."

THE MUTINY

WHEN you have been shipwrecked, and, sole survivor of the crew, have tramped through the African jungle seven days on the food you can pick from the bushes; when your clothing is in rags and ribbons, your feet blistered and bleeding, and your stomach in a state of unstable equilibrium, you are likely, on touching the coast again, to welcome the sight of a brig at anchor in the bay, and to more than welcome the offer of a berth from a man who sculls ashore at your hail, especially so when he imparts the information that the nearest settlement is still two hundred miles farther on. That is why I shipped with Captain Bruggles.

He was the largest man I had ever seen—almost seven feet tall. But, unlike most tall men, his development was perfect. There was nearly a thirty-inch stretch across his back from shoulder to shoulder; his arm was as large as an ordinary leg; his leg could not have been gartered by an average woman's belt; and his clinched fist would hardly have gone into my hat, had I possessed one. Over this massive framework of bone and muscle towered a leonine head with an uncut shock of coarse, brown hair. His face was not displeasing, but in repose it took on the grim dignity of a lion's; and this, with his great size, gave him a personality rather oppressive, especially when his steady, gray eyes were fixed upon you. He wore no hat, and was clothed merely in sockless shoes, extremely dirty trousers, and flannel shirt—the latter unbuttoned, exposing a forest of hair on his chest. Down deep in this chest he seemed to keep his voice, and it came forth in rumbling intonations. But his words were well chosen—those of an educated man.

"I'll give you a passage," he said, when I had told him my trouble; "but you might as well ship with me; you sail first mate, you say. I want a mate who can cook for the crew, or a cook who can navigate and keep the crew in shape. I don't care which."

"Of course I'll try it, captain," I answered, eagerly; "but isn't it difficult for a mate to boss sailors and cook for them, too?"

"Not aboard my vessel. Galley's forward, but the bill of fare is simple. Come aboard."

As I was too exhausted to be of use at an oar, he sculled the boat out to the brig, while I sat upon a bow-thwart, blessed my good luck, and studied the craft I had shipped in. She was about four hundred tons' register, and, judging by her sheer, the tautness of her standing rigging, and a general smoothness, was not very old; but braces and halyards hung in bights, and there was a week's work for a full crew, scraping and painting. Truly, she needed a mate, and I was about to say as much when a hoarse, roaring growl sounded from the brig, and echoed back from the forest on the beach.

"What is it?" I asked, in astonishment.

"One of my crew," answered the captain. "He's hungry."

I said no more. He sculled rapidly up to the side ladder, told me to toss up the painter, and sang out: "Hillee ho, boy, on deck! Pull rope, pull rope, pull rope!"

I threw the coiled painter over the rail, and a huge, hairy face with red eyes, wide, grinning mouth, and fang-like teeth looked down on me. Then a hairy paw as large as Captain Bruggles's hand caught the rope and pulled it taut.

"Up you go!" said he.

"Not much!" I exclaimed, reaching for an oar. "That's an orang-outang, isn't it? And he's loose."

"They're all young and tame. Follow me up. Leave the oar alone. There's no danger, and you mustn't hit one unless he deserves it. That only spoils 'em."

He climbed up and stepped inboard. I cautiously followed, but remained on the side steps while I inspected the deck. The big brute who had taken the painter had belayed it, and was slouching forward, looking back at Captain Bruggles, who had seated himself on the mizzen-hatch. Squatted on deck forward and crouching over the windlass were four others of the ungainly beasts, and in a strong iron cage amidships was a sixth, undoubtedly the hungry one, for he shook his bars and bellowed at us.

"Climb in," said the captain. "You're all right. Come in, and I'll explain this. No doubt it looks queer to you."

"If you don't mind, captain," I answered, a little huskily, "I'll stay here a few minutes, until I'm more accustomed to it. I can hear you. Is this your crew—that I'm to oversee and cook for?"

"This is my crew. I've trained 'em from babies. They're not able-seamen yet—that is, they can't paint and scrape and splice like a man; but they can do twenty men's work shortening sail, and cost me nothing in wages and very little in grub. But, I admit, I can't keep a mate; and there's no good reason for it, either. All it needs is a little nerve and common sense and firmness, and a mate'll have no trouble with 'em. I think you're the man for me. You'll only have to cook their mush for 'em once a day, and give 'em orders same as I do. My daughter cooks for the cabin. Got a galley down aft."

"Your daughter!" I exclaimed, in astonishment. "A woman aboard with these brutes?"

"Yes," he bawled. "She's not used to 'em yet, and stays below." He nodded toward the cabin. "By the way, you must be hungry. Come down below and fill up. Then we can talk things over better."

He arose and approached the companionway, and, with my heart beating painfully, I stepped to the deck and followed. A growl of protest arose from the combined throats of the six, and the prisoner rattled his bars furiously. I hastened my steps, looking back, ready to spring overboard if need be, but Captain Bruggles quelled the uproar by halting, lifting his hand, and uttering the one word, "Hush!"

He called through the closed door, and bolts slid back on the inner side. When it opened we descended, and I saw a slim girl in the half-light of the passage.

"Father!" she sobbed; "oh, father, don't leave me again! I'll die if you leave me alone again. They were crawling around looking down the skylight."

"Were they?" he answered, sternly. "And I told them not to. All right. I'll 'tend to 'em. This is a new man, going mate with us, Jessie. Let's see —your name's Fleming, isn't it? Mr. Fleming, Jessie; this is my daughter, Mr.—"

"Rob! Rob! Oh, Rob!" she screamed, and in a

second I had my arms around her, while she kissed me as I never was kissed before, and most certainly never expected to be kissed by her. She was the girl that every man knows—the girl who said " no "; and we had parted under the moonlight three years before at a certain swinging gate near the end of a lane four thousand miles from this brig and its horrible crew—I to go back to the sea and forget, if I could; she to continue her even life and—so it seemed now—to remember.

" What's all this? " asked the father, sternly, and I released her.

" Why, it's—it's Robert Fleming," she answered, in some confusion; " I told you about him, didn't I, father? We're old friends."

" Lovers, I should say, if I'm a judge. Well, no more o' this. Young man, you want a berth, I want a mate; but I want no son-in-law, and I do want my girl for a while. Understand this at once."

" Very well, sir. I understand," I said, while Jessie drew away from me, " and whatever scruples I had about taking this berth have disappeared. I'll ship at going wages."

" All right. We go down to Frenchtown, on the Pango River, for a cargo of animals, snakes, and birds—whatever my agents have collected. That's my trade—procuring wild creatures to supply the menageries. And as I'd been to sea before I learned it, I combine both ends. Your work, of course, is to stand watch like any mate, rig tackles for cargo-work, and, in short, do everything that my boys forrard can't do. You won't have to cook for 'em long, because I'm training the oldest and most intelligent to light a fire forrard, and he can soon cook the mush. The rest of their grub is fruit, yams, and such, which they help themselves to. Here, I forgot. Jessie, get something for Mr. Fleming to eat."

Jessie had listened with a strained look of terror in her face while her father talked, and I noticed how her pretty features had changed from what they were when I knew her at home; she had aged ten years. And I did not doubt that the aging process had begun when she joined her father.

She immediately began setting the table, and soon had a cold meal ready for me, which I attacked as a starved man will. Meanwhile an uproar on deck had called the captain away from us, and when I had eaten enough to be able to speak between mouthfuls, she said:

"You must not go in this vessel as mate. Insist upon it. The last mate was killed, and, I believe, the one before the last. Father is the only man in the world who can control them. They will kill you, too—they will kill you, Rob. And then—what will I do?"

"I agreed to, Jessie. I can't go back on it."

"Run away to-night. Take the boat, and take me with you. I am dying of terror. I cannot bear it. Oh, Rob, take me away from this vessel!"

She buried her face in her arms and sobbed like a child.

"There are wild beasts ashore, Jessie," I said, gently; "and we would have to tramp two hundred miles. You cannot do it. I only shipped to be with you. Wait until we make a port. What manner of man is this father of yours, anyway, to condemn a girl like you to this?"

"He is a man without human sympathy," she said, lifting her tear-stained face. "He left me at home when I was little, but paid my way; and six months ago he sent me passage-money and instructions to join him at St. Louis on the *Senegal*. He cannot understand fear—he has never felt it; he boasts that he can conquer any wild beast in the world with his hands, and wonders why others are afraid. He is kind to me—though I tell him frankly that I do not care for him as a daughter should—but, when he is in liquor he is a fiend."

"Drinks, does he? I should think a man in his trade would not."

"He drinks at every port when the work is done—that is, when all the animals are disposed of. The noise is frightful, and he is the worst—a greater beast than any."

"I'll stand by you, Jessie," I said, as I arose. "I'll get you out of this scrape if I can. And "—I leaned over her—" you'll stand by me, won't you—you'll say yes instead of no? "

"Yes, yes, Rob, of course. Oh, forgive me for that. I didn't know—I thought you were going to stay home. I thought I'd see you again."

Her father's heavy footsteps sounded on deck, but there was time for one kiss, and I took it; then he called down the skylight for me to come up. I obeyed, noticing as I closed the companion-door and turned to face him on the poop what I had not noticed when I entered the cabin—that over the companion was a steel cage, or grating, which could be secured from the inside, and that the skylight and after companion each held a similar arrangement.

"I put 'em on to satisfy Jessie," he said, as he observed my glance. "Now, come down to the mizzen-hatch and I'll introduce you; but, first, I want to know your relations with my daughter."

"I met her at home," I answered, firmly, as we

seated ourselves. "She and my sisters were great friends, and I asked her to be my wife. She declined at the time, but reversed her decision two minutes ago. I shall marry your daughter at the first opportunity, Captain Bruggles; and she herself will satisfy you that she will not suffer. I am one of those rare men who go to sea for pleasure; but, with a wife, I will remain ashore and live on my own property."

"I care nothing for your property, Mr. Fleming"—his voice was almost a growl—"but I do for my girl. I've waited twenty years for her to grow up. So, let her alone. I've warned you. Now we'll talk business. Get two handspikes out o' the rack."

A little nervously, while the huge brutes forward watched me, I stepped amidships and secured the handspikes; he took one from me, leaving me the other, and told me to stand beside him on the hatch.

"You're to give each one in his turn a thump on the head after I hit him. Strike about as hard as you'd hit a nail with a hammer; it won't hurt 'em."

"Now, boys!" he called to them, "hillee-ho, boys! Come talk—come talk—come talk. Hillee-ho!"

"You must learn my calls," he said, turning to me. "They're used to 'em."

"I'll want a little time for that, sir," I said, holding hard to my six-foot club. I was a large, heavy man myself, and had borne myself well in a great many rough-and-tumble fights, but I had never fought an orang-outang, and the sight of those half-dozen monsters lumbering toward me was weakening. The smallest of the six—for the prisoner was released—when standing erect would top my height by more than an inch, while the largest nearly ap-

proached the giant at my side in size and weight.
But they were not always erect; their usual mode of
progress being a swinging walk on all-fours, and
when they would lift their immense heads and shoulders, bearing their weight on the hind legs, the long,
hairy arms would continue the walking motion, just
clearing the deck as they swung. They stepped upon
the outside edge of the foot, the unsightly toes curl-
ing under, and their lips would draw back in con-
vulsive grins, exposing the yellow fangs; then the
wide mouths would close and an expression of fierce
gravity occupy their ugly faces until the next emotion prompted a change. They squatted before us
in a row, breathing hoarsely and blinking hideously.

"Haeckel," said the captain, to the fellow on the
right, "come!" The big ape scrambled toward
him.

"Look," he said, and the blinking eyes were turned
on me.

"Mate, mate, mate. See, boy," and the captain
pointed at me. Then he shoved his big finger into
the beast's face and said, impressively, "Work, work,
work." This formula was repeated three times,
while Haeckel blinked his respects to me. Next the
captain brought his handspike down on his head
with force enough to have cracked the skull of a
Hottentot, but Haeckel only winked faster and
grinned.

"Hit him yourself, now—a love-tap, not too
hard."

I was very careful not to. Haeckel grinned again,
and took his place at the end of the line, fully acquainted with his chief officer.

In the same manner, gathering courage and confidence from the amicable grins I received, I was in-

troduced to Darwin, Huxley, Tyndall, Spencer, and Marsh.

"I've named 'em after the leading evolutionists," said the captain, as we returned to the poop; "but I doubt that they'd feel complimented."

I was too weak in my knees and dizzy in my head to ask whether he meant the scientists or his pets; the reaction of feeling following my interview with the brutes had come, and I barely escaped fainting. Jessie's white face and wide-open gray eyes, looking at me through the skylight—where she had probably climbed to watch us—was what nerved me to hold my senses; for I knew that I would need all my store of courage and strength to get her away from that brig and her unnatural father.

"You see," he said, when we had seated ourselves on the quarter-rail, "it's utter nonsense to say that animals can be controlled by kindness alone. You can't do it. Their nature will assert itself once in a while. And, by the same token, you can't control 'em by severity alone; it makes 'em ugly, and they break out when they dare. But, combine the two, and you have the working rule which made the Christian religion the greatest force for civilization the world has known—hope of reward and fear of punishment. It will civilize a devil out o' hell."

"Practical, I admit," I answered, "in your case. But how may a man of my size inspire them with fear?"

"They fear you now—all but Spencer, the one who was locked up—and you must see that they continue. Never hesitate to strike if they are ugly, and, when they work well, praise them."

"How about Spencer? How shall I put fear into him?"

" He'll be in my watch. You will have Haeckel, Darwin, and Tyndall."

"How about Spencer, when all hands are up? I must be among them all."

" He's just a little ugly lately, but'll get over it. I'll bring him around myself. Only, don't pick a row with him."

" No fear, captain. And will you tell me how the last mate was killed, so that I'll know more about what not to do."

" Damnation!" he growled. " Damn a babbling hussy! He was killed because he was a damned fool and disobeyed instructions. Spencer is the oldest, and has one privilege over the others—he gets his mush in a separate kid, a habit he formed when he was alone with me. You must remember to give him his share before you serve the others. The last mate forgot it."

" Cheerful prospect for me," I said, rather bitterly, " when I can't tell them apart."

" We won't sail till you do know 'em and until you know all the calls and tricks. I came in here to get a little sleep, and wouldn't object to a few nights more. I stood both watches for two weeks—am badly used up."

" Then the mate was killed on this passage? "

" Two days out. It was Spencer."

" I'll take particular care to learn Spencer's face and habits. That is, unless I can make another deal with you. I'll buy this brig of you at your own figure, and give you passage to the nearest consular port, provided you drop your crew overboard and help work ship."

" Have the money with you? "

" No, I'll send for it through any consulate."

" No good."

" Very well, captain. I have my choice, then, of another trip in the jungle or a berth here where I will probably die. I take the chance; but, though I mean to obey your injunction in regard to your daughter while aboard, it is only fair to you and myself that I say now that it is on her account that I stay. You have taken her from a quiet country home—"

" Never mind, never mind what I've done. It's my business, and she's my girl. Don't broach this subject again."

" Very well, sir."

" There'll be work enough to keep your mind busy here, without concerning yourself with my family affairs. Come forward, and I'll show you how far Spencer has gone in his trade."

He spoke dispassionately, even though, being angry myself, I had give him cause for extreme anger. But, as I followed him, I came to the conclusion that this remarkable man had seldom felt the need of so cheap an emotion; one of his size and strength could have his own sweet will and way without it.

Just abaft the foremast was a newly built bed of stones and mortar, and resting on this an iron tripod supporting a pot the size of a washtub. Here we halted and Captain Bruggles sang out:

" Spencer, come. Fire, fire—cook, cook."

Spencer came from the group at the windlass. He was the largest brute of all, though I had not remarked it in my embarrassment when being introduced. Looking for other characteristics by which I might know him in the darkness, I noticed the absence of his right ear—possibly lost in some argument with his fellows. As he approached I drew back, for the monster rose up on his legs squarely before the captain, bared his yellow teeth, and growled.

"He's still ugly," said the captain, quietly, to me. Then he drew his clinched right fist quickly backward to a level with his shoulder and launched it forward, following with a heave of his whole mighty body. Never in my life had I seen such a knockdown; the fist, impacting on the protruding chin of the grinning beast, lifted him off his feet and turned him nearly over in the air. He came down on his head, floundered to the deck, and lay quiet. It was a knock-out. The others jabbered excitedly, but remained where they were.

"Now's your time, Mr. Fleming," said the captain; "get a handspike, say 'Fire—cook' to him when he comes to, and bat him with the club. You'll never have a better chance to impress him."

I was not anxious for the experiment, but preferred the risk to the almost certain death which would come of failure to impress Spencer. I secured a handspike, stood over the brute, and, when he groaned, moved, and sat up, I knocked him back.

"Fire—cook!" I ordered, sternly, and the captain repeated it.

Spencer sat up again, grinned at me, and went back to the deck. When he arose he blinked, and, without striking him now, I again gave the order. Blinking steadily, he arose to all-fours and lumbered toward a pile of boards near the fore rigging. Selecting one, he picked it to kindling-wood with his hands and feet. I had seen feats of strength at circuses on shore, but never, perhaps, such an awful display of muscular force as this—unless, perhaps, it was that knock-down. When he had made a pile he carried it to the pot and arranged it carefully underneath. Then he disappeared down the fore-hatch and returned with a flint-and-steel and a piece of tinder.

"Spencer," said the captain, gently, "water, water."

The ape arose, grinned ever so slightly, secured a draw-bucket and drew a bucketful from over the side. This he poured in the pot.

"He don't like the touch of water," said the captain. "When he can handle it cheerfully, I'll give him fresh water and teach him to stir the mush."

Spencer was now striking fire from the steel and blowing on the punk. Soon it caught; he arranged small slivers to feed it, added larger ones, and, when the fire was burning well, squatted before it with an expression on his face of fascinated admiration.

"That'll do, Spencer. Put out, put out, put out," ordered the captain. The pot was not heated yet, and Spencer arose, tilted it, and deluged the flames. Then he was patted on the head, and praised—in which ceremony I, perforce, did my share.

"He can light a fire all right," said Captain Brug-gles, as we walked aft; "but when he burns himself he is apt to knock the whole business overboard. Then, too, he must get used to the water."

"How do they steer?" I asked. "Do they know the compass?"

"No; but if you set the course for 'em they can hold her to it fairly well; and steering by the wind is easy for 'em. Sometimes, too, when their nat-ural intelligence don't tell 'em what rope to pull, you may have to put it into their hands. On a dark night a topgallant buntline is the same to them as a topsail buntline. Of course, it delays matters a

little, but I make it a point to begin shortening sail
early."

He led me below, where I signed his articles at the
bottom of a long list of "mates," and received an
outfit from his slop-chest; then he showed me my
room, Spencer's bucket, and the bin of meal for the
making of mush.

As darkness was closing down I performed this
part of my duty, cooking the mush in sight of them
all, and with my handspike within reach; but nothing unpleasant occurred, Spencer coming at my call
and blinking gratefully as I served him, while the rest
waited expectantly, and ate their portion together
out of a wash-deck tub.

I fought orang-outangs all through the night, but
wakened in the morning much improved in spirits
and vitality, and convinced that the only safe plan
of action was to refrain from all open communication with Jessie, to simulate the greatest interest in
my work that was possible, and to appeal to the
first consul or man-of-war that we met; for Captain
Bruggles was most certainly violating the maritime
laws of all nations. At breakfast, when for a moment I was alone with Jessie, I outlined this plan
and she agreed to it.

The day was spent in completing my acquaintance
with the crew; but, beyond a slight fretfulness at the
disagreeable washing-down of deck in the morning,
there was no trouble, or promise of it; they evidently
classed me in with their masterful captain, and did
not compel me to assert myself. Next morning we weighed anchor, set the canvas, and went
to sea.

To me, accustomed to see a whole crew manning
a topsail halyard and mastheading the yard to the

music of a chantey, it was an uncanny spectacle—
that getting under way. There were cleats nailed
to the deck abaft the leading-blocks, and—three at
the fore, three at the main—the monsters would
scramble along these cleats in all postures, sometimes face upward, again face downward, with the
halyards gripped by one hand or one foot, or their
teeth, while the yard went aloft in jerks. When up
to its place we nippered the halyards at the block
and they stopped pulling and belayed. All up-and-
down running rigging led through leading-blocks on
deck, so that they could use their immense strength
rather than their mere weight. Two could sheet
home and hoist a topgallant-sail, one could set a
royal, and, when it came to stowing the anchor,
Haeckel and Spencer did it—by hand.

The passage down the coast was uneventful. My
nervousness wore off after a few night-watches alone
with them, and I found that they welcomed my approval of tasks well performed as they feared my
occasional demonstrations with a capstan-bar. But
Spencer made no headway with his cooking; in spite
of all we could do, he would not touch the draw-
bucket unless told to, and even showed as great a
repugnance to carrying fresh water from the tank in
a bucket, though in the morning washing-down of
the deck he took his share of the splashing without
unusual protest.

With Captain Bruggles my relations were serene
and even friendly. Having uttered his commands
with regard to his daughter, he seemed confident that
they would be obeyed; and as Jessie never left the
cabin, and I was very careful not to arouse his sus-
picions, my relations with her had not developed past
what they were on our first meeting by the time we

had sailed up the muddy little Pango River and anchored off Frenchtown—a cluster of thatched huts, a trading-station, and a rickety wharf. There was no government, no consulate, no post-office, no other craft in the river.

Ordering me to rig cargo-whips and strike out all empty water-casks, Captain Bruggles went ashore in the one boat, and I enjoyed my first long talk with Jessie, which contained little of value to this story, except our conclusion that nothing could be done here in the way of escaping. When he returned I was innocently busy with the work, and he informed me that various cages of different brutes, birds, and reptiles would come off soon on floats. He himself would stow them in the hold, and on the passage up the coast would feed and care for them. That day and on the three following natives from the shore floated out a holdful of large and small cages—boxed in (I suppose to prevent excitement among our crew)—and I struck them down the hatches as fast as they arrived. What they contained I could not guess, but, all being aboard, we hoisted over the prison-cage amidships, which went ashore and returned, boxed in like the others. There was no doubt of the occupant of this—another ape. The roaring and growling from within and the answers of the crew were unmistakable evidence. We stowed it on the main-hatch again, but left the boards on for the present, while Captain Bruggles clubbed his agitated pets down the fore-hatch and covered them.

" It's a female of their breed," he remarked to me; " and we'll have to keep her closed for a while, until they're used to her presence."

Another cage had come off with this last load,

which the captain opened on deck, disclosing a four-foot snake of species unknown to me, but possessing the triangular head of all poisonous serpents. This creature, he explained, was a rarity, and, being valuable, he would stow it in the cabin—which he did, in spite of Jessie's protest. A few other packages and bundles came off, which he also took below, and I surmised, by the odor of his breath at supper-time, that there was whisky among them. There was; he was drunk before dark, and a greater change in a man I never saw produced by the stuff.

His face took on the color of a ripe tomato, and the sacs of flesh under his eyes puffed out and half closed the lids. His gray eyes, darker from the obscuration, glittered through two horizontal slits, giving a hideous expression of ferocity to his face, while his rumbling voice became an almost inarticulate growl. While I was stirring the mush for the crew he roared continually at me from the poop, and as I could not understand a word that he said, and would not leave the supper to burn, my inattention brought him forward in a fury of rage. He collared me, lifted me clear of the deck, and shook me as a terrier does a rat, then dropped me. I was not injured—though very angry—and managed to understand that he would feed the brutes himself that evening. He stirred violently while I nursed my wrath, and, when the mush was cooked and I had doused the fire with a bucket of water, he lifted the fore-hatch.

Up they came, and as I looked on their faces and heard their snarls I retreated toward the handspike-rack, secured one, and went aft; then calling to Jessie to fasten them, I closed down the iron gratings over the skylight and companions.

"There may be trouble to-night, Jessie," I said,

when she appeared at the forward door, " and I may have to jump over and swim; but, if there's a gun to be had ashore, I won't be gone long."

Her answer was drowned in a storm of abuse from her father. He had filled Spencer's bucket and kicked it out of the way; now, with a large dipper, he was spooning the last of the mush into the wash-deck tub, and squinting viciously at me. But the crew were paying no attention to their supper; they were creeping around the big box amidships, sniffing, grinning, and growling, and, as the captain brushed past them on his way toward me, three of them followed menacingly a few feet.

" What are you saying to my girl? " he bellowed, as he approached. " Didn't I tell you to let her alone? "

" Captain Bruggles," I answered, raising my handspike, " don't lay hands on me again. I won't have it. If you were not so drunk you'd not think it necessary. We'll have our hands full with the crew to-night. As for your daughter, I was telling her to fasten the gratings."

" What for? Who told you to drop the gratings? "

" Never mind that now," I answered. " Look forward—look at them."

My manner impressed him and he turned. I meant no trick; the brutes were ripping the planking off the cage, and two of them—Tyndall and Spencer—were fighting. Captain Bruggles ran forward, seizing a handspike as he went, and charged among them. He used his six-foot club one-handed, as I would have handled a belaying-pin, separating the combatants, and driving them forward to the windlass, where they jabbered and snarled at him, and rubbed the sore spots; but they were conquered for the time. Then, telling them to stay where they were, he came aft and finished the demolition of the cage-covering, disclosing an undersized brute, a full sister to those forward, but only half-grown. He studied her for a few moments, while she grinned and chattered at him, then he burst into a roar of drunken laughter, and, slapping his thighs, came aft to me. His mood had changed; he seemed to have completely forgotten our quarrel, and this alone prevented me from going overboard to seek aid for Jessie on shore.

"Ain't it fun?" he chuckled, before he had reached the mainmast. "Ain't she a beauty, and ain't they all in love? Let's turn her loose. Come on." He turned back.

"Captain Bruggles," I called, running after him, "I beg of you not to. You will never get them under control again. Take my advice and box up that cage again—or I'll do it, and you keep the rest back."

It was almost too dark now to see the expression of his face, but I knew by his steadfast stare that I had angered him.

"You coward!" he said, thickly; "and five minutes ago you dared face *me*, and I thought I could like you; but you're a coward, after all."

"Father!" came Jessie's pleading voice from the companion. "Father, do as he advises, please do!"

"Shut up, you mincing trollop," he roared at her. "You're too sympathetic, by Gawd, you two." He turned and pounced on me. I had left the handspike aft, but had I possessed it I could not have used it after he had seized me.

"What is there between you two?" he bellowed in my ear as he held me by the arm. "Hey! tell me; what is there between you?"

"I have already told you, captain," I answered. "There is nothing, and will be nothing between us while we are both here. When we get ashore I shall want her for my wife."

"You will, hey! Want her for your wife, will you? I'll give you a wife, by the Lord—I'll give you a wife!"

Struggle as I could, while Jessie screamed from the cabin, he dragged me to the cage, slipped the bar, opened the door, and thrust me in. Then he closed the door and rebarred it. The female snarled at me, but made no attempt to resent the intrusion, and I possessed myself of a piece of planking which lay half through the bars. Crazy with mingled fear and rage, I jabbed it at the captain's face as he stood near the door, but he dodged and drew back out of reach.

"There's a wife for you," he said, with as much sarcasm as his drunken voice would express. Then followed a volley of personal abuse.

"Oh, if I get out of here alive," I answered, insanely, "I'll kill you for this, you devil!" Then I turned to watch my fellow-prisoner. She was paying me no attention, being more interested in the movements of her admirers outside. They were coming aft in a body, swinging their huge shoulders from side to side, beating their chests, and growling angrily. Whatever may have been their state of mind before, they were certainly in a most jealous rage now, possibly at me, who had obtained precedence over them, but directed for the time at Captain Bruggles, whom they had seen favor me. The giant Spencer was in the van, and he made straight for the captain.

"Back, boys!" he thundered. "Back!—go back! go back!—go back!"

Spencer, with a blood-curdling, booming roar, sprang high in the air and came down on his enemy, who staggered under the load, but maintained his footing. Then began the mightiest single combat which, I believe, ever took place on earth. A full moon was now rising over the eastern hills, but there was not yet sufficient light to see clearly their outlines—only their combined bulks, surging back and forth in the shadows, a blacker darkness. There was no growling nor snarling, but a continuous wheezing in short, jerky notes. They reeled and whirled, sometimes falling together with a thud which shook the deck, but arising tightly locked, and slowly drifted aft past the mainmast and mizzen-hatch. Then I saw them separate, one staggering over against the rail, and I heard the captain's voice, in thick, broken accents:

"Jessie, Jessie, loose the snake!—quick! Turn the snake out on deck! I'm bitten—crippled!" He was sober now.

But his appeal was answered by Spencer's snarl of rage, and again they clinched. I heard no answer from Jessie, and my attention was drawn to my immediate neighbors, two of whom had locked and were fighting as deadly a battle as the other; the other three were fumbling about the cage, and my main fear now—inasmuch as the young lady was watching them with amiable curiosity—was that they would unbar the door—which might let me out, of course; but I felt safer at present where I was. Two of them attempted it, but the bar was keyed by a vertical bolt which baffled their intelligence; yet, fearing accidental success on their part, I stabbed viciously with my splinter at their hairy paws as they worked, and the result was satisfying. Each uttered angry snarls of pain, and each, possibly, thinking the other the assailant, a third murderous battle began, and the female jabbered approvingly, moving over toward the side of the cage nearest the last fighters. This brought her uncomfortably close to me, and I moved to the other corner. The cage was about eight feet square, and the bars were too close together to admit the passage of a paw, so, unless my cagemate began demonstrations, I was in no danger. Though undersized, she was large and strong enough to have broken my back with a blow, or bitten my arm off, had she cared to; but she was docile and happy, dividing her interest between the combats in her behalf and the remaining brute without, who was improving his time by getting acquainted.

A terrible cry rang out from the pair at the mizzen-hatch, and at first I could not make out whether it came from Spencer or the captain. It was a death-cry, containing every note of mental and physical agony, and was repeated again and again. At last it became articulate.

"Fleming! Fleming!—Jessie!—the snake!"

"Loose the snake, Jessie, if you can!" I called; and then, "I can't help you, captain; I'm locked in."

The moonlight was stronger now, and I could see them huddled on the deck, still but for the movement of Spencer's immense head. He was uppermost, and his furious growls, coming half choked from his throat, told of his victory. The cries of the captain had ceased, but awful sounds of huge teeth snapping and grating and crunching, as the monster bit and burrowed, made a horrid accompaniment to the vengeful snarls. Then there was quiet for a moment, but for the noise of combat forward, and Spencer lifted his huge, ungainly shape—a black silhouette against the white paint work of the cabin-trunk—threw himself into a sudden contortion, and something passed over the cage, scattering warm, sticky drops of liquid, a few of which struck my hand. Then, sounding his humming, booming roar of challenge, he bounded forward and pounced upon the lovers at the bars.

I do not know which one it was, Spencer being the only one I had recognized in the darkness, but believe that it must have been Huxley, the next largest, from the vigorous resistance which he made; there were a few preliminary blows with their long, powerful arms, then they locked, whirled forward, and from this on they were indistinguishable from the others. Three separate struggles for life and love were now going on before my eyes, but I had little chance to observe them, for the female, angry at the interruption to the *tête-à-tête*, and evidently considering me responsible, was facing me, erect, with mouth wide open, eyes half closed, and hoarse growling barks coming from her throat.

Suddenly she extended both long arms high above her head and sprang. I dodged, and avoided the direct impact of the brute, but could not escape a glancing blow on the head from one heavy fist, which sent me reeling into a corner. When my wits came back I was crouched on my knees, still gripping my splinter of wood, and with my brain throbbing in a splitting headache. In the opposite corner, as high as she could climb, was the female, looking back over one shoulder as she clung to the bars and whis-

pering excitedly. In the middle of the cage was the
cause of her agitation—the snake. It was coiled, and
its head rose from the middle of the coil, waving like
a reversed pendulum, and darting forward and back
while it hissed steadily; but it was not threatening
me, and I regained my feet with the hope that,
having saved my life once, it would continue the
service, and with this hope came the hope that the
brutes without would kill one another, when Jessie,
if she had escaped madness or death from fright,
could liberate me.

The moon was much brighter and higher in the
sky, proving that I must have lain at least an hour
unconscious; and in this hour results had come to
two of the duelists, for in the starboard scuppers
was one quiet form, and on the edge of the fore-
hatch another. Either they had fought to the death
and separated to die, or they were the vanquished of
two battles, the victors in which had later come together. Two were fighting furiously near the port
fore rigging, and the other two were aloft; but this
was a flight and pursuit—not a fight. They had
reached the foretop as I looked, and the leader, uttering grunts of pain and protest, reached for the main
topmast stay, and went up it, hand over hand. The
other followed, growling menacingly. Up the main
topgallant rigging they went, out the topgallant
yard, up the lift, and then straight up to the
royal masthead, where the rigging ended; then
they slid down the main-royal stay to the fore
topgallant masthead, and from this their descent
was a zigzag by lifts and foot-ropes until they
reached the top, when they again started up the main
topmast stay; but the pursuer had gained steadily,
and just as they were half-way up—directly over

the cage—he caught his quarry by the leg. The
fight was resumed in midair. Hanging by one paw
as often as two or more, they swung about the stay,
tangling themselves in the staysail halyards, striking,
kicking, and biting, until one, with a human cry of
agony, let go and fell, head downward. He struck
with a crash on the starboard upper edge of the cage,
clung a moment, and fell to the deck, where he quivered, gasped, rolled over, and lay still. Another was
dead.

But his death had produced results within the
cage. Why the snake should have held me responsible for the jarring and shaking of the cage when the
great beast struck it I do not know, unless it was
because its eyes were on the female in the opposite
corner, who was manifestly innocent. It was within
easy striking distance, and chance alone saved me,
my splinter of wood, held before me like a cane, receiving the impact of its open jaws as it launched
toward my leg. It writhed about the flooring for a
second or two, then coiled, lifted its head for another
spring at me and—went down under the blows of my
stick. I nearly decapitated the reptile with the first
sweep, and followed up my advantage until it ceased
to writhe, by which time I was in a nausea of fear,
trembling in every limb, and wet with perspiration;
for I had not bettered matters. But, as the orang-
outang opposite slowly descended the bars, I des-
perately imitated the hissing of the snake, and she
scrambled up. So hope again rose in my heart. I
kept her there by hissing, and by occasionally moving the dead snake with my stick.

A loud, wailing shriek sounded from the two at
the fore rigging. They were huddled on the deck,
and I did not doubt that one had felt the death-bite.

Again it rang out, echoing among the hills, and again; then there was silence, but for that horrid crunching sound, and at last one of them arose, just in time to meet the descending weight of the victor up aloft— who had descended the stay to the dead-eye and sprung at him from the rigging.

Fervently hoping that they were evenly matched, and that this last battle would be a draw, ending in death for both, I watched them, hissing the while, as they lunged and careered along the deck. But it was not to be; one of them was Spencer, as I knew by a momentary inspection of the right side of his face as they passed the cage, and the other was certainly not Huxley, the next in prowess, for Huxley must be the one beside the cage. It was one of the others, and though once, perhaps twice, a victor that night, he had no chance with the giant Spencer. This struggle was short; it ended at the main rigging, where they fell in a heap, and it ended as had the others, with the fearful cry of agony, the choked growling, and the crunching. Then Spencer, survival of the fittest, arose to his feet and roared his challenge to the universe—the booming, humming, barking growl of an angry orang-outang; and, with hysterical flightiness, I answered with my hiss—to which he paid no attention.

He came toward the cage, pouncing upon and mangling the body of Huxley for a few moments on his way, and squatted before the female, jabbering hoarsely and pawing the bars with his huge hands. What impression he made upon her was beyond my understanding; but she chattered in return, and at last, as though understanding her fear, he stalked slowly around the edge to my corner, grinning hideously. I picked up the dead snake, wriggled it in the air, hissed to the best of my ability, and poked the battered head of the reptile through the bars. Spencer sprang six feet away, then, making a détour along the rail, returned to the safer side of the cage, where he squatted and began the grimacing and mumbling and jabbering of simian courtship.

And thus I passed the rest of that horrid night, keeping the female in order by occasional hissing, but making no strong impression on the doughty Spencer. I called repeatedly to Jessie, but was not answered until daylight broke, and then came a voice which I did not know from the companion:

" Rob, are you there? "

" Jessie! " I answered, joyously; " yes, I'm all right for the present. Don't come out. I've got the female under control with the dead snake, and they're all dead but Spencer. How are you? How have you made out? "

" Where is father? Oh! " she screamed, " it's horrid. They've killed him, Rob. What will I do? What can I do? "

I looked aft, and in the gathering light made out the headless body of Captain Bruggles alongside the mizzen-hatch, and knew then what had passed over my head early in the night.

" Don't look, Jessie! " I called. " Go below, and some of the natives may come out. They must have heard the noise."

" I loosed the snake, Rob, when father told me to, and then I fainted, I think. What has happened? "

" They've killed one another—all but Spencer and the female. Don't come on deck. Some one will be off soon from shore."

She said no more, and I watched the antics of Spencer. His grotesque grimacing seemed to fail of

satisfactory results—even though every square inch
of his hairy body was damp with the clotted blood of
his rivals, he could not win the favor of the frightened young lady in the cage. She paid more attention to the snake than to him, and maintained her
position of safety, high on the bars. At last Spencer
changed his tactics; he began to " show off."

Attacking the pile of boards at the rail, he produced a good supply of kindling-wood, which he arranged under the iron pot; then, procuring the flint-
and-steel, he started the fire; but he neglected, as
usual, to fill the pot with water to the result that
when he had enthusiastically piled on the fuel, the
pot became red-hot. And still he worked insanely,
launching whole boards at the flames, and creating,
perhaps, the most successful fire that he had ever
seen. Jabbering and grunting, and occasionally
scampering to the cage to welcome the first signs
of approval, he soon had a roaring bonfire which
ignited the tarred mainstay and the staysail just
above. A flickering flame crept up to the mainmast head, and I knew that the brig was doomed.

" Water, Spencer!" I called, loudly and peremp-
torily. " Water!—draw water!"

To this day I do not know why that excited brute,
possessed as he was by primitive instinct and passion, obeyed my order. It may have been reason,
but I doubt it. It may have been the force of
habit, yet he hated water; but whatever the motive,
he obeyed me. He seized the draw-bucket, lowered
it over the side, and brought it up brimming. This
he launched at the fire. It struck the red-hot pot
squarely, and the result was a shattering of the re-
ceptacle to pieces, some of which went one side, some
the other, and one of which dropped on Spencer's

toes, sending him forward, howling with pain. The others burned their way into the deck, and flames sprang up, ate their way to the rails and fiferail, and crept aloft on the tarred rigging. Spencer remained forward, grunting over his sore foot, and soon there was a roaring barricade between us. The female turned her back to the heat and would have descended, but I remonstrated with the dead snake and persuaded her to remain where she was.

" Jessie! " I called. " Jessie! come out now— quick ! "

She showed herself at the door and answered me.

" Come out, and slip the bar—quick! It's all safe now. Spencer can't get aft, and this one is afraid of the snake. There's no danger now, only from the fire."

She opened the grating and came out of the cabin, looked at each dead body on the deck, and crept forward to the cage.

" Lift out that bolt in the bar, Jessie," I called, encouragingly, for she was tottering, " and then run aft to the taffrail—to get into the boat when I join you."

She did so. I moved toward the door, shaking the snake at the female and hissing her out of my way, and, when Jessie had sped aft, I opened my prison and closed the door behind me. Then I thought for a second or two, and obeyed a prompting that I am not ashamed of to this day. Jessie was perched upon the taffrail, ready to slip down into the boat towing astern; she was safe, and so was I, with that potential snake still in my hands. I opened wide the door and hurried aft.

Jessie was in the boat before I reached the taffrail, and when I descended on two parts of the painter—

so as to be able to slip it—I found her in a dead faint.

"No wonder," I mused, as, while the boat drifted down stream, I dashed water in her face. But when she opened her eyes, and smiled weakly, and called me by name, I knew that sanity was left her.

"Look at the brig, Jessie," I said, as I lifted her. "There's Spencer out on the jib-boom, and the female on the spanker-boom. It's a horrible courtship."

But she would not look; instead, she stared down stream, and I followed her gaze.

Rounding the next point in the river-bank was a French schooner-of-war—one of the slave-trade police of the African coast—and from her peak floated a homeward-bound pennant.

THE END